The Lion of the South

*"If you loved The Scarlet Pimpernel,
then you are going to love this book."*

— Rebecca Hill, *A Tale of Two Pages*

I0561741

Praise for Jessica James Books

"Explores the War Between the States in a way that will touch you like no other work of fiction."
— THE BOOK CONNECTION

"Andrea and Hunter are like a Virginian, Civil War-era Elizabeth and Mr. Darcy."
— LITERARILY BLOG

"I didn't want to put it down. I told myself 'just one more chapter' at least half a dozen times."
— BECKY'S READS

"I think it is the best Civil War fiction book since Cold Mountain."
— JAMES D. BIBB
Sons of Confederate Veterans, Trimble Camp 1836

"[Emotions] seem to transcend the pages to settle in the very marrow of the reader's bones."
— BOOK PLEASURES

"I haven't enjoyed a book so much in years! Shades of Gray is an incredible achievement and a treasure."
— VIRGINIA MORTON
Author and Historian

"One of the most moving Civil War stories I have ever read. I had to remind myself this was fiction. Do not walk, run to your nearest bookstore for your copy of Shades of Gray."
— REVIEW YOUR BOOKS

"Not since reading *Gone With the Wind* have I enjoyed a book so much! I could not put Shades of Gray down, from start to finish!"
— SARAH WINCH

This stunning story captures the reader's attention from the start."
— RT REVIEWS

Other Books by Jessica James

Romantic Suspense
DEAD LINE (Book 1 Phantom Force Tactical)
FINE LINE (Book 2 Phantom Force Tactical)
FRONT LINE (Book 3 Phantom Force Tactical)

Meant To Be: A Novel of Honor and Duty

Historical Fiction
Noble Cause (Book 1 Heroes Through History)
(An alternative ending to Shades of Gray)

Above and Beyond (Book 2 Heroes Through History)
Liberty and Destiny (Book 3 Heroes Through History)

Shades of Gray: A Novel of the Civil War in Virginia

Non-Fiction
The Gray Ghost of Civil War Virginia: John Singleton Mosby
From the Heart: Love Stories and Letters from the Civil War

www.jessicajamesbooks.com

The
LI🦁N
of the
South

Jessica James

The Lion of the South
Copyright 2018 by JESSICA JAMES
www.jessicajamesbooks.com

ISBN: 978-1-941020-16-6
Library of Congress Control Number: 2017958320

Edited by Literally Addicted to Detail Services
Cover Design: Historical Fiction Book Covers
Cover Art: Courtesy of Morven Park (morvenpark.org)
Interior Design: Patriot Press

April 2018

Proudly Printed in the United States of America

Special Thanks to Morven Park (Cover Image)

Morven Park, located in Leesburg, Virginia, is a 1,000-acre historic estate and equestrian center.

Once the home of Westmoreland Davis, governor of Virginia (1918-1922), and Thomas Swann, Jr., Governor of Maryland during the Civil War, Morven Park attracts 200,000 visitors each year, enticed by the site's exquisite scenery, formal gardens, equestrian center, athletic fields, museum collections, hiking and riding trails, and of course, the iconic Davis mansion, which is featured on the cover.

The mansion began as a small fieldstone house (built circa 1780) and was expanded upon through the decades until it became the 22-room Greek revival mansion seen today.

The Park is open daily for visitors, and tours of the mansion are available. More information can be found at MorvenPark.org.

"Do your duty in all things. You cannot do more, you should never wish to do less."

— Robert E. Lee

Prologue

A layer of smoke rises and drifts across the open fields like a giant gray blanket, stinging the eyes and blurring all vision. The sun seems reluctant to throw its rays upon the horrid scene, preferring instead to hide behind an impenetrable veil of clouds.

Perhaps it is a sympathetic God who leaves the details of the gory battle hidden from view. The once-fertile land, now ravaged and burned by war, is better left unseen; the bodies, broken and dying, better left only to the imagination.

During the greater part of the afternoon, the guns blazed away, diligently executing their ghastly work. Sunset has now hushed the land, and both sides have fallen back, licking their wounds and burying their dead. Tomorrow, as soon as the sun has tinged the sky, the bloody work shall begin anew.

It's been a year and a half now, and daily, hourly, the hostile conflict claims its many victims: young men, old men—and countless others who are mere boys.

Those who wear gray recognize this sacrifice as a duty—an honorable one—but they know the carnage cannot continue for long at such a pace. The protracted duration of the war has already taken a toll on the Confederacy's vitality, causing it to be in mortal peril of exhaustion and collapse. Arms—and the men to carry them—have dwindled from a flood to a trickle.

Starved, nearly bankrupt, thousands of her best soldiers sitting in prison or killed in battle, the South has nowhere to turn.

But perhaps all is not yet lost.

In times of war, there are always those who do not hide from the terrible calamity that spreads across the land. Soldiers, of course—but others, too, who fight without the prospect of reward or even recognition.

Just such a figure has stepped forth from the shadows, blowing the smoldering embers of defiance into a bright flame. The depleted—yet dedicated—soldiers have begun to raise their heads with a newfound spirit of resistance, and to fight with revitalized strength.

Truth? Myth? Fact? Fabrication? No one is sure. Yet all are eager to embrace the Confederacy's last, great hope…the mysterious legend who has begun to tip the scales in their favor.

The Lion of the South.

Chapter 1

January 1863

The sun cast its last rays of the day across the western horizon, creating a spectacular display of color in the process. But the three riders hidden in the trees overlooking the Union camp did not see it. They focused their attention on the white tents below them, and the long shadows creeping like fingers toward their objective.

They did not talk. Their eyes were the only things that moved as they waited, watched, and listened. From the intensity of their expressions as they stared down at the Federal encampment, one would think they were closely evaluating the next move in a chess game.

Most of the activity below appeared to be concentrated in a large, canvas tent, so there was not much to see—but there was plenty to hear. The din emanating from within the enclosure's folds had increased substantially over the past two hours; the strains of music pealing forth, and the offbeat clapping of hands, suggested a lively celebration had been underway for quite some time.

When an elegant carriage arrived in front of the tent, the men still did not move or display the slightest inclination to react. But the moment the fiddle stopped playing, they seemed to collectively hold their breath, and lean forward in anticipation.

An uproar of laughter soon replaced the sound of music—at a level so raucous as to provoke a dog to bark in alarm at the disturbance. It was clear the party was breaking up, just as the encroaching shadows created by the setting sun reached the encampment.

As figures began to appear, all three men on the hillside concentrated on the scene with hawk-like intensity. Union soldiers, mostly officers, spilled out like a dark blue stream and promptly melted away into the shadows. The gentle buzz of voices drifting on the breeze created a general hum, making individual conversations impossible to discern, no matter how hard the horsemen strained.

Within moments, two elegantly dressed civilian men and a commanding officer walked into view. They moved at a leisurely—and unsteady—pace to the carriage, where they paused to converse, just as two more shadows materialized in the doorway.

A screech owl chose that moment to emit its eerie call from above, but still, the riders did not move. Even their mounts stood alert, yet motionless, as the soft glow of light radiating from the tent illuminated the first figure. It was a woman—an elderly lady of distinction, if one could judge from the twist of gray hair, the elegant attire, and the high position of her chin.

Three sets of eyes immediately shifted to the next figure, another woman, but she had raised the hood of her lavish cloak before walking into the light, making it impossible to distinguish her age or any identifiable characteristics.

The gentlemen helped the ladies into the carriage before climbing in behind them, causing the conveyance to rock precariously, and the horses to pull impatiently. The older woman leaned out and took the general's hand. Her distinct voice carried easily.

"Thank you so much for your hospitality, General Carlyle."

"My pleasure." The officer inclined his head into the coach, appearing to talk to the other woman. "I expect to hear from you soon...about my proposal."

The voice that answered was that of a young female, soft in tone, and full of mirth in attitude. Her reply drifted up the hillside. "I shall not keep you in suspense for long, General. In the meantime, please accept my gratitude for your kindness in allowing me to accompany you to the picket line today. It was a delightful diversion, and an honor to ride such a spirited horse."

"It was my pleasure, my dear. My pleasure."

Two Federal outriders cantered up just then to escort the conveyance as far as the pickets, bringing the conversation—or at least any sound of it—to an end. As the carriage pulled away, the men on the hillside backed their horses into the tree line.

One of the men leaned close and whispered to his leader, "Did you see what you came to see?"

The man questioned did not answer, but the expression on his face as he stared in the direction of the disappearing carriage made it clear he had seen something he had *not* wished to see.

Without another word, he turned his horse and spurred it into the darkness. The other two riders swiftly followed.

Chapter 2

C harles J. Thorpe, chief detective of the Union Intelligence Service, walked down the long corridor with hurried strides, muttering and grumbling with every step.

Anyone who saw the detective's corpulent figure stomping along knew enough to move out of his way. The hallway was narrow, and Thorpe's temper, like his waistline, was bigger than anything around it.

The spring of discontent had descended upon the Army of the Potomac with little warning and no respite. The bloody sacrifices of the past two years had been offset by the timid, vacillating leadership of those to whom the highest commands had been entrusted. McClellan—the worst of them—could not be induced to attack unless his force was overwhelmingly superior and victory was assured. The President had at last replaced him, but little had changed.

Months ago, Thorpe had been certain the war would be brought to a conclusive end within weeks, but since then, the winds of war had changed. A new leader—an antagonistic, lawless villain—had stepped forward and transferred the conflict into the shadows. Every move Union forces made, every advance, and every strike, was anticipated by the enemy and used against the

North. Still worse, prisoners were disappearing by the dozens. Not all at one time, mind you—only a few here and a handful there. Just enough to be considered a singular incident, and not a big one at that.

In the past few weeks, the enterprising escapades had become more frequent and singularly daring—and the prisoners of higher value. Just last week, two Confederate officers had disappeared from the prison at Point Lookout. The week before that, three colonels and a major vanished into thin air while being transported to a prison in New York.

The incidents had sparked the rise of curious rumors. Incredible stories spread like wildfire as the people in Washington grew increasingly excited—and simultaneously terrified. In fact, on the streets and at home, in open society and in private conversation—the inhabitants spoke of little else.

The facts, according to local gossip, were that a gang of ruffians from the countryside had organized the raids and recruited others to take part under threat of death. Even those convalescing in Confederate hospitals were not exempt from being drafted to assist the vigilante band's nefarious endeavors. They reportedly slipped out at night, bandages and all, only to be found recuperating once again in their beds by morning.

As winter continued with little actual fighting, the feats performed by the meddlesome band of reprobates had increased in frequency—and grown more cunning and creative. Who they were, and where exactly they'd come from was not yet clear, but it was widely accepted they were under the leadership of a man whose brazenness and fearlessness were almost too bold to be possible.

Stories of his stealth, his daring, and his bravery were magnified and enhanced as they passed from ear to ear, so that now the troupe of traitors was never spoken of without a superstitious shudder.

And why not? The blatant impudence of the insolent rebels knew no bounds. Not only did they carry out their midnight mischief, they had the audacity to mock the Union forces once the deed had been done. After an unexpected defeat in battle or the loss of valuable prisoners, the Federals would receive a communication—sometimes in the form of an official dispatch, but just as often a slip of paper mysteriously discovered in an officer's coat, or an ominous warning scratched out in the ashes of a burned-out campfire.

The message always contained a brief notice that the crew of ruffians was at work, and it was always stamped with a wax seal depicting the figure of a winged lion.

Everyone took the symbol as it was no doubt intended. The lion, of course, was a courageous animal—noble, regal, majestic. The wings symbolized the evil-doer's ability to fly away unseen—as he so often did.

One thing was for certain. This irreverent troublemaker knew the most effectual way to injure the enemy. With a vigilance hard to escape, the Lion would pounce upon messengers bearing important dispatches between the War Department and the officers in the field. As a result, the Lion's band of miscreants captured papers of great importance and left Union commanders feeling insecure about advancing or even retreating, resulting in no movement or action in any direction.

Fear, rather than sense, ruled the deliberations of the federal government, and terror was greatly felt by those serving in the field. Although outright attacks by the unknown foe were seldom waged, the results, when they occurred, were always the same. The brave bandit would launch his riders like a gust of wind, striking Union forces with unbridled ferocity. A peaceful hush would follow, like the stillness that follows a sudden storm, and the battlefield would be littered with the fallen.

Mostly as a way to protect himself and his job, Detective Thorpe took great pains to diminish the significance of the miraculous feats pulled off by the Lion. He blamed the officers in charge, or the prison wardens under whose failed leadership the events occurred.

Still, he took the threat seriously. Within the last few weeks, he had doubled the number of his assistant detectives and spies, and flaunted liberal rewards to the ailing country people for their help in capturing the elusive and insolent cad. One thousand dollars in U.S. gold was promised to the man or woman who revealed the identity of the mysterious and elusive *Lion of the South*.

Thorpe prided himself on his reputation for craftiness, but recognized that his ability to corner and capture the Lion would take more than just guile. He needed an ally in the field to help sway public opinion against this enterprising daredevil—and he knew just the man for the job.

Unfortunately, it was too late to prevent the Lion from getting fresh accolades. News of the infuriating foe's latest triumph had obviously reached the White House, and Thorpe knew where the blame was going to fall. He knocked once on an ornate, wooden door before entering and found, as he expected, about a dozen high-level officers sitting around a large table. Aides and orderlies stood awkwardly along the wall or were seated in the few extra chairs scattered throughout the chamber.

"Nice of you to join us. I suppose you've heard the news." The Secretary of War did not bother to greet Thorpe with salutations, nor did anyone else in the room.

"I've caught wind of some of it, sir." Thorpe stood beside

a chair apparently reserved for him, gasping and wheezing as he tried to catch his breath after the short, brisk walk. "Surely, it can't be as bad as they say."

"Can't be as bad as they say?" The secretary's fist hit the table. "It is *worse* than what they say. I want to make it clear that this scoundrel must be caught, and he must be apprehended soon." The official calmed himself by taking a deep breath and then opened a folder to pass out the papers contained within. "Now that Detective Thorpe is here, I won't keep this under wraps any longer. You have all probably guessed, the Lion of the South has struck once more."

"Did he make off with prisoners again?" one of the men asked.

"Or was it horses this time?" A man in civilian dress, sitting with arms crossed and looking bored, waited for the papers to be distributed.

"Gads," Thorpe grumbled as he hurriedly scanned the report. "I tell you…that man, Captain O'Keefe, must be a fool! That meddlesome bandit wouldn't get by *my* men unless he be the devil himself."

The secretary ignored the comments as he stood and began to pace with his hands locked behind his back. "As you can see," he said, shaking his head as if still trying to come to terms with the exploit himself, "a lone rider galloped headlong toward the pickets at O'Keefe's outpost near the Chain Bridge last night, waving a white flag and yelling at the top of his lungs."

"Military protocol would require that they stop him." An officer at the far end of the room stretched impatiently for a copy of the report that had not yet reached him. "It's inconceivable to think any foe would dare come this close to the defenses of our nation's capital."

"Oh, yes. They stopped him."

The room grew quiet as the men concentrated on the single sheet of paper in their hands.

"As you can see in the report," the secretary said, "the rider, all red-faced and out of breath, told the pickets he was a local farmer and that he'd run across the Lion and his men, encamped in a nearby grove of trees."

"Then what happened?" A wide-eyed young man who was apparently an aide to one of the important people at the table—and therefore not privy to the report—leaned forward in innocent anticipation.

"I'm getting to that." The secretary shot the man a punishing look for speaking. "Captain O'Keefe gathered his men and sent them spurring out of the camp, all in a flurry and armed to the teeth, certain, no doubt, that he would be the one to snag the Lion and the reward." The official shot a scathing rebuke toward Thorpe.

"And was he there?" The young man was too anxious to hear the rest of the story to heed proper protocol and remain quiet.

"Oh, he was there all right."

"So, he's been captured?" The soldier slapped his leg.

"No, you stupid jackanape. He wasn't captured."

A soldier wearing the stars of a general shook the paper in his hand. "'Twas a trick! The Lion's men, and a whole lot more of them damned rebels, were *waiting* in the woods."

"That's right." The secretary finished the story, hitting the table with his hand again as he did so. "They gobbled O'Keefe's men right up. Not a shot fired. The entire regiment swept away to a Southern prison, probably never to be seen again."

The entire circle of men fell silent after a seemingly shared exhalation of breath. The story certainly lent itself to something of supernatural proportions and left them awestruck. Truly, the Lion must be the devil himself to have ventured right to their doorstep. Surely, this will-o'-the-wisp was aware that the gaping mouths of hundreds of cannon were aimed at that bridge, and thousands of armed men were within hailing distance.

Yet each was also aware that no effort, or next to none at any rate, had been made to guard against such flagrant brazenness; such blatant, deliberate impudence. Who indeed would dare such a foolish and dangerous act of diversion?

"If those of you in this room cannot do the job, I will find those who can." The Secretary of War spoke in a clipped, angry tone that told everyone he meant business, and that their livelihoods were at stake. "This rebel is toying with us, laughing at us. The constant aggravation he causes is either through a lack of exertion on your part or a preponderance of perceptiveness on his!"

The group remained seated, silent and sullen, either staring out the window or eyeing one another warily, wondering whom the Lion could be.

"The impertinence," one finally said.

"The insolence," said another.

"The courage…"

Chapter 3

A ll was astir at the usually quiet Welbourne Manor. Set among the rolling hills of Virginia, less than fifty miles from the outskirts of the nation's capital, the home was striking in both size and magnificence. Even the most casual observer could ascertain that the owner of the property was not only a prosperous man, but one who valued taste and refinement.

The sprawling plantation house that dominated the property presented a sight of regal splendor, yet reflected an old-fashioned image of character and grace. Beautiful sculptures and statues embellished the vast gardens, and white marble fountains rose in small clearings among the rich foliage. In every direction, one could see horses grazing in lush pastures that rose and fell in an undulating landscape for miles.

As for the dwelling itself, four massive, cathedral-like columns accentuated the front porch and welcomed guests with great stateliness. Two large windows bookmarked the front door, and a balcony overhead added a touch of sophisticated charm to the scene. The house and its grounds could certainly compete with any palace in the world for its attractiveness and expression of bygone glory.

The interior of the grand home was no less magnificent—yet not ostentatious in the least. Dark, wooden floors gleamed with polish, and ornate silver candelabras in the foyer shone like new. The ceilings were of an impressive height, and the decorative plaster corbels in the doorframes displayed a high level of intricacy and elegance. Wealth, combined with excellent taste and class, were in evidence everywhere, making it clear no reasonable wish or necessity would be left unfulfilled.

March had opened in its usual way to those who were accustomed to such things in this section of the country. One could begin to go outdoors without a cumbersome overcoat, yet few would venture to do so. The roads were at their deepest in mud, and even the constant wind was not of sufficient strength to dry them. Today, just like the one before, raindrops pounded against the windows and ran in torrents down the panes.

But when the sound of carriage wheels settled on the ears of those within the house, the gloominess instantly dissipated. A general air of excitement rose and a charge of energy sent each person running to the foyer to greet the arrivals.

Within mere moments, two smiling, laughing, and exceedingly wet young ladies burst through the door, shaking their cloaks and wiping their feet.

"Miss Sallie, take off that wet coat," said a stout woman with a round face. "You'll catch your death of cold."

"Oh, Aunt Mazie," the sopping girl said, "it is so good to be home once again. Wet or not!"

As the girls removed their coats with much hugging and fanfare among the servants, it was clear neither of them was a stranger to the household.

Sallie, a petite young lady with rosy cheeks and abundant curls in her auburn hair, seemed particularly excited to at last be home.

Her companion, a graceful, refined figure, elegant despite her look of fatigue, had uttered nothing as yet. But her eyes, a beautiful shade of blue and full of warmth, swept the surroundings. "It feels like I'm home," she said, gazing around with childlike interest at the large foyer and the surrounding jovial faces. "It's as if nothing has changed."

"Why, is this our Miss Julia?" Aunt Mazie stood with her hands on her hips, and a smile that beamed like a light in contrast to her dark skin. Despite her portly figure, she ran to the girl and clutched her against her ample chest. "Why, you all growed up."

"She deserves a scolding." Sallie wiped her feet one more time. "It's been more than six years since we last saw her here."

"Why you go stayin' away for so long, Miss Julia?" A handsome black man with gray hair and whiskers was the next to step forward.

"Oh, Spencer, look at you." Julia wrapped her arms around him. "You don't look a day older."

"Aww. You're just tryin' to get on my good side."

"That's right. I want you to saddle the fastest horse Landon owns just as soon as the weather allows."

At the mention of Landon, the happiness and excitement exited the room in one great surge.

Sallie paused and glanced around. "Where *is* Landon? Isn't he home?"

Spencer stepped forward. "Mister Landon is feeling under the weather today."

Sallie's face fell with disappointment, and her brows creased with concern. "Locked in his quarters?"

Everyone looked down. Then Spencer cleared his throat. "It appears so, miss."

Julia tried to lighten the mood. "I will have plenty of time to see Landon, I'm sure."

"He's going to be so excited to see you." Sallie grabbed Julia's arm and led her to an adjoining room that contained a blazing fire. "I wrote him that I intended to bring along a surprise."

Chapter 4

Julia Dandridge walked into the large parlor and gazed lovingly at the familiar room where so many memories had been made. Not much had changed here either. Three large, comfortable chairs sat in a half circle in front of a fireplace that snapped and spit with a newly laid log. An elaborately decorated grandfather clock stood in one corner, its constant ticking adding to the ambiance of the room. Another settee and two more chairs sat in another corner by a large, floor-to-ceiling window that gazed out over the gardens.

The room was lighted with two silver candelabras that reflected and flickered off the large gilt-framed portraits of four generations of Grahams that graced the walls. The presence of the stern faces looking down from their positions of honor brought a sense of formality to a room that was otherwise cozy and comfortable.

As Sallie continued to chat about their journey, they both held their hands close to the roaring fire. It wasn't until some minutes later that Julia was overcome with the feeling she was being watched.

Turning her head slightly, she discovered a man standing—or rather, *leaning*—in the doorway with his shoulder resting casually against the frame. At first glance, it seemed she'd caught a look of intense interest—or perhaps scrutiny—upon his face. But on closer inspection, she found his eyes dull and distant, as if he were staring at nothing at all.

Sallie perceived her silence and turned to see what had caused it. "Landon! There you are."

The man took an unsteady step forward and set an empty glass down on a nearby table. "I dare say, you look like a pair of half-drowned kittens," he drawled in a lazy, languid tone. It was then that Julia noticed how disheveled he appeared. Stretched across his broad shoulders was a coat that showed signs of having been slept in, and though he wore a vest, as all well-bred Southern gentlemen did, his shirt was undone at the collar.

Perhaps little else at Welbourne had changed, but Sallie's brother was barely recognizable as the handsome young man Julia remembered. Tall, above average even for a Virginian, Landon Graham had raven-black hair and penetrating eyes of a similar color. He could still be considered very handsome, as long as one could look past his rumpled appearance and the tired, detached—almost despondent—expression on his face.

Julia did her best to suppress any outward display of disappointment. Although the man standing before her was much taller and broader than she remembered, he had aged as though by several decades. He appeared reserved, taciturn—some might say, haggard—with at least a day's growth of stubble on his face, and wild, unruly hair. Even his eyes were duller now, stark and desolate, as if they'd lost their spirit. The light in them had burned out.

"I wish I had known you were coming." He spoke with a slight slur to his words, yet his tone indicated a touch of irritation.

"Wish you had known?" Sallie laughed as she went to him with outstretched arms. "I sent you word a week ago."

Landon studied his sister with a tilted head as if trying to remember. "Oh, yes. Perhaps you did," he said before enveloping her in his arms.

For an instant, as his eyes closed with his sister pressed against his chest, Julia could plainly see the devotion and love he felt for her stamped on the lines of his face. But it lasted only a moment.

As soon as he released Sallie, he turned his attention to Julia, and distinct displeasure marked his voice. "You did not tell me you were bringing a guest." His gaze swept over her in a way that conveyed little cordiality, and no warmth.

Sallie's voice rang out in laughter, but it was too loud to be considered natural. "I wouldn't call Julia a *guest*. Can't you see? It's Julia Dandridge."

Landon tilted his head and squinted again in concentration. He seemed to be flipping through the pages of time in his thoughts, trying to reconcile that the young woman before him was the same girl with whom he had shared so many adventures in his youth—or perhaps he was simply pretending to do so, for Sallie's sake. "This is little Julia?"

When he lifted his gaze and met Julia's, she imagined she saw a glimmer of welcome, but if she did, it vanished in an instant.

Sallie giggled. "Well, not so little anymore."

"I see that." He bowed slightly, but upon losing his balance, reached for the back of a chair to steady himself. "A pleasure to see you again, I'm sure."

Julia stood motionless, speechless, her brain numb as she stared into a face that was as stern and unemotional as marble. She had dreamed about this moment hundreds of times over the years—perhaps even thousands—but never had it unfolded like this. A warm embrace. A whispered expression of affection—or at least a word of greeting—would have lessened the severity of this transformation.

"How is Gideon?" Landon's tone was as cold as his expression, and the atmosphere in the room crackled with tension.

"He is well…last I heard." Julia's voice quaked a little. "He expressed his deepest sympathy for your loss—as do I."

"Last you heard?" Landon ignored the expression of condolence for his only brother. "Oh, yes, I suppose it would be difficult for him to get word to you. If my memory serves, you still reside in Washington City. Isn't that so?"

Julia looked down, not sure how to respond. He had spat the name of the nation's capital as if it were some type of incurable disease, a place worse than Hell itself.

Sallie discerned her hesitation and took a step forward. "Yes, she's been in Washington. And Gideon is facing the enemy, defending Virginia. Let's leave it at that."

"Yes, indeed." Landon did not acknowledge the disparaging comment from his sister about his own situation. "Let's leave it at that."

It had been about a year now since Landon and Sallie's brother was lost to the war. Soon after that, Landon had relinquished command of the small regiment he led. Despite being from one of the most notable families in Virginia—and among the richest—it was strikingly clear he had not yet recovered from either incident.

"I hope you enjoy your visit, Miss Dandridge."

Landon turned stiffly toward the door and spoke over his shoulder to Sallie. "You should find Spencer to stir up the fire. Your friend appears cold and uncomfortable."

Sallie shot her brother a scornful look. "It is most likely your disdainful and derisive attitude that chills her, not the room."

Landon did not respond. He squared his broad shoulders and went to exit the room, but cut the corner too short and hit his arm on the doorframe. After grabbing the molding with both hands to steady himself, he continued on his way without a second glance back.

Chapter 5

The room fell silent upon Landon's departure. Julia didn't move. She continued to stare at the empty doorway, trying to reconcile that the lost soul she had just seen was the same young man with whom she'd dashed wildly around the plantation in her youth. The man who'd just exited was lost. Haunted. In no way did he resemble the cavalier, confident figure she had thought she would see again...had *hoped* to see again.

"I'm sorry." Sallie finally spoke, her voice trembling. "I should have told you."

"Told me what?"

Sallie spoke rapidly as if laying down a heavy burden. "I was so hoping that things had changed since I was last home. I thought my months away would..." She stopped and covered her face with her hands, shaking her head as if unable to continue.

"Don't cry. I'm sure it is nothing." Julia took a step closer to her friend, but she glanced nervously over her shoulder to make sure Landon had not returned.

A single tear ran down Sallie's face as she talked, staring now into the fire. "The war has changed him so."

Julia took her friend's hand and helped her to the couch. "Heavens. I thought him a perfect gentleman. You don't have to explain anything to me."

"But I must." She heaved in a huge breath. "He feels responsible for Sawyer's death, but I never blamed him. Nobody did."

"I'm so sorry about Sawyer." Julia sat down next to Sallie and threw her arm over her friend's shoulder. "It was so horrible. So devastating. And you being his twin… Oh, I don't know what I'd do if it were Gideon." Julia closed her eyes at the thought of losing her own brother, as if that would take away the image of such a terrible ordeal.

"I don't believe Landon will ever recover from the horror of it."

"I know they were very devoted to each another." Julia could think of no words to take away the pain.

"I thought Sawyer's death would bring Landon and me closer, but it has only torn us apart. Landon hates everything and everyone."

"Including himself," Julia whispered as she stared idly at the doorway where the man had disappeared. She had been in his presence only a few minutes, but the only emotions she'd read on his face seemed to be anger and disdain.

"Yes. I'm afraid so. When Landon received word of Sawyer's death, he began drinking. He was no longer fit for command. You can only imagine what they are saying about him."

Despite his wealth and social status, Landon had been among the first to answer the call of duty, ready to sacrifice and devote all to the cause. He had organized troops and led them on the field, and by all accounts, had established a reputation that was beyond reproach.

"I read his name often in the paper." Julia shook her head. "Why, the Yankees were terrified of him."

"Truly?" Sallie sounded surprised. "He told me he was just another soldier, and not much of one at that." She stood and began to pace. "Anyway, after Sawyer died, he came home on a furlough, and he never left. He locks himself away in his chambers and allows no one to enter—not even Spencer half the time. There are periods when no one sees him for days."

Julia could scarcely picture the fun-loving young man she had known in this new light. When Julia's father was killed serving in the military out west, their mother had done everything she could to raise her two children. But Mrs. Dandridge had always been weak and in ill health. She had succumbed to a fever soon after her husband's death, when Julia was just nine, and Gideon, fourteen.

When Landon's father heard that the two children of his childhood friend were alone, he'd welcomed them into his home. Julia remembered the gray-haired Mr. Graham as a person who was as kindhearted and gentle as he was rich. He was a quiet man—some might say somber—but always patient and gentle.

Unfortunately, his wife was not nearly as welcoming, and could often be downright cruel. She'd put up with the orphaned children living in her grand home, but did not hesitate to make it clear that the difference in status between the two families rendered the arrangement nigh intolerable.

"He rarely goes to town these days. Hardly even leaves the house, except when necessary for business." Sallie sat back down. "When he retires to his quarters, no one can venture there except at his express command or invitation."

"He communicates with no one?"

"Very few. The schoolmaster, occasionally. And a couple of the men from his old regiment who are home on furlough or recovering from injuries. You remember Judson McGuire, don't you?"

"Jud?" Julia's eyes opened wide. "The boy who used to sit behind me and dip my pigtails in ink?"

Sallie laughed. "Yes, that is the one. But he is the schoolmaster now, having to punish the young boys who are as devilish as he was."

"It's hard to believe we are all grown up. It happened so fast."

"Yes, with the war, I think we all had to grow up fast." Sallie sighed. "Poor Matthew Sweeney is another one who has not turned his back on Landon."

"Sweeney served with Landon, didn't he?"

"Yes." Sallie paused. "But he lost a leg at Antietam. He helps where he can at the local hospital."

"Oh, I didn't know." Julia stared into the fire, thinking of her younger, carefree days once again, and then turned her attention back to Sallie. "It's nice to know old friends can still be counted on to come visit Landon."

Sallie's voice lowered to a whisper. "It's not really to visit. All they do is drink and play cards."

"Oh-h. I see."

"And then, there's Priscilla…still trying to get her claws into him."

"Priscilla?" Julia's head jerked up. "I thought she had married."

Sallie shook her head. "She did, but her husband was an older gentleman and died recently of the fever. I'm afraid she has set her sights once again on Landon."

"As I recall, your mother thought it a good match."

Sallie sighed. "She only saw what prestige the union would bring to the family, and went to her grave believing it would take place. She never considered Landon's feelings on the matter."

"And what does Landon think of the idea?" Julia succeeded in keeping her voice from sounding too interested in the topic. "I always thought he would concede to your mother's wishes."

"It's hard to tell what Landon is thinking. Certainly, *I've* never been able to do it anyway."

Julia remembered the day Mrs. Graham had informed her that Landon and Priscilla were betrothed. After months of anguish and despair, she'd discovered it wasn't true. But by then, she was living in Washington with an aunt and uncle she had never met before and didn't like once she did.

It had been a distressing and traumatic event for both Julia and her brother to be uprooted from a loving home, and taken away by relatives who were estranged from the family. Julia had been too young to understand the details of the family dispute, but she knew that her mother despised Aunt Abigail, and would never have consented to the arrangement.

The series of events that led to that plight had occurred swiftly and with no warning. Mr. Graham was not even cold in his grave before Julia and Gideon were sent away. As fate would have it, Mrs. Graham's health took a sudden turn for the worse shortly after that. She'd followed her husband to the grave within a year, leaving Landon to care for the estate and the twins.

The sound of Sallie's voice jolted Julia from her recollections.

"The worst of it is, Landon pretends nothing is wrong right now—because he is too inebriated to know that it is."

Julia did not know what to say. Her own heart selfishly ached at what she had seen. She had sought this place as a refuge, hoping to find solace in the company of the man she remembered from her youth. She had assumed he would be happy to provide assistance in her time of need.

But now that gentle, sweet friend was a sullen, miserable recluse who would not allow anyone close to him. The man who had embodied sacred principles and stood above all others for cause and country, no longer even wore the uniform of his beloved South.

Landon's spirit was nothing more than the smoking remnants of what had once been a brilliant flame. Julia had idolized him for his passionate nature, and relied upon him for encouragement and support. But he was secretive and angry now. Brooding. Withdrawn.

The man who had exited the room earlier was a mere shadow of the one she remembered.

Julia blinked to keep tears of bitterness and pain from falling. She had come here for help from the only people she had thought could provide it. Now, she was as alone as she had been in Washington. How silly she'd been to think she could come back here after six years and just pick up where she'd left off—as if there were no war.

The strong, fragrant aroma of spring flowers from the hall wafted into the room, triggering sweet memories of the past, and replacing those of the present. Neither imagination nor dream could conjure up a more pleasant spot or a more perfect childhood.

But then again, perhaps Julia's mind played tricks on her. Maybe Landon wasn't the larger-than-life guardian she remembered. Perhaps time and distance had colored her recollections of the man who was nine years her senior. The person she recalled had always been kind and patient, had always shown up when she least expected—but most needed—it. She had once gone so far as to think he enjoyed her company.

It appeared now he had only tolerated it.

"I thought by bringing you here, he might try to stop drinking. You and he were always so close."

"It does not appear I helped the situation in the least." Julia stared idly out the window. "He seemed very angry."

"Yes. Angry at himself. Angry at the war." Sallie wiped a tear from her cheek. "Angry at the world."

Chapter 6

Times were hard and growing worse.

The elation that followed the triumph of Manassas back in '61 had long ago faded. The pageantry, mystique, and gallantry of war had vanished—along with the expectation of a speedy conclusion.

In the beginning, young men had dreamed of marching off to fight, believing in their hearts they would be contributing to a great cause. Preparing for battle was considered a glorious duty, and the demands of camp life were deemed mere romantic adventures.

It did not take long to discover they were in error. War was dreadful. And there was no end in sight.

It was now the spring of '63. The winter lull had ended, and soon the new fury of the storm would begin. The condition of the roads prevented any general engagement, but hardly a night passed that the flurry of pounding feet was not heard, as troops raced from one threatened spot to another.

Even the most ardent secessionist realized winning would not be easy. Those who had clung obstinately to the conviction that England would intervene on the side of the South inwardly doubted such a feat would occur—at least not before it was too late.

Those early successes were perhaps the cause for so much

discontent now. The soldiers thought themselves invincible, and the women who loved them believed them capable of defeating any enemy—big or small. A generous helping of patriotic spirit, mixed with resolute courage in officers and men, was assumed to be a military combination that could not fail.

But as the war dragged on, the body count piled up, and nerves began to fray. Soldiers were no longer the only ones to suffer through this catastrophic event. In every direction, homes lay wrecked, and hearts overflowed with an intensifying feeling of despair. Fathers, husbands, and brothers were gone. Homes, barns, and mills were burned. Livestock was driven away or slaughtered. Food and crops were stolen or destroyed.

Nowadays, everyone—no matter the amount of influence or wealth—suffered from the lack of goods caused by the squeeze of the blockade. Even the simplest necessities like cloth, needles, calico, and sugar, were considered luxuries. Coffee had risen to thirty cents a pound, and tea was nearly impossible to find at any price.

The country folk could survive on what they grew, but in cities like Richmond, food was scarce and very dear. Meat that was fit to eat was an indulgence of the past, and any fresh fruit that made it through the blockade went straight to the hospitals for the wounded. Provisions attained had to be paid for with the ever-increasing price of blood.

All normal habits of life had been suspended once the struggle began. Parties, balls, and afternoon teas were replaced by the arduous task of making socks or pulling lint for bandages. The once familiar sound of the hounds in full chase—and the large, extravagant breakfasts that followed the hunt—were now extinct in all but memory.

Yet, strangely enough, smoke, fire, and the blood of heroes

deluging the land were now such common occurrences as to barely draw attention or remark.

Even the news that Union General Patrick Carlyle was headed their way no longer caused the chaos and commotion it once had. That ruthless, callous character had already committed every possible outrage against the region. They had no recourse but to ignore the atrocities he perpetrated as best they could and go about their business.

Dismayed and discouraged by a series of disasters in the west, the Confederacy craved a hero that would take its mind off the inevitable reality it faced. The mysterious Lion had not been seen or heard from since his last great feat the previous month. His unpredictable nature continued to cast a shadow on the enemy, but those in the south began to worry. Could he lay dead in a trench on some lonely battlefield? Or worse yet, have been captured? Never to return?

Anxiety ran high as supplies ran low. Breathless with anticipation, the citizens of the Confederate states scoured the papers and waited for news in every village and town. Though chances were growing slimmer by the day, they yearned for a report that showed the tide was turning. In those days of gloom and despair, a nation's fate, a people's rescue, were staked on one man's greatness of soul.

Optimism was beginning to falter—but not courage.

Hope was fading, but it was not yet completely dead.

Chapter 7

J ulia and Sallie slept soundly their first night at Welbourne and did little but eat and reminisce the next few days, since the conditions outside remained quite wretched. The sky seemed reluctant to rain or clear up, so the grounds remained wet and muddy.

On her third day at the old homestead, Julia opened her eyes to bright rays of golden light stabbing through the slot between the drapes. For a few minutes, she remained in a trance—not quite asleep, yet not fully awake, as she tried to grasp why she felt so relaxed and comfortable. Why was everything so peaceful and quiet?

As the cobwebs of slumber fell away, Julia sat straight up, and then bounded out of bed. Running to the window, she brushed the curtains aside and lifted her face to the radiant rays of the sun. She had obviously overslept, yet, unlike in Washington, there were no bands playing on the streets. She heard no tramping of feet, no shouted orders, or trumpet calls. Turning here head to the left, then to the right, she saw not a soldier in sight. A profusion of birds of every variety provided the only music outside her window.

Washington had never been a quaint or quiet town, but with the onset of the war, it had swelled into a chaotic, transient city, filled with a veritable labyrinth of quartermaster storehouses, commissaries, and shops. Churches, public buildings, and abandoned mansions were converted into hospitals, prisons, and headquarters, adding to the general tumult of the city.

Many of the city's inhabitants who were loyal to the Confederacy had fled before the conflict even began. At times, those who remained found themselves living under martial law, virtual captives in a town now surrounded by a smattering of Union forts.

As the war dragged on, the capital turned even more into a city under siege. Julia had awakened to reveille and retired to the sound of taps. The reverberation of drums, along with an endless supply of trains either coming or going, seemingly filled every moment in between.

Union troops by the thousands crowded the streets, setting up their supply depots and camps. The banner of black smoke created by the profusion of campfires seemed to hang over the area by day, and the smell of it was inescapable even at night.

The month before Julia left, all had been in a great flurry over the Lion of the South, who had reportedly ridden to the very outskirts of the defenses and captured an entire regiment. How he had accomplished such a feat, no one understood. How indeed had a Confederate soldier—as the Lion was rumored to be—gotten through the lines? Still more perplexing...how had he gotten *out* with an entire contingent of Union troops in tow without a shot being fired?

Dressing hurriedly, Julia plaited her hair to the side, and crept out of her room. She moved quietly as she made her way through the hallway and down the wide, curving staircase. There had been no sign of Landon since their initial meeting, and she wished to avoid an encounter with him now. Pausing once to listen, she heard nothing except some low voices and singing coming from the kitchen in the back. The hum of an active household had a soothing effect that Julia found reassuring and comforting.

Passing through a dimly lit hallway, she entered her favorite room in the house and stood motionless in the doorway, her gaze moving fondly from one familiar object to another. It was an appealing space that displayed good taste and money, yet it was inviting and welcoming.

Floor-to-ceiling bookcases were built into the walls on one side, while light flooded into the room from the large windows adorned with sweeping damask curtains. Julia gazed musingly at the solid walls and massive timbers that represented strength and solidity more than elegance or refinement.

Her thoughts drifted back to the carefree days spent here, and the vibrant memories she had clung to while in Washington. A thousand incidents, pleasing to remember, flooded her mind—roused by the mere act of standing in this room.

As her gaze fell upon the large sofa, a smile formed on her lips. She recalled the many cozy mornings spent curled up there, close to the fire. The twins, Sawyer and Sallie, always sat on one side of the massive couch, with Julia's brother Gideon in the middle, and she and Landon on the other side. She remembered how brilliantly the winter sunbeams sparkled through the curtains onto the mantel, and how inviting it appeared when adorned with pine garlands at Christmas.

The fireplace always seemed to be generously filled with logs, radiating a glow that wrapped the room in warmth. Laughter and joy filled the space to capacity. Relationships she'd assumed would last forever had been forged.

Julia's gaze drifted to the large window and wide sill on which she used to sit and daydream. Walking to it, she ran her hand along the dark wood, rough with age and full of sweet recollections. Then she turned her attention to the view outside, so welcoming to her tired spirit.

The Virginia countryside was beautiful, in spite of the un-willingness of winter to release her clinging grasp. Gently rolling hills, and trees ready to burst with their spring attire, greeted her hungry eyes. The gardens in front of her budded with the prom-ise of new life, and the small lake beyond was shiny as glass. The blue expanse of cloudless sky made her think of long ago, when her pulse had thrilled with the magical fullness of life.

And a good life it had been. Despite his wealth and position in society, Mr. Graham had put few restrictions on young Julia when she and her brother came to live with them. Sallie was his little girl—his princess—and Julia was what he'd called his *untamable*.

Those thoughts made her wonder if there had ever been any-thing but a dazzling sun shining overhead, and birds singing mu-sically in the trees. Like a perfect fairytale, she recalled no shadow, no sorrow, no burden ever crossing her pathway. Those days had come and gone, filling her with pleasant memories and joy, leaving no dark spot behind.

Could it have been real? Was it possible to have experienced nothing but happy, carefree days spent in infinite peace? No evil sight or sound to break the spell? Could providence have shielded her so tenderly in her younger years—only to balance those days with the torment of the present?

Julia closed her eyes and reveled in the warmth of the brilliant sunlight on her face, trying to cast away the dark thoughts that threatened. She was safe here. Happy. She sighed heavily. She was glad she had come.

"Enjoying the view?"

Julia whirled around, and then nervously smoothed out her dress as a way to conceal the initial sensation coursing through her, which was equal parts joy and distress.

"M-Mr. Graham, you startled me."

Landon's bold, intimidating gaze assessed her frankly. "That doesn't answer my question."

"Oh…yes," she finally responded. "And the memories."

His gaze locked on hers, just for a moment, but long enough for her to notice the bloodshot, tired eyes. He looked exhausted, as if he'd been up for days. Or perhaps it was just an unspoken pain that made him appear so somber and solemn.

Though taken aback by his cold indifference, Julia did not fail to notice the impressive change in his appearance from their first meeting. He was clean-shaven today, and impeccably dressed in knee-high leather boots and a crisp, white shirt.

In fact, he seemed so very proper now, so formal and refined, she found it hard to imagine the young man galloping over the countryside and teasing her endlessly.

"Mr. Graham? Come now, Julia. That is what you used to call my father. Why so formal?" He strode across the room toward a serving board and reached for a crystal decanter in the back. His movements were just as Julia remembered them—effortless, poised, measured. Yet now his hand had a slight tremor in it, barely perceptible, yet noticeable to her.

"You said you were thinking of the sweet, bygone days at Welbourne. Surely, we are well enough acquainted that you may call me Landon."

Julia wasn't sure how to respond. Instead of feeling relaxed and at ease with an old friend as she had imagined she would, she felt intimidated by his attitude and demeanor. She had set her hopes on confiding in Landon—and those hopes were now dashed.

"The past is something I will always remember with plea-sure…and gratitude—"

"*But...*" He continued the sentence for her and cocked his head questioningly as if fully expecting a qualification.

"But...it's just that...well, things have changed since then."

"Oh, yes. Things have certainly changed." Landon removed an ornate stopper from the decanter he held and sighed heavily, like a release of pain. "Sawyer is dead." The carafe clanked against the edge of his glass multiple times as he tried to pour a drink. "Dear Sawyer is dead," he repeated under his breath, and then, seeming to remember that someone else was in the room, turned toward Julia and held up the bottle. "I'm sorry. Something for you?"

When she shook her head, he held up his glass. "No? Well, cheers." He downed the entire contents with an unsteady hand and then closed one eye in a grimace as the fluid went down. "In any event, you may call me, Landon."

A tumble of confused thoughts and feelings assailed Julia as she caught a glimpse of the tortured dullness of loss in his dark depths. She remembered a young man with piercing eyes, one whose commanding presence and manner inspired both fear and respect in everyone he met. She abruptly turned back to the window. "As you wish." She heard the glass hit the table behind her as Landon set it down.

Strangely enough, the unexpected turn of events did not elicit pity or regret. It made her angry. Yes, the loss of Sawyer was a tragedy, but thousands of families in the South had suffered a similar fate. Perhaps Landon wasn't the strong, faultless man she had conjured in her mind. The man she remembered—or at least the man she had imagined and dreamed of—would never fall prey to alcohol. The blow of his brother's death would have only made him stronger.

"I imagine the loss of Sawyer hit you hard, too." He was

suddenly right behind her again, though she hadn't heard his approach. "You and my brother spent a great deal of time together." His words were gentle enough, but his manner and his voice were official, cold.

Julia smiled as she thought about the young, rough-and-tumble boy who had been her playmate as a child. Sawyer was gregarious and devilish, enjoyed being a clown. She remembered him as one of the happiest, frolicking, carefree young men she had ever met. His personality, and his light hair and freckles, made him the exact opposite of the man standing behind her.

Although closer in age to Sawyer than Landon, Julia had preferred Landon's company. He had an undeniable force of energy about him, and a patient ability to overlook and accept Julia's wildness. Then again, how could he not? He was the most untamed man she'd ever met.

"I suppose that is what you were daydreaming about when I came in." Landon stared out the window as he spoke as if it pained him to talk about his brother. "Those untroubled days you spent with Sawyer and Sallie, roaming the fields and woods."

The tone of his voice caused Julia to turn around and study him more closely. The expression on his face was one of somber thoughtfulness, and it confused her.

Julia remembered Sawyer with fondness, but it wasn't Sawyer who had taught her how to ride a strong horse or climb a tree. And it wasn't Sawyer who'd been her protector, hugging her when she needed it, but pushing her most of the time to accomplish things she didn't think she was capable of. No, it was Landon who had watched over her with the most tender and patient care.

As the eldest son, Landon carried a heavy weight of responsibility on his shoulders. He traveled with his father on business trips, and took an active role in running the plantation—duties that made him quiet, sensitive, and wise, even as a youth. Julia loved his composed, unruffled demeanor, and he seemed to enjoy her wild, fervent, unrestrained manner, in return.

For a moment, Julia almost wished she were a child again, and could run into Landon's arms for comfort and security. Yet from the looks of him, he needed someone to lean on more than she did.

"You must think me the devil himself," he said, staring broodingly at the floor. "Seeing me like this."

"Does it matter what I think?"

This seemed to stop him. He paused and stared at her with an expression that was a mixture of tenderness and regret. "There was a time when it would have."

Julia thought she heard the slightest catch in his voice, but he turned away to revisit the serving board.

The words hit Julia hard. Not because he'd disclosed he didn't care what she thought, but because he admitted that he once had.

"You may have noticed, I don't have interest in much of anything at the moment."

"Yes. But I don't understand why."

"You don't?" The decanter hit the glass as he poured another drink. "Sawyer is dead. I was his commander."

When he turned to her, she saw the raw hurt that glittered in his eyes.

"The two are not necessarily connected. Had someone else been in command, he would still be gone."

"Perhaps." He paused with his glass halfway to his lips. "But we can never know for sure, can we?" He emptied the glass in one swallow and then stared at it contemplatively as if it held all the answers. "I would gladly accept a physical wound of the body—in fact I yearn for that type of pain." He raised his gaze to meet hers.

"But not this. Not Sawyer."

The heartrending look of grief in his eyes told Julia more than any words and caused her heart to hammer violently. She didn't know what to say. What *could* she say? Not only had he lost his beloved brother, he felt *responsible*. No wonder it had affected him so deeply.

Julia fought for the right words to soothe his conscience, but a sudden rustle of fabric coming through the doorway interrupted the conversation.

Chapter 8

"Look what a courier brought this morning." Sallie stood just inside the room, holding a piece of paper high in the air.

"What is it?"

"It's news of another successful exploit of the Lion and his men—just last night. Oh, you just won't believe what he did."

Landon turned his back. "Truly? Must we hear of that enigmatic fellow?"

"I do believe you are jealous, Landon."

"Jealous?" He walked toward the fireplace. "I'm not sure the man exists. He is simply the figment of multiple imaginations."

"Oh, he exists." Sallie's voice turned scornful. "And a more courageous, intrepid, valiant man has never been born." She held the piece of paper to her breast and twirled around in a circle. "Never has so much been achieved against odds so terrible. The world has never known truer greatness or a character more pure and chivalrous."

"What did he do?" Julia took a step toward Sallie.

"You just won't believe it. It doesn't seem possible." She ran her gaze over the paper again. "It says that almost two dozen Confederate prisoners escaped from a camp. The Yankees sent out the cavalry immediately but found no trace of them."

"Oh, dear. Then how do they know it was the Lion?"

"Truly, Julia." Sallie rolled her eyes expressively. "Who else would attempt such a feat?"

"But did he leave his mark as he so often does?"

"It says here, the only thing found was a scrap of paper."

"I knew it." Julia smiled and stared at the chandelier overhead. "No doubt it included a winged lion."

"No." Sallie shook her head. "Scrawled on the paper were the words: *1 Peter 5:8.*"

"I don't recall the verse. What does it say?"

Both women ran over to the family Bible and began flipping through the pages. "Here it is."

Julia marked the spot with her finger. "It says, *Be sober, be vigilant; because your adversary the devil, as a roaring lion, walketh about, seeking whom he may devour.*"

The two of them fell silent, and then Sallie whispered, "Oh, how romantic. It *was* the Lion. The hero of hundreds of battles and thousands of hearts."

"Come now, girls. You don't believe in this fairytale, do you?"

Sallie squinted at her brother as she held the paper up and shook it at him. "The Lion is not a fairytale. He is a man of flesh and blood." She wrapped her arms around herself and closed her eyes. "Such a man he must be to have attempted such an act as this. No one will ever be his superior."

She came out of her trance and gazed at Julia. "They say he's wealthy. Perhaps from an old, aristocratic family."

"Wealthy? Is that so?" Landon's brow furrowed. "Wherever did you hear such a thing?"

"I don't know. Everyone has a theory as to what he's like or whom he might resemble."

"It would be more reasonable to believe he is a farmer's son or a lowly merchant." Landon spoke in a grave voice.

"How so?" Sallie's brows knitted in confusion.

"Money and titles are hereditary." He lifted his glass to his lips but paused before drinking. "Brains and courage are not."

"What do *you* think of this mythical Lion character, Julia?" Sallie's voice remained animated, seemingly determined to ignore Landon.

"Yes. Have you ever heard of such a tale as this?" Landon turned to Julia. "Do the people in Washington City believe in this storybook fellow?"

"Oh, yes. I've heard talk of him and admire him very much."

"Admire him? For what? His courage? His craftiness?" Landon's penetrating gaze swept over her.

Julia took a moment to think about it. "Of course, his courage is commendable, and his craftiness most praiseworthy, but there is more to it than that."

"Go on.'"

"The fact that he operates under the cloak of anonymity is a most admirable trait. No one knows his name or what he looks like, yet he freely risks his life for others." Julia sighed. "Yes, it is character that tells—"

"Character?" Landon sounded bored by the conversation. "You mean, like courage?"

"No," Julia said, shaking her head. "Many a man has that. What I mean is a firm, steady substance of soul. Being kindhearted as much as courageous. The Lion demonstrates concern and compassion in the duty he performs."

"A bit like St. Nicholas at Christmas, spreading joy and goodwill," Landon retorted with a sarcastic tone.

"True." Julia ignored the jab. "He has given everyone the gift of hope, a treasure far more powerful to the South than weapons or supplies."

Julia could only dream of what the man must be like to possess all the qualities necessary to undertake such feats. She was familiar enough with military leadership to recognize that a great commander had to be a genius for detail—and not just in fighting battles. A great leader had to be wise in the selection of his men and skilled in reading his adversary's mind and character.

On top of that, the Lion's actions proved he possessed other rare qualities of heart and soul—those with which all truly great men are endowed. Honor. Selflessness. Generosity. Patriotism.

"Indeed. Quite a *noble* fellow." Landon's tone sounded mocking and derisive, not sincere in the least.

"But he *must* be," Sallie exclaimed. "To have men follow him on such dangerous and perilous excursions, sworn to secrecy, and accepting duties that might cost their very lives."

Landon laughed, but it sounded forced. "Surely, there are more important things to concern yourself with than this imaginary man."

"Yes, like breakfast." Julia turned to Sallie and motioned with her eyes toward the door, hoping her friend would take the hint. Then, she turned back to Landon. "Will you join us?" She only asked the question in order to be polite, but desperately hoped he would decline.

"Breakfast?" Landon glanced at the clock on the mantel. "I've been up for hours and have already eaten. You girls run along."

"Wait." Sallie stamped her foot in agitation. "As to your earlier question—yes, there is something more important to concern ourselves with." She turned toward Julia. "The packet also included an invitation." Sallie brought the paper closer to read the communication aloud, although it was clear she had already studied it so long, she knew it by heart.

"The Chancefords humbly request your attendance at a charity horse race on Saturday next, to be followed by a ball." She stopped reading and then did a jig across the room. "Do you know how long it's

been since I attended a ball—or a horserace for that matter?" She grabbed Julia's arms and swung her around. "It will be so much fun! You'll be able to meet everyone."

"Meet them? Don't I already know most of them?"

"Mostly, I suppose. But it's been six years. Surely, they have changed."

"There are definitely *fewer* of them since you were here last." Landon's voice sounded solemn and cold.

Both girls had forgotten he was in the room.

"Landon, what a terrible thing to say!" Sallie whirled around and admonished her brother. "Why must you be so insidiously and constantly cruel?"

"I'm merely stating a fact, Sallie." He shrugged indifferently. "Lots of our boys went away and never came home." He regarded Julia with an expression of stone. "And those who remain might be suspicious of a young woman who suddenly reappears after living among those who *caused* the untimely disappearance of so many good men."

"Landon. Stop this instant." Sallie stomped her foot. "I do not like what you are insinuating."

There was a short pause as Landon took a sip of his drink. "Still, it bears consideration."

The icy sarcasm and unfriendly behavior of a man Julia thought she knew—and knew well—caught her off guard. She quickly lowered her lashes to hide the hurt, but his words instantly extinguished any spark of hope that there might be a reconciliation between them. She stood silently, staring at the floor in cold shock, waiting for an idea or clue regarding how to react. He was a complete stranger to her.

Finally, too confused and humiliated to say anything, she picked up her skirt and fled the room.

Chapter 9

"Are you happy now?" Sallie stood with her hands on her hips, eyeing her brother angrily.

"Do I look happy?" Landon raised the glass to his lips.

"No. You look miserable. And you seem intent on making everyone in the household the same." She let out her breath in exasperation. "You are the wealthiest man in the region, yet you insist on being wretched and unhappy."

"Being wealthy does not rescue one from misfortune, dear sister," he responded forcefully. "Surely, you are aware of that."

"I still don't understand what would possess you to say such a thing."

"And I don't understand what would possess *you* to bring her here."

Sallie gasped. "What do you mean? We met unexpectedly at an affair in Alexandria after six long years. Why would I not?"

"Are you sure it was *unexpected?*"

"Landon Graham, I don't even know you." Sallie's face turned red with emotion. "You are suspicious for the mere reason she was forced to live with relatives in Washington? Obligated to leave with an aunt and uncle she'd never met, and who didn't even know she existed until Mother contacted them? Is that justification enough to turn our backs on her? She, who's been like a sister to me?"

"She has reached her majority. She does not need permission to leave a place she finds objectionable." The tensing of his jaw betrayed his deep annoyance. "One might reason that she did not find Washington disagreeable at all."

"She has friends there now. Ties. She could not just leave."

"Many fled at the first sign of war. Thousands more after Manassas."

This time, Sallie simply laughed. "I would say I believe you are tipsy, but there is no need." She lowered her gaze to his glass with a sullen look of disgust and then raised it again.

"Do you have something else you wish to say?" Landon seemed to have read her look.

"I shouldn't need to say anything. Everyone in Virginia knows you have a drinking problem."

Landon put his head back and laughed majestically. "I beg your pardon. A drinking problem? Me?" He took an unsteady step forward. and held the glass he had recently refilled out for her to see. "Watch. I'll prove to you once and for all that I do not have any drinking problem." With that, he lifted the glass to his lips and emptied its contents once again. "See?" He gazed at her, smiling mischievously. "No problem drinking, whatsoever."

Sallie stamped her foot in agitation. "I'm serious, Landon. How dare you think our Julia is not loyal to Virginia. That is preposterous."

"*Our dear Julia* has more blood relatives on the northern side of the Mason-Dixon Line than this one. How can you be so sure?"

"That is outrageous. Her own brother serves in the Confederate army. He, who is dearer to her than life itself. She would *never* do anything to put him in harm's way. To infer that is an affront to her Southern background."

"Their ancestral roots are not Southern, only their upbringing. Here."

"I don't care what you think of her, Landon, but you must stop humiliating me in my own home and in front of my guest."

"Is that an order?" He raised one eyebrow as a glint of humor crossed his face.

In response, Sallie crossed her arms and turned her back on him in exasperation.

"You are too trusting, dear sister. It's been years since you last saw her. People change."

Sallie glanced at him over her shoulder. "Oh, yes. I know people *change*." She seemed ready to say something more but instead bit her lip and glared.

The insinuation, coupled with her silence, caused the humor to fade from Landon's expression, more so than any words could have done. "You have no right to bring her into my home without permission."

Sallie whirled around. "*Your* home? Is this not my home, as well?"

"You know what I mean. I cannot afford to have my reputation sullied by a—"

"Surely, I am not the first to inform you that your reputation has already been sullied beyond repair." Sallie was sorry the instant the words left her mouth, but when she saw the pathetic look on her brother's face at her cruel comment, she was doubly remorseful. "I'm sorry. I didn't mean that."

Landon stared straight ahead as if unable to look her in the eyes, but she could see his chest rising and falling as if he were suppressing a response.

She walked over and took his hand. "I'm sorry, Landon. Please forgive me."

In an instant, just like the Landon of old, he reestablished his control. "What is there to forgive, little sister? You speak the truth."

Sallie made a desperate attempt to change the mood. "It is so beautiful outside, and I have missed Welbourne so. Will you walk with me to the lake like we used to do?"

Chapter 10

With a gallant bow, Landon held out his arm and walked with Sallie out to the wide back veranda. She paused and took a deep breath. "Nowhere on Earth smells as pleasant as Welbourne."

"You may be a little prejudiced in your observation, Sallie." Landon's whole attitude had changed. His dark eyes were glowing, and he appeared relaxed and content at having his sister home with him.

The Graham children had flourished as a tight-knit family, thanks to a kind but stern father who kept their cold and domineering mother in check, when he wasn't traveling on business. Since Landon's birth came some six years before the arrival of the twins, Sallie and Sawyer, he had grown to become more protector than brother—and in later years, their guardian and disciplinarian.

As a result, Sallie had become accustomed to her wiser, older sibling coming to the rescue. No matter the circumstance or dilemma, she relied on Landon to step in and expeditiously take care of the problem. Sometimes, he accomplished this through tact and common sense. Other times, by his strength or diplomacy. In any event, he was continuously there and always knew what to do.

Perhaps that was why it was so distressing he could not cope with the tragedy that had befallen the family and the country at large. Instead of being a caring and comforting brother, he was now a detached and aloof stranger, seeming not to care about anything or anyone—including himself.

Sallie pushed away the unhappy thoughts and looped her arm with Landon's while leaning her head against his shoulder, just as she used to do as a child. The months of separation while she had been away visiting friends had caused a deep fissure of distance between them. The same intense devotion was still there on both sides, but each had now built a wall the other dared not penetrate.

The war had constructed that barrier, and it was that which now dictated what they dared talk about. Sallie could not speak to her brother about the pain in her heart over the loss of her twin. She knew it would only cause Landon more torment. And to discuss anything that related to the conflict was also out of the question. The political aspect of the country changed almost daily, the rumors and stories so vicious—and often fictitious—made it wise not to comment one way or the other.

Silence stretched between them as they strolled across the wide expanse of lawn, arms linked together, both having so much to say but neither having the ability to communicate it. As they approached the shores of the great lake, a gaggle of geese glided soundlessly through the water away from them, creating ripples that sparkled like millions of jewels in the sun.

When they reached the far side of the body of water, Sallie turned and gazed at the home behind her. Built by her ancestors four generations earlier, the house stood three stories high and contained four chimneys and sixteen fireplaces of various sizes. The walls were more than two feet in thickness, and most of the windows ran from ceiling to floor. Those that did not, had wide, welcoming sills to perch upon.

Surrounding the mansion were a number of outbuildings, all

orderly and neat, and further beyond lay gardens and orchards encompassing twelve acres. Near the lake and off to the east was a little strip of land covered with a grove of live oaks, a spot known as the park. The entire property was welcoming and attractive, especially this morning with the white paint of the main house glowing in the sun, and the rest of nature seeming to sparkle with new life.

"So, how did you like your time away from Welbourne?" Landon's voice sounded sincere and more like the brother Sallie remembered, as he strolled beside her. "You are probably much too sophisticated for the slow way of life here now."

"I admit, I loved traveling, but I missed you and—" She almost said *Sawyer*, but changed it at the last moment. "—the house, and Spencer, and Aunt Mazie, and everyone."

She pulled him to a stop. "Truly, Landon. I missed you so much. I missed this... Walks with you. Talking."

"I missed you, too, little sis." He looked her up and down. "Although it appears I can't call you that anymore. You're much too grown up."

"I don't feel grown up at all." She held onto his arm and stared at the ground. "It's so hard...the war...and all the pain it's caused." She brushed a tear away before he could see it.

"Perhaps the tide will turn."

She lifted her head, took a deep breath, and sighed. "Are you saying you believe in the Lion, after all? That the course of the war is changing?" She gazed into eyes that seemed to be filled with faith and optimism. Coming from Landon, the words—and the assurance in them—meant something.

"I'm saying you don't need to worry yourself about such things as the war. You are safe here at Welbourne."

"That's what I told Julia."

At mention of the young woman's name, Landon stiffened as if he'd been struck, not even bothering to conceal his reaction. "I wish you had told me you were bringing her here."

"But why? She was so excited to see you. I wanted it to be a surprise."

"Things are different." He bent down, picked up a stone, and sent it skimming across the water. "Those days are behind us."

"Why can't we pretend it's the same as it was back then?" Sallie pouted. "We had so much fun. And you have to admit, you and Julia were very close. She followed your every move." She laughed under her breath. "I dare say she idolized you."

A strange look passed across Landon's face before he spoke. "She was a child."

"She was almost sixteen when she left." Sallie stared at her brother curiously. "Hardly a child."

"You have me on that point," he responded coldly. "She was old enough to make up her own mind, and she chose to leave— while I was away on a business trip, I might add. Never to be heard from again...until now."

"But you've spoken to Gideon. He explained it all to you... that Mother arranged for them to leave when Father fell ill, and you were away. When their aunt and uncle arrived to pick them up, what choice did they have?"

"Yes. At the time, of course, it had all the aspects of an innocent and unavoidable situation. Now, she is part of the very fabric of society that we are at war with."

"You needn't be so harsh. Mother told her to go, and she went. Imagine how she dreaded the idea of living in the city among strangers when she loved living here so. Poor girl. I pity her. She seemed so lonely there."

"Lonely? She had plenty of suitors, I'm sure." There was a

touch of curiosity in his tone.

"Yes. Her beauty was much admired—or at least much re-marked on." Sallie was silent for a moment. "But I don't think she liked it there."

"Why do you say that?"

Sallie shrugged. "She doesn't talk about it, but she seems sad. Dejected. I get the feeling she lost her one true love."

Landon bent down and picked up another stone, which he studied a moment before sending it across the water. "Well, I see they were successful in teaching her how to wear shoes."

Sallie smiled at his attempt to lighten the mood. "Yes. She was a bit of a tomboy, wasn't she? I remember Mother throwing up her hands in complete exasperation whenever Julia came gallop-ing down the lane with you, her pigtails flying."

For a moment, Landon seemed lost in the recollection. His eyes softened, and the muscles in his face relaxed as his attention focused on something out over the water.

Sallie reached for his sleeve and touched his arm gently. "You don't really suspect her of anything, do you, Landon? Not our Julia."

His eyes darkened. "Perhaps *suspect* is too strong of a word."

"But you do not trust her."

He stared over her shoulder with a solemn look of torment. "My brother is dead. Murdered by an enemy that did not have the decency to return his body." He returned his attention to Sallie, and his eyes were aflame with emotion. "No, I do not trust some-one who has lived among them and has done nothing to escape from their evil clutches during these long years of war."

"But she had no means! No—"

Landon held up his hand to stop her. "Even Gideon has dis-tanced himself from her."

Sallie took a step back and shook her head, refusing to believe what Landon was telling her. "He is an officer in the Confederate cavalry, and she resides in Washington. I'm sure it's by necessity, not intention. Surely, he...surely, he has no reason to distrust her."

"I can think of a number of reasons." Landon swept his coat back and stuffed his hands deep into his pockets as he paced upon a patch of lush grass. "It is my understanding that at the outbreak of the war, she was urged by friends to leave the city—as any number of other women with Southern sympathies did without hesitation." He stopped and stared at Sallie. "She was even offered an escort south directly after Manassas, but resolved to remain; apparently, with no regard for her own reputation or those of her Southern acquaintances."

"But perhaps she felt she had nowhere to go. Nowhere to turn. I feel she is somehow in grave trouble."

Landon scoffed at the idea. "That is nonsense. She knew she would be welcome at Welbourne."

"But she's not welcome," Sallie murmured. "You've made that quite clear."

"It's different now. I don't want a stranger here to meddle in our affairs."

"A stranger? How can you be so cold? *I* was the one who insisted she come. I thought it would help you—"

Landon's jaw tightened. "No matter your intentions. I must protest her presence."

Sallie crossed her arms and eyed him angrily. "If you feel so strongly about it, why did you allow me to go visiting? I was a stone's throw from Washington."

"I wanted you to be safe. I was afraid the war would come here...perhaps it was a mistake." His voice cracked a little, but then it turned angry. "Anyway, you were only there for a few months. She's shown no inclination to leave Washington, even after the long years of war. Apparently, she enjoys the high-society life."

"Not Julia. She's not like that."

That is what *I* thought," Landon said glumly. "But popularity and power can go to one's head."

"What do you mean?"

"Come now. You must have been made aware of her status in the city. Her family and so-called friends have associations with cabinet officials and military officers. She is the dinner guest of diplomats and judges, and she mingles socially with everyone from newspapermen and merchants, to lawyers and bankers."

Sallie shook her head as if to stop him, but he continued.

"The house where she resides has recently been occupied by a number of Federal officers. She *lives* with them."

Sallie came to a stop. "How do you know all of this?"

"Her uncle is an employee of the very government sent out to destroy us." Landon looked away. "It's common knowledge."

Sallie swallowed hard and studied a cloud drifting overhead. "Still, I pity her. She was teased mercilessly for her poor means, was always made to feel inadequate, and constantly called a backwoods child. I think that is why she distanced herself from the required etiquette, revolted against the rules, and spent so much time with you."

"Yes, a child of hazard, blindly blown about by the wind of circumstance."

Sallie couldn't tell if her brother was being sincere or sarcastic, so she ignored him altogether. "After being treated like an outsider for so long, I suppose it's possible she relishes the attention now."

"Believe me, Sallie. I wish it were not so." Landon's jaw tightened and a look of pain descended upon his countenance. "The

Julia I knew would not wish to remain in such a place and under such circumstances, but the facts are the facts. Every day was a choice. Every delay a confirmation."

"But…"

He held up his hand. "Here's another fact. Her uncle's brother-in-law is in the Treasury. *His* brother works in the Department of War, and a nephew has joined a New York cavalry unit."

"What has that to do with any—?"

"And then out of the blue, you run into her…by *accident* you say."

"Yes. I had no idea—"

"At Mrs. Dupree's house in Alexandria."

"It seemed quite natural. Mrs. Dupree teaches music now that her husband is gone. She invited some girls who were visiting to attend a recital."

"But you had never met this woman, this Mrs. Dupree before, is that not right?"

"That's correct, but a friend of mine—"

"And Julia just happened to be invited, as well." He interrupted her again.

"Yes. Of course. Apparently, she is well acquainted with the widow."

A nerve in Landon's cheek twitched. "Interesting."

"Why is that interesting? Mrs. Dupree simply moves in the same social circles as Julia's family."

"That is a convenient explanation. But it's interesting because Mrs. Dupree's son is sitting in one of our prisons."

Sallie tilted her head. "I didn't know she had a son. So he is a soldier?"

"Not really." Landon bent down and snagged a piece of tall grass. "He's a spy."

Sallie came to a stop. "A spy? What do you mean?"

"I mean, he was caught pretending to be a merchant in one of our camps. Someone got suspicious and followed him as he tried to get back through the lines—"

"But you can't be sure he was trying to do anything!" This time, it was Sallie who interrupted.

"They discovered enough on his person to know. There is no question about it. So you see, that is the type of *friend* Julia Dandridge now has. And yet she unexpectedly meets you at such a place, and you help her obtain a pass to accompany you here? Did you ever stop to think that perhaps *you* were the only way she could travel back into the Confederacy?"

"No." Sallie shook her head so hard her curls flew back and forth. "I arranged to travel with her, but she already had a pass to get through the lines."

Landon came to a sudden stop, and his entire body stiffened. He remained facing straight ahead, not bothering to look at his sister. "I beg your pardon?"

"I said—"

"She already had a pass?" He didn't allow her to finish and now stared broodingly back at the house, his black eyes mere slits. "Signed by whom?"

"I don't know. I didn't ask. I—" Sallie covered her eyes and shook her head. "Oh, this awful war has left me so confused."

"Yes, the war." Landon stood with his hands thrust deeply into his pockets as if to keep them still as he continued to stare pensively back at the manor. "Enemies without, and traitors within. Friend and foe alike disguised."

Landon had murmured the last words so softly, Sallie did not quite hear them—but something about his mood warned her not to question him further. Her brother was usually a reserved and quiet man, but those who witnessed his anger were not inclined to rouse it again. "I'm sorry. I did not know these things."

Throwing his arm over her shoulder as if the entire conversation had been forgotten, Landon gave her a squeeze. "And why should you? You have other things to worry about besides the fate of our country. Now, tell me about your latest suitors."

Sallie giggled, glad he was back to the charming man she remembered so well. "Who says I have any suitors?"

"Of course, you do." He began to walk with his arm still hanging over her shoulder. "I can think of at least one right now."

She regarded him with a curious smile. "You can? And who might that be?"

"Thomas Cunningham. He asks about you every time I see him."

Sallie diverted her eyes. "He's probably just trying to be polite."

"No. I believe he's completely smitten."

"I look forward to seeing him again," Sallie said noncommittally. "And everyone in the neighborhood."

"Just so you know, your beaus will have to meet my approval."

"Then I fear I will never marry." Sallie's brown eyes sparkled with humor. "You will never think anyone good enough for your sister."

"True. You will live here with me as a spinster for the rest of your life." He walked a few steps in silence. "It *is* just the two of us now."

"How strange that is." Sallie shook her head. "I thought that by inviting Julia, it would make the house feel more like old times...when we were all together and happy." She paused and tried again to gauge Landon's mindset. "I hope you are not too angry with me."

"I'm not angry, but you have to understand we can't just pick up where we left off." He bent down and swiped a piece of grass from the bank, which he then stuck between his teeth. "We have to start anew."

Sallie nodded in understanding. "Very well, but can we at least endeavor to make her feel welcome while she is here?"

"If that is your desire, dear sister, I will try."

Sallie grasped his arm again and laid her head against it. "Thank you, Landon."

"It's good to have you home, Sallie."

She could tell by the deep, tremulous tone of his voice he meant it.

Chapter 11

Julia stood at the window and watched in painful silence as the brother and sister talked with animated gestures while strolling around the lake. Although she could not hear the words, she could guess the topic, making her wonder if she should just start packing. The last thing she wished to do was cause consternation in the household of Welbourne.

This was a sanctuary to her, a place of refuge, the only true home she had ever known. But now she realized she'd been naïve to think she could come back here and be accepted...just pick up where she had left off. Since the war had begun, it seemed like no place on Earth was safe or not full of turmoil. Everything had been turned upside down.

Completely worn out by excitement and anxiety, Julia sank into a chair and leaned on the windowsill, her chin resting in the palm of one hand as she gazed thoughtfully out over the wide expanse of field, forest, and stream. The sun rested on the wooded crests that rose from the back of the orchard, casting shadows on the wide lawn. Other than the droning flight of insects and the soft chirp of birds, all was silent and peaceful.

It was so different from the place she'd left. No trumpet calls or thunder of cannon. And no dinner parties. No afternoon teas. No pretending to be something she was not.

The endless time she'd spent away in utter solitude seemed

like an eternity. Even though she'd been surrounded by relatives and acquaintances, attended parties, and socialized with many of Washington's most elite, she'd been utterly alone.

Julia took a deep breath and sighed as her gaze continued to follow the man outside. In many ways, at least from this distance, Landon had not changed at all. He was still calm and composed, with the same dark, brooding, imperturbable eyes she remembered so well. He still moved with fluid ease and strength, conveying the confidence of a man indifferent to danger. Yet something about him was lacking, making him appear subdued, helpless, and lost. Perhaps it was his brother's soul crossing too soon into the dark mystery of eternity that had caused the profound change in him.

Julia's gazed rested on him with a kind of fascination and growing sympathy. As a child, she had been devoted to Landon... worshiped him with an adoration she knew would horrify him if he understood its intensity. Worse yet, those feelings of high regard had only increased over her long absence. She had thought it only natural. *Absence makes the heart grow fonder.* But Landon had made it clear there was no reciprocation of those sentiments.

Then again, perhaps it was not *he* who had changed—just her memory of him. Even when Landon was young, he'd rarely manifested any outward emotion, and seldom felt the need to speak. He didn't judge, and he didn't condemn. He just accepted her.

Despite their difference in age, he'd been gentle and patient, yet demanding and unyielding at the same time. It had been Landon's hand Julia had so often sought for comfort—firm and strong, and always there when she needed it. She missed the person she had once known, and wondered if he was gone forever... or if he had actually existed. This man was different. Unfamiliar. Bitter. Cold.

Her eyes continued to follow the dashing figure as he skipped a stone across the lake, just as he used to do in his youth. Julia felt her breath catch. Was the sensation in her chest caused by her heart breaking? Or healing?

Laying her head down on her arms, Julia forced her thoughts away from Landon to her only sibling, Gideon. Their parents had died when he was still a youth and she a child, so they shared an almost inseparable bond. Gideon, some five years her senior, had stepped in as father, brother, and friend, strengthening their already close relationship.

He never treated her like a bothersome youngster, but rather confided in her, helped her, and cared for her, especially when they were utterly alone the first few days after their mother's death. Julia had cherished his brotherly companionship, which was constant, and his love, which was boundless.

How surreal it all seemed now. Were the memories of her time at Welbourne real? Or a fantasy she had conjured to get through her dark, dismal days in Washington?

With both of their parents gone, she and Gideon had become children of neglect and poverty. When Landon's father saw the squalor in which they lived, he'd generously taken them under his wing, moving them from a small, two-room cabin to the magnificence of Welbourne.

As Julia watched Landon and Sallie, now walking arm-in-arm, her heart ached for her own brother. *Where are you, Gideon?*

She had not heard from him in months, and hadn't seen him in a year. A part of her was missing, and she could not rest until she got it back. Deep inside, she knew he was not dead. She could still feel his spirit. But where was he, and why had he not contacted her for so very long?

Julia sighed wistfully. She'd returned to Welbourne for a number of reasons, one of which was to find answers. But Landon's reaction to her arrival had not gone as expected. She dared not question him more fully, or let him know how worried she was for Gideon's safety. He would only use her estrangement as a reason to be suspicious.

A tear made it halfway down her cheek before she wiped it away. The picture-perfect past she had hoped to rediscover was not to be. Her uncertainty about returning had been well founded. The war, and Sawyer's tragic death, had changed everything—more than she had even imagined.

When Julia's gaze fell on her own reflection in the glass pane, she winced at the image. The secrets she had to keep, the demanding duty that had been laid upon her young shoulders in Washington, were taking their toll. She, too, appeared to be growing older by years each day. The tiny lines around her mouth and the dark circles around her eyes told the tale of the heavy burden she carried.

Should she have come in the first place? Should she go now? She yearned for a light to guide her in determining her future course. But no mater how hard she tried, no easy answer appeared before her.

All the years of pent-up agony and grief released within Julia in a great surge of emotion that took her breath away. Sinking to her knees, Julia poured out her feelings in the solitude of the room, her hands clasped together as tightly as her eyes were closed.

I am here, not knowing what destiny awaits me. Show me my path and give me the strength to follow it…Amen.

Chapter 12

General Patrick Carlyle read the dispatch from Detective Thorpe with a disbelieving expression on his face, his mouth agape. When he was finished, he snapped his jaw shut and crumpled the report into a ball before tossing it into the fire.

"Taylor!"

"Yes, sir." A young lieutenant, who had been standing guard outside the door, rushed into the room looking anxious and alarmed.

"Gather my escort and alert the men. We're moving."

"Yes, sir." The man saluted and then paused. "To where, sir?"

"Just inform them we're leaving!"

The lieutenant nodded and ran from the room to obey the order.

General Carlyle paced in front of his large, wooden desk with a scowl on his face. He could not answer the man's question about where they were going because he hadn't figured that out yet. All he knew was that he could not let anything like the Chain Bridge incident, or the terrible event of two nights earlier, happen to *him*. It would end his career. It would ruin his life.

Why, Captain O'Keefe is the laughing stock of the entire army. How could he have fallen so easily for the Lion's treachery? And now, more prison-

ers escaped? Heads will surely roll.

Carlyle paced and simmered, his mind working feverishly to develop a plan to move his men to safety and then capture, if not kill, this worrisome devil. Yes, he was a fighting man and had the reputation—if not the record—to prove it. But Carlyle knew he had to be careful. Think things through. The Lion was maniacal. Worse than that, he was alert, daring, and devoted to his duty.

Dammit. He must be stopped!

In spite of the Union general's experience and capabilities as a commander, the elusive Lion produced in his mind a grave distrust regarding the security of his location. He suddenly felt insecure about where he had placed his advanced troops, and was completely uncertain in regard to adequate protection to his rear.

The damnable Lion had scampered too many times to still be considered a minor nuisance. No, he was a genuine threat and had to be dealt with—in a decisive and meaningful way—from a place of utter safety.

The general's worst fear was that his conniving foe would make a rush past his outpost with thousands of men, all scream-ing that incredible blood-curdling rebel yell at the top of their lungs. His sentries could never stand against such strength and numbers. They could hardly be expected to resist such violence and uncivilized ferocity. These tactics were perfectly barbarous and completely unjustifiable. This type of warfare was sanctioned by neither policy, nor propriety. Carlyle was ready to fight to the last man, of course—but this was too much to ask of anyone.

To ensure that he would not fall prey to the Lion's tactics of swiftness and surprise, outposts had been positioned on every road around his camp, and his men were ordered to be on high alert at all times. As an added precaution, Carlyle besieged the war department with dispatches, urgently entreating them to send reinforcements—immediately and in great numbers.

In his mind, the Lion could have no higher ambition than to capture and carry off a person such as himself to Richmond, and he would sooner be shot than fall into the hands of the Confederacy—so he said.

A few weeks earlier, General Carlyle had been called upon by Detective Thorpe to help devise a plan to stop this antagonistic madman. It now began to play upon Carlyle's mind that the Lion had caught wind of their efforts. Maybe the escape of the prisoners was meant to serve as a warning that the Lion was active and ready to pounce again. Perhaps the treacherous traitor had read the newspapers, and discerned there was an orchestrated effort afoot to paint his escapades in a negative light.

It was no secret, after all, that General Carlyle enjoyed close ties to the most influential newspaper reporters in the region. It was therefore not beyond the realm of possibility the Lion had uncovered the fact that Carlyle and Detective Thorpe were attempting to sway public opinion against the daredevil and his nefarious schemes.

The Lion would no doubt be outraged. Incensed. General Carlyle, more so than anyone else, was in imminent danger and needed to be on guard at all times. But with his sights set on a future political run, it was necessary for the general to display a calm, composed exterior at all times, and demonstrate his superior, intellectual military savvy—even if he must pretend a confidence he did not feel.

The officer threw his shoulders back and stared at the handsome figure he made in a mirror. With his hands on his hips, he moved into a position that would better reflect his glistening high boots and gleaming spurs. "You will not find *me* capitulating to the Lion," he said to the image. "Submission and surrender are not matters to which *I* will comply."

Yet now was not the time for recklessness or rashness. There would surely be ample opportunity to show his own intrepidness and prove his heroism at a later date. No, General Carlyle knew far too much of Southern tenacity to let loose his troops on the enemy's front or be lured into an outright contest. His best course of action was, most assuredly, to lie low.

Only an impetuous, imprudent man would attempt to confront the Lion head-on. Why, everyone knew the Lion fought with a total and reckless disregard for human life; that his vigilance was an instinct that never allowed repose. Like a lightning strike, his men would converge with revolvers flashing, deal their deadly blow, and then disappear, leaving nothing but a memory by the time the Federal forces could react. The notorious renegade had perpetrated a number of atrocities that any civilized race would blush to commit.

Consequently, it would be senseless for Carlyle to initiate an attack upon a man who was so well known for his energy and daring. The Lion would never be taken without a fight to the death. If one were to rely on rumors, the infamous outlaw possessed combat experience and had the perplexing reputation of leading from the front. The loss Carlyle was sure to suffer in an outright offensive move would never justify the gain. The enemy—the Lion—was within Carlyle's reach and his power to conquer, but he would have to use extraordinary guile to snare him.

In the future, the general could perhaps find a fortified position from which to unleash the full fury of his men on the irritable foe. For now, it would be good martial strategy to let the Lion take the initiative and show his hand. It was only a matter of time until he made a mistake.

Of course, the most difficult element of this entire enterprise would be discovering the Lion's identity. So far, the masked marauder had eluded all efforts to ascertain his name—or any of his merry men, for that matter. The reason was simple. Everyone in the region was either devoutly loyal to him—or deathly afraid of him. No community on the face of the planet was as united in thought and feeling as this region of Virginia, and no amount of coercion or threats would convince the citizens of the commonwealth to divulge any secrets.

Carlyle rubbed his chin as he pondered the problem. He needed to find someone who disliked the Lion—or was far enough away so as not to be influenced by him. A difficult proposition indeed, but surely not an impossible one. Money could always be offered to loosen some tongues. The people in Virginia, and all over the South, were starving, destitute.

Carlyle paced and pondered. Then again, it would take a great sum of gold to get anyone to turn against one of their own. Those Southern people seemed to draw strength from danger, and hope from despair. They were emboldened by destruction and remained proud even in defeat.

No, perhaps instead of paying someone, he could *encourage* them. Yes. Someone with ties to the area, who was yet a patriot to the country. Money was not the only way to loosen lips. Beautiful women had long been known to use their ingenuity to swing the pendulum of a nation's fate.

The general stopped in the middle of the room. He knew just the woman for the job. He'd been awed by her beauty and charisma when he met her and had since formed a closer bond. The seeds of this plot had already been planted. It would take but a slight nudge to set it fully in motion.

It seemed logical to use a woman for his ploy since the current military tactics had not yet proved fruitful—nor did it appear they would do so in the near future. How could they? The Lion seldom lingered long in one spot. He arrived with the force of a hurricane wind and left whenever he chose to do so.

This policy of constant activity and enterprise baffled the Union command, but the general simply scoffed at such unreasonable and crude tactics. The Lion's fighting strategy was unjust and barbaric. He did not fight fairly.

The general paused when he caught a glimpse of his martial figure in the glass windowpane, and instinctively fixed the collar of his coat. "The Lion has met his match." He spoke to the reflection, raising his head a notch higher and throwing his shoulders back a bit further.

Despite the Lion's record of unsurpassed valor, and his unyielding resolve in every crisis, he would be no match for the wit and craftiness of one General Patrick Carlyle.

The officer's eyes glazed over as he stared out the window. What would it be like to haul the infamous Lion to jail—or better yet, drag him through the streets of Washington in chains to the gallows? There would be a media circus, of course. Probably parades, bands, speeches. And as the hero of the historic event, Carlyle would be the most venerated man in the country.

He rubbed his hands together excitedly as images of the future played before his eyes. In time, the Lion would skulk back to his lair at the very mention of General Carlyle's name. He pictured it now... the Lion and his men running for the hills. It would not be an orderly retirement, mind you, but a retreat conducted in dire confusion and alarm. Dignity and courage—traits for which the Lion was so well known—would not be demonstrated *that* day.

Carlyle emitted a low cackle as he visualized the attack that would place the coveted prize in his possession.

The general himself would lead the thundering charge of cavalry against this pathetic foe, his handsome form dominating the scene, his fine, lean figure leaning low over the neck of a fearless warhorse, his polished sword stretched toward Heaven…

***

As Carlyle set forth plans to change his location, the officials in Washington were busy doing everything they could to ramp up the defenses of the nation's capital. Every road was picketed, every lane guarded, and the villages surrounding the city were occupied by outposts of both cavalry and infantry.

Yet, even with the strength of the patrols and the vigilance of their scouts, those in front were well aware of the risk for a surprise raid. The Lion had become notorious for making rounds at night and in bad weather, and he was estimated to have anywhere from one to fifty thousand men at his disposal. The Union troops along the front were inclined to believe the latter number was far more probable, making picket duty a detested and fearful duty.

Common sense—mixed with a good dose of terror—dictated that the number of men in league with the Lion, most certainly ranged in the high thousands. How else could the chief agitator and his followers appear and disappear at will, striking here one day…twenty miles away the next? As soon as one Union regiment was reinforced, another was attacked. Just when more troops were rushed to that particular area, another, somewhere else, would fall prey to the midnight crusaders.

Little did these Federal commanders and troops know that a mere two dozen men was all it took to keep Union troops in their constant state of suspense and anxiety.

The incessant strain, coupled with the whispering and gossiping about the Lion's latest exploits, served to increase the angst among those who were forced to stand guard against this mysterious foe. Many of the Yankee soldiers dreaded the thought of being a part of the Lion's next feat, and the nervous anticipation of such a treacherous event occurring drove some of them to the brink of madness.

Many of the most notable Federal officers would go so far as to admit that the Lion was a dangerous and talented rival, but General Carlyle was not among them. He enjoyed the prominence of his position, and the overwhelming sense of security that his entourage of aides brought him. He did not believe he needed to change his flamboyant and extravagant lifestyle for this anonymous rival—only his place of operation.

Indeed, it was his belief that the country would suffer if he put too much distance between himself and Washington. All the journalists in the capital depended on him to provide military tidbits, battle snippets, and just enough scandal to make his gossip intriguing. The sensational stories that flowed from Carlyle's lips filled columns of news pages week after week.

Of course, much of what he provided was an embellishment of the facts, but his position provided the opportunity to paint himself in the most glowing terms without fear of contradiction.

If the general reestablished his headquarters too far away, the newspapers would suffer, and consequently, the citizenry of the entire region. No, he was too much a patriot to cause widespread consternation by moving away from his current base of operations.

This was the conundrum. He would need to set up an impregnable camp—close enough to Washington to be able to get supplies, yet far enough away to give the appearance he was making strides to discover the whereabouts of the intrepid Lion and his gang of miscreants.

The laurels such a feat would bring him were impossible to quantify. His name would be on the lips of all the fair maidens, and his reputation as a soldier would be recorded in the annals of history. He could see it now—lounging soldiers jumping to their feet and touching their caps in respect. Women throwing flowers along his path and swooning at the mere sight of him.

Why, he could run for Congress as a war hero—a veritable living legend—and would be impossible to defeat.

As Carlyle continued to muse, the scowl on his face twisted into a smile. Why had he not thought of this sooner? He would move his men to the town of Fairview. It was the county seat, easily defensible, and close enough to Washington to send for additional reinforcements—if such a situation were to urgently arise.

Additionally, the houses were large and lavish. His men could be lodged in the comfort they had come to expect and treated to the luxuries to which they were accustomed.

Fairview had one other promising feature that could not be ignored—plenty of adoring women who loved co-mingling with the men in blue—particularly high-ranking officers such as he.

Carlyle rubbed his hands together as his plan began to fall into place. They could make it to Fairview by nightfall and set up a perimeter of pickets so tight, not even a ghost could squeeze through. Then, he would send for his friend Detective Thorpe, and together, they would re-work their plan to rid the Union of the troublesome Lion. Though he had thought the group would be easily wiped away by force, he had since come to the conclusion it would take ingenuity and resourcefulness to accomplish the deed.

With a little help from Detective Thorpe and an acquaintance of mine, I am just the man to accomplish it.

Carlyle's face looked almost gleeful now as he thought of the simplicity of the scheme and the end result. No doubt, he would be made a major general, at which time, he would request a position in the White House as an advisor to the President. There would be no more worrying about midnight attacks from unsavory characters like the Lion.

Best of all, he'd no longer be forced to listen to the bleating of women and children when their homes and barns were set aflame by his men. It wasn't their cursed bawling he detested so much as the odor of that black, billowing smoke. It burned his eyes for hours and clung to his clothes for days.

Considering what had been accomplished in the past year, it wasn't as if the scorched earth policy he'd adopted to drive the Lion from his den had been successful. On the contrary, those damned proud Confederates seemed to absorb faith and fortitude from the flames of their own homes.

The general paced in front of his desk, his chin resting in one of his hands. There was only one problem. Would it appear he was retreating? Running away when no identifiable enemy was known to be near or threatened him?

Bah. No one will believe such a thing.

But just in case, he would leak a story to *The Herald*, just to make sure his logic for the move was well known, and that his courage in this time of crisis was unquestioned.

Carlyle clapped and turned to his desk. He would request that Detective Thorpe bring his nephew along. That handsome rascal could talk a dog off a meat wagon. No wonder Thorpe had taken him under his wing.

Even more importantly, the young man was a well-to-do merchant, so he could travel anywhere without risk of increasing suspicion. And the nephew's striking good looks made him a favorite among the ladies-be they from the North or the South.

Between them, they could concoct a story certain to insult the Lion and bring him out of his lair. Then, they would devise a trap for him, lure him nearer to Washington and seize him—while Carlyle lay safe and sound in his haven of Fairview.

Chapter 13

L andon Graham stood facing the hearth, his legs spread apart, hands in his pockets, staring vacantly at the ornate andirons and embers of a fire that had burned low. Welbourne was his, and his father's before him, and his grandfather's and great-grandfather's too, for that matter. It had come into his possession much sooner than he expected when his father had fallen ill and died while traveling. His mother had followed him to the grave not long after, leaving Landon alone to care for the twins, Sallie and Sawyer.

The library where he stood was a place that roused many memories of the past, and as a result, he rarely stepped foot in it. He did not like to look back. He saw no point in remembering things gone forever.

But something had drawn him here, something vague, like a whispered voice or a hazy dream that could not quite be recalled. As he gazed around, the dull ache of memory began to seep into his soul, triggering images that rekindled feelings he'd long ago cast aside. There was something special about this room, so comfortable and calming in its simplicity. Perhaps that was why it had always been Julia's favorite. The mere thought of her caused his jaw to tighten and his brow to crease with irritation.

Landon didn't like the memories that surfaced, so he turned

away, causing his gaze to fall on a chair facing the window. She must have been here recently, sitting in that seat, perhaps reminiscing. He could picture the scene as he had so often witnessed it. Her head bent over a book in the evening, her unbound hair falling around her shoulders and cascading down her back like a waterfall.

Those blue eyes had invaded his unwilling thoughts quite often over the years, but despite his effort to keep a distance between the past and the present now, a smile tugged at his lips. When she was in a room, there was no need of sun to light it. Julia, with the wind-whipped hair, wild and fearless, was always trying to match her determined stride to his.

Landon remembered many days when this parlor had echoed with nothing but the sound of their breathing. Strange perhaps, that he could recall so very little conversation between them. Somehow, they'd both been adept at the language of silence, able to communicate with little more than a look or a touch.

Yet words had been spoken. His eyes swept his surroundings. In this very room. Words that could not be repeated or forgotten. Those moments were engraved upon his memory in detail, and no lapse of time could ever efface them.

His hands clenched into fists by his sides as other images assailed him. He remembered everything and could think of nothing else. Though some parts had faded over time, most were as clear as a vivid dream—as if someone had tossed a lighted match into his heart, causing flames of memory to dance and flit through his mind. He recalled the mischief in her twinkling blue eyes when she bested him in a horse race, and her constant watchful curiosity that made everything he did of interest to her.

Julia possessed a vitality all her own, a fiery, impulsive spirit that remained unmatched by any woman he'd met since. Landon had grown accustomed to the inevitable loneliness her departure had wrought, and thought he'd successfully dealt with it. But now, as the fresh memories assaulted his brain, and the enduring pain seized his heart, a troubling admission struck him. The feelings he'd thought extinguished were perhaps just buried deep. The sensations welling up in him were too intense and painful to be considered entirely vanquished. In spite of his long separation from Julia, his heart now pulsed in a way he'd thought long dead.

The reminiscences rushed through him like a rain-swollen stream no matter where his gaze rested in the room. It disturbed him that the impact of her memory was not just emotional. The bewildering web of attraction that had intensified between them as they matured was now a physical thing, as tangible as the touch of a small hand in his, as perceptible as the sensation of soft hair against his cheek. He found these unexpected emotions perplexing and painful, full of wonder, rife with uncertainty, but filled too, with unforeseen possibilities.

As he reflected on the magical enchantment of the past, those thoughts of pleasure shifted like a flash into gut-wrenching pain. The agony of their parting came back to him like a sharp, sudden wound, amplifying his misery and gloom. Those days could not be brought back and relived. He had done the right thing, did what he had to do. There was nothing to do now but move forward and forget.

Why then did he feel this terrible emptiness?

Unable to stand the direction of his thoughts, Landon turned to leave. He had to let go of the past, an action that was easier said than done. Because when it came right down to it, he wasn't sure which was stronger—his longing or his regret.

When he was halfway across the room, Landon heard the sound of bubbling laughter drifting in from the hall. A few moments after that, the sound of silk skirts could be heard swishing toward the doorway.

"Landon?" Both girls stopped in the threshold as if unsure whether to enter.

"You needn't sound so surprised." He gave a sweeping gesture with his arm, even though his body recoiled at the idea. "Come in."

Sallie laughed and tried to cover her obvious shock. "If Julia had known you were here, I'm sure she would have had Spencer saddle two horses and galloped away without a second thought about me."

Landon shifted his gaze to Julia and watched her cheeks blossom before she looked away. Her sun-kissed hair hung loosely over her shoulders and shimmered in the light surging through the windows. Her feminine frame was alluringly draped in a rich azure gown that accented the beauty of her glowing blue eyes. With the blindness of childhood familiarity, he had never envisioned or realized how stunning a woman she would grow up to be.

"We've just come from the barn." His sister didn't seem to notice his distraction and continued talking while shaking the bottom of her muddy skirt. "Look at my dress. Julia just had to go and give the horses some treats, never considering the awful conditions or the depth of the mud. Then I had to hear about Brazen's wonderful qualities and how she would give anything to ride—"

"Sallie." Julia interrupted, instinctively knowing Landon would allow no one to ride his favorite horse.

"If there is any woman who could handle him, I have no doubt it would be Julia." Landon's gaze shifted from his sister to Julia, who was looking down, her long lashes resting on her cheekbones. "Unfortunately, he is quite strong, so I am not willing to indulge you in that respect. I'm sure Spencer can find you a more suitable mount."

Landon turned back to the fireplace as a way to keep his gaze from resting on her. Just then, Aunt Mazie bustled through the door with a silver tray and set it down on an end table, puffing and out of breath. "Here's the tea and warm bread you wanted, miss," she said to Sallie. "Tilda is calling me back to the kitchen."

"Oh, my hands are too cold to pour." Sallie opened and closed her fingers and then walked to the fireplace and stuck them close, even though there was little warmth emanating from the embers. Landon turned his attention to Julia, certain she would not wish to perform the task. She had always been unwilling to learn such mundane domestic duties as pouring tea, despite the constant demands from his mother that she do so.

"Would you like some, Landon?" Julia walked confidently to the tray and lifted the dainty pot with long, slender fingers, her features a mixture of delicacy and strength. Landon had no desire for tea—he already had a drink sitting on the mantel—but he found himself nodding. "If you please."

He lowered himself stiffly into a nearby chair and tried to hide the twinge of pain it caused. Then he regarded Julia with somber curiosity as she poured the steaming brew into three dainty cups, revealing no perceptible unsteadiness or timidity whatsoever. In fact, she displayed the grace, composure, and proficiency of a queen, as if she had been raised in a palace among the very well-to-do and was perfectly comfortable navigating the intricacies of high-class society.

He watched in curious silence as she walked over to Sallie with a fragile cup and saucer, exhibiting beautiful posture and fluid movements as she handed them to his sister. His eyes slid up to her face, to the relaxed, easygoing smile that showed no trace of discomfort or unease.

This could not be same girl who'd yearned for the wide-open sky; the child who'd danced like a sunshine beam through the barn, so full of unbound joy and energy that she had to be reminded to walk, not run. Her slender hand gave every impression of delicacy, yet he could recall the calluses of one who always had a set of reins in her hands. Illuminated by the soft glow of sunlight and a few candles, she appeared tranquil and angelic—a complete contradiction to her usual character.

No. This was not the force of nature he remembered...The one with skinned elbows and scraped knees. This could not be the girl who enjoyed any endeavor that involved peril and danger, who would take any risk on the strength of a dare.

Something had changed—or been transformed—in her. She was beauty and mystery, her seeming fragility and innocence in no way matching Landon's memory of her.

Who was this demure, dignified, sophisticated woman so at ease with the rituals of a cultured life?

More importantly, why was she *here*?

Landon studied her subtle smile as she glided across the room with apparent ease and nonchalance. Her blue eyes sparkled with life—and a hint of something else—because in spite of her feigned cheerfulness, he could tell that some sort of burden or pain weighed her down.

The contradictions between his memory of her and this moment continued to confuse him. Was this the same person who was always in motion? Constantly out of breath? Pigtails forever sailing horizontally behind her?

Was this really Julia with the honey-tanned face and hair streaked with gold, who could climb a tree as well as any boy and ride a horse much better than most men?

Maybe that behavior had been his fault. She'd been just nine when her parents had died, and didn't fit in with the older twins as easily as her brother Gideon had. Sallie, Sawyer, and Gideon had all been young teens, and formed an immediate bond of friendship.

As the youngest, Julia had been left to her own devices, and as a result, was frequently found on Landon's heels. At first, he'd found it annoying to have a little girl tagging along behind him. But since she didn't bother him with incessant chatter as most girls her age did, he'd gotten rather accustomed to her company.

Landon had eventually taken her under his protective wing, and taught her how to shoot and fish, and even ride astride— much to his mother's dismay. Julia had been quick to learn every lesson and was always grateful to be taught. Despite his being seven years her senior, she'd always seemed sensible—and wise— enough to bridge the gap.

Still, this had to be quite an elaborate charade for her. Somehow, somewhere, the rough edges had been polished smooth and shined to a gloss. He'd never dreamed it possible that Julia Dandridge could appear domesticated, let alone traverse the complex intricacies of high-society etiquette. The change in her confused and surprised him—and served to increase his suspicions.

Without intending to do so, Landon studied her alert, observant motions. How strange that since their sudden parting, she had lived a normal life: attending parties, making friends, learning the decorum and proprieties of acting like a lady. And how odd that *he* could sit here looking so composed on the outside when there was a hammer pounding crazily in his chest. Regardless of how hard he tried to keep his distance, he could not deny that some alluring magnetism drew him to her.

Yes, she appeared prim and proper now, a lady of uncommon

dignity and presence. But he remembered a time when those long, graceful fingers had been entwined with his; when the smoldering depths of those blue eyes had been aflame with desire and devotion.

His heart quivered at the recollection and caused him to look away. The truth was, even without this noticeable alteration, Julia's unexpected appearance at Welbourne had been a shocking event. The turmoil he'd felt the moment he recognized her had been such that he'd forgotten his exhaustion, and it had been many an hour until he finally fell asleep.

As he pondered the reason for his current muddled state, Landon decided it wasn't because she brought back memories of his past or emotions of anger or confusion over their last meeting. And it wasn't her disarming, shy smile, or her eyes that still carried a hint of an affectionate flame.

No, it jolted because there was no going back. Decisions that had been made long ago could not be changed. Incidents that had occurred could not be altered. Deep down inside, he felt a jarring pang of regret that sparked a misery so acute it felt like a physical pain. It distressed him that she should see him like this, but he swiftly pushed aside those troubling thoughts. The war had changed all that. He needed to be on his guard with her, not reminiscing about the past...or what might have been.

"Here's your tea, Landon." Julia interrupted his musings as she handed him a cup and saucer with smooth, graceful ease. The sound of her voice affected him deeply, causing an explosive current to pulse through his veins.

"I will take Spencer's recommendation for a mount," she said, standing close enough that he could smell the sweet scent of lavender in her hair. "It has been a long time since I've ridden."

Landon glanced into her eyes to see if they appeared as sincere as her words had in stating a fact he knew was untrue, and then studied her smile of deception. "I'm sure it will come back to you easily."

He looked away as he recalled how her blue eyes used to gaze into his with faith, trust, uncertainty, and yearning. He wasn't sure what he saw there now, but he suddenly found it difficult to breathe for the pain in his heart.

"I'm looking forward to it." She brought the dainty cup of tea to her lips but spoke before taking a sip of its contents. "Brazen looked rather docile this morning, but I'm sure he can be a handful when well rested."

Landon tilted his head to see if she were merely making conversation—or implying something deeper. He could decipher nothing from her expression. She seemed to be making an innocent statement, not suggesting a hidden meaning—yet he knew she was not the type of person to speak without intention.

Chapter 14

March was not living up to its promise of coming in like a lion and going out like a lamb. It had certainly roared in like a noble beast, but there was still no sign of the weather softening or consenting to embrace the moderating aspect of spring.

Dreary, gray skies repeated themselves day after day, deepening the gloom along the tented slopes of Washington and beyond. There was little to be happy about, and nothing to celebrate. Disease had joined with winter to kill soldiers by the hundreds, and not a day passed without at least a dribble of casualties from the field.

With the roads buried deeply in the mud of spring, new campaigns were curtailed or abandoned. The inaction, indecision, and delay amplified the overall misery in mood, and wrecked any efforts to make progress. Rumors began to spread that even the sun had succumbed to the morose atmosphere. Why else would it be so reluctant to peek its dazzling face from behind the seemingly perpetual bank of clouds?

Pessimism and depression were especially prevalent throughout the capital city, and testiness was mounting among those in charge. More than two years of war, and they were right back where they started. Nothing of consequence was happening on the front lines, yet officers who needed even the briefest leave of absence found it hard to get. No one was to leave their post for any reason, and all orders to the contrary were denied.

The reason was simple. Every man was needed to guard communications, support the outposts, protect supplies, secure the safety of couriers, and fortify the front—just in case the Lion decided to strike again. Nothing was spared to defend the city against the clever and daring foe who had proven more than once he possessed an utter disregard for danger and death.

Hysteria intensified in the streets of Washington, and rumors ran wild. Merciless stories of the Lion's military prowess increased the horrors the Union officers feared he could inflict. For nearly two weeks, there had been an almost constant clamor and scurry down the roads. Every day, several squadrons of Union cavalry swept across the bridge at a rapid trot, their trumpets echoing, while the main body that defended Washington remained busy reorganizing, training, and placing new sentinels.

The Federals were discouraged, angry even, but not yet completely demoralized. It was a simple fact that the conflict was an utterly unequal one and would eventually end in the surrender of the entire Confederate force. That it had lasted this long was a matter of enraged surprise on their side, and wondering exultation on the other.

But the public perception was different as civilians watched the wounded and the sick pour in, and the hospitals overflow. Like the rain that would not stop, the dripping stream of loaded ambulances never seemed to slacken. Still, the officers in charge did not stop their valiant boasting about their invincible army, and the journalists continued to print the fanciful tales of victory as if they were verifiable truths.

As far as the U.S. government was concerned, one man alone could be blamed for prolonging the contest for such a duration and with such unexpected results. Though they didn't know his name or identity, they knew he led with the caution of a veteran fighter and the confidence of a well-bred soldier. His unpredictable and troublesome attacks were like the lightning bolts that flickered around the edges of a thundercloud. Silent, yet menacing…sudden and brilliant—and possibly deadly.

They recognized that no matter the incredible resources brought against him, the Lion's successes were keeping the sacred fire of his country's liberties alive and bright.

And they intended to stop him. *No matter the cost.*

***

On the other side of the Potomac, the gray and colorless days were brightened only by hope. Even though the soil of Virginia had been drenched with the bravest blood of both armies over the past two years, most nevertheless believed that victory could be wrung from the devastation surrounding them.

Faith remained strong, and confidence was growing, but there was still enough misery to go around. In every town and on every street corner, the people huddled, relying on each other for strength to get through the storm, and imploring Heaven to bless those who risked all to save them from the foul invader. News penetrated to those in the country, but grudgingly. The citizens lived from mail to mail, yet dreaded what sad news it would bring.

The women kept themselves occupied in sewing circles, meeting in churches or each other's homes, to work over uniform cloth, tenting, and flannel until their fingers swelled and bled. To rest their weary hands, they knitted socks and scarves, and talked with great enthusiasm about the intrepidness of their Southern heroes.

As the candles burned down to their ends, they reflected on the reasons they had for hope and how little cause they had for fear—and told stories of a time when their countryside was not one vast military camp.

The social gatherings generated no shortage of conversation, except that now and again, here and there, a woman could be seen staring blankly at nothing at all. Her sudden silence and moist, yearning eyes indicated thoughts of loved ones far away from home. And then the discussion would change somewhat, to remind those who were grieving that the cost of victory could not be measured by what it took to procure it.

As sunlight dwindled and light became scarce, the topic would inevitably turn to the days of plenty, causing sighs and groans to arise throughout the room. The women would reminisce about the not-so-distant past when it was nothing to have ham and beef—pink slices cut thin as shavings—and sugar plum pudding with little iced cakes and rosy apples—all laid out on tables of snowy damask, complete with shining silver and stylish porcelain.

In the year of 1863, they were happy to have a little salt pork or rice and beans. Every crumb of food better than the ordinary—every orange and apple, every drop of wine—went straight to the hospitals. They were a people bound by a common tie of patriotism and sympathy, and they tolerated no assumption of superiority among them.

Although the Southern people remained true to their cause, one could see there was also a longing for peace. The speed with which a rumor would be grasped and disseminated, no matter how absurd or contradictory, proved the intense desire they had to end the conflict.

One report, widely rumored to be true, was that France and England had recognized the independence of the Confederacy and declared war against the United States. Yet another was that Lincoln and Congress had agreed to recognize the Confederacy, with the understanding that both the North and South would join forces against Maximilian in Mexico.

Back when the war was new, such rumors and prayers had not been so direly needed. The Confederate army had gained a vast superiority over the enemy and often achieved great victories in spite of the inequality of arms and numbers.

But as the strength of the army dwindled with death and disease, nothing but valor was left to keep the flag flying against an enemy who was superior in everything but courage. Bright episodes in the spring of sorrow were few and far between. The present and the future were so replete with danger that the past was almost forgotten, edged out by thoughts of what might happen at any hour.

Not until the emergence of the mysterious Lion did the people begin to have reassurance again. The tactics he used were ingenious, his power of destruction tremendous. So great was the enemy's fear of him that a simple demonstration on the part of his men was sufficient to scatter the Yankees to the winds.

North or South, people rarely spoke without mentioning the Lion's countless successes, his boundless influence over the people, and the impressive audacity with which he gained his victories. And despite the peril of his exploits, the boldness of his tactics, and the dangerous risks he took to achieve success, there was no shortage of men striving to join him.

All over the Confederacy, but particularly in Virginia, his was a name known and revered in every household. The Lion, they said, was restless and ruthless, elusive and bold. To those who had the unfortunate duty of trying to stop him, it seemed he never slept. He was at all times warring or preparing for war. His courage was legendary. His boldness renowned. With a mere glance, he could put courage into a coward and fear into a foe.

As for the people who idolized him, they had begun to sleep a little more soundly at night, and hold their heads a little higher by day. Thus far, the Lion had been perfectly capable of staying at least one step ahead of the enemy. It was only a matter of time until the noble warrior achieved peace for the Confederacy and victory for the South.

Chapter 15

Three horsemen sat casually across the path, their silhouettes appearing only as a dim, smudgy outline of horse and man in the faint moonlight. The Union courier had been riding as rapidly as the condition of his horse and the narrow road would warrant, so he didn't see the obstruction until he was just a few feet away. He pulled his startled steed to a sliding halt in front of the group.

"Fed or reb?" one of them said in a low, threatening tone.

The courier peered into the darkness, trying to distinguish the color of the men's uniforms in the little light the moon and stars afforded. The sound of three revolvers clicking almost in unison settled the matter for him. None of the three riders spoke again, but the seriousness of their duty and haste were evident.

One pointed toward a slight trail off to his right, and the two others moved in to follow. After that, they rode at a reckless pace through the darkness, placing scarcely any restraint upon their reins. Apparently, they were no strangers to this remote trail.

The courier's heart began to rattle in its cage at the thought he was being taken to the Lion's den. It was well known that the Lion's successful enterprises were due in large part to the selection of skillful and intelligent guides, men familiar with the section of country in which the Lion operated. Those loyal followers knew all the little roads and cow paths, and could creep through the

dense undergrowth or dark ravines like foxes, unobserved. If discovered, they easily eluded pursuit.

After traipsing for quite some time through the woods on
little more than a deer path, the riders arrived at a clearing where
a small campfire burned. A horseman stood deep in the shadows,
talking in whispered tones with a few other men. His horse was
puffing and splattered with mire, suggesting the man had been
in the saddle for untold hours and ridden over muddy roads for
many miles.

The courier's escort rode forward to join the assembly, followed by a brief interchange among the group. The rider in the
shadows, a man of military erectness and strong stature, spoke in
low tones before backing his horse even deeper into the canopy
of trees. At last, through some unseen communication, one of
the other men stepped forward and spoke to the Union courier.
"What is your name, and where are you bound?"

The messenger remained stoically silent—or more accurately,
fearfully so. The solemn forest, the grave voice that addressed
him, and the broad-shouldered silhouette of a man who did not
speak, made him uncharacteristically alarmed.

As the threatening silence bore on, the frenzied buzzing of
insects became deafening. The Union soldier could feel the eyes
of the man in the woods intensely studying him, yet the figure
was so deep in the shadows as to remain unidentifiable to him. He
could make out no details other than a lethal calmness with how
he sat his horse, and the noticeable eagerness of the men around
him to obey his every word. It had rained earlier, and the trees still
dripped, but the man seemed unconscious of—or unconcerned
with—his dousing.

After emptying the messenger's saddlebag and reading the
contents by the fire, one of the men walked toward the myste-

rious figure. "It's a communication for Union General Hanley, telling of the approximate number and disposition of our troops at the river."

The man in the shadows studied the paper, though it was obviously too dark to read. "Very well," he said in a low voice. "Have Riley exchange uniforms with this gentleman. They're about the same size."

He handed the note back. "And send Jenkins to me. I have a *new* dispatch I need him to write."

The Confederate soldier's face broke into a wide grin as he began to grasp his leader's plan. "Yes, sir." Away he went through the woods, crashing through the brush with an impetuosity that displayed his determination.

Meanwhile, the Union courier grasped the plan, as well, and stood in awe of the quick thinking and swift response by the mysterious man in the woods. He had no doubt the new dispatch—the one that would be delivered by the man named Riley—would be written in such a way as to deceive his commander, General Hanley. An attack would be made under the false assumption of a light enemy force—and the Lion would be celebrating a new triumph by the end of the next day.

Chapter 16

Julia walked through the meadow, the high grass brushing her knees, and a smile playing on her lips. The air was chilly, but the sun, with its caressing warmth on her back, eased her mind and caused her spirits to soar. A host of birds added to the serenity of the scene by serenading her with their mesmerizing melodies. As far as she could see, wildflowers carpeted the glade, and the sky above it all was so blue, it gave the scene the impression of a painting.

But it wasn't long until unsettling thoughts came cascading back. Julia had not expected the overwhelming flood of emotions at seeing Landon again—or the terrible emptiness that had consumed her at *his* reaction to seeing *her*.

She kicked a stone out of the way as if it had caused all her problems. Landon was not the first to have a dear brother killed in the war.

Perhaps it was the way Sawyer had died that stung worse than the loss itself. The young lieutenant had been captured by General Patrick Carlyle, an officer known for his brutality and ruthlessness. Instead of being exchanged, as was the normal protocol at the time, Landon's younger brother had been imprisoned—a place from which he'd never returned.

To add insult to injury, the Yankees had refused to return his body, so the family was forced to mourn without being able to properly say goodbye. They claimed his life had been blotted out by the poisonous breath of disease, but there was no way to know for sure how long he had suffered or from what he had succumbed. The whole affair had put a tremendous strain on Landon and Sallie's relationship, and still stood as a wall between them.

Julia paused and raised her head to get her bearings while on the top of a small knoll. Memories lingered around the edges of her mind as she gazed at the countryside spread out before her longing eyes.

The Virginia afternoon had spent its early heat, and a wandering breeze, laden with the odors of spring, came up from the water's edge. Below her ran the sparkling tributary that branched off the river. Wildflowers grew in abundance there, and she recalled many peaceful hours spent braiding the vibrant blossoms into her hair while Landon cast his line.

As Julia began walking again, she caught a glimpse of movement near the water's edge. Without realizing it, her lips turned to a smile. Landon Graham stood on the bank with his hands on his hips, staring vacantly into the deep pool. His massive horse, Brazen, stood nearby, ripping green shoots from a patch of fresh grass.

Julia waited until she was near him to speak. "Going fishing?"

Landon turned slightly, and cast her a disapproving look as if she were intruding. "Not today."

Although she yearned to see the rapt, reverential gaze with which he used to greet her, Julia accepted his remote reply, and began to pick the early spring blooms that stretched out in colorful array before her. "Look. Flowers everywhere. Just like they used to be."

His gaze followed her movements broodingly, but he did not speak.

When she looked up at his silence, her eyes fell upon something directly over his shoulder. "Oh, look. Is that our tree?" She felt the heat rise in her cheeks at her outburst. "I mean, is that the tree we used to sit in?"

Landon turned around and gazed where she pointed. "I think perhaps it is." He walked toward the oak with long, effortless strides, as Julia struggled to keep up. He paused once to swipe a blade of grass, which he characteristically put into his mouth.

The tree stood out from the others because the trunk had split in two when it was a sapling. As it grew, a flat hump had formed in one of the trunks, making the perfect seat for a child. The opposite trunk had a similar malformation, but not as large, making it a resting place for small feet. Julia had spent many an hour in that tree, reading or watching Landon fish.

They both stood at the base now, looking up at the seat that had once been near the ground. "It's grown." Julia's voice was full of disappointment.

"Yes. It has changed."

"Just like everything else, I suppose." Julia's voice sounded more wistful and disappointed than she'd intended.

Instead of replying, Landon laced his fingers together and held them out. "Here. I'll help you up."

Julia took a step back in utter surprise. "No. I'm too old for such things."

"Too old? Or too prim and proper?" He tilted his head and stared at her, but she could not read the look on his face.

"That's silly." Julia cleared her throat. "I don't climb trees anymore."

"Just as I thought." Landon laughed and placed one hand on the tree, as he leaned down to gaze directly into her eyes. "Julia Dandridge is too sophisticated to do anything that would get her hands dirty. Things have changed indeed."

Julia felt her cheeks grow warm, and knew she must be blushing profusely.

Landon didn't give her time to make an excuse. He crossed his arms and raised his eyebrows questioningly. "Or *maybe* it's just that you're afraid of heights in your old age."

Seeming to know how she would react to such a challenge, he held out his hands again. Without saying a word, Julia slipped off one shoe and lifted her foot. Landon hoisted her up into the makeshift seat and handed her the shoe. After replacing it, she leaned her head back to rest it against the bark. "This part hasn't changed. It's still a perfect fit."

"Looks like there's room for two now." Landon stepped into the crotch of the tree and pulled himself up. As he settled in beside her, they both grew quiet—but it was not an uncomfortable silence. It was the hush of two friends, neither of whom was willing to interrupt the perfect feeling of being entirely isolated from the world and its troubles. Once again they seemed able to communicate without saying a word. Just like the old days, they were comfortable and content with each other's presence.

For a few long minutes, neither ventured to break the delightful calm or the sanctity of the surroundings with speech. They were bound by nothing, yet attached at every level. They were as familiar with each other as they were with their own siblings... able once again to read each other's thoughts, if not their words.

Julia closed her eyes, trying to feel as carefree and untroubled as she had when sitting in this tree as a child. When she reopened them, her gaze fell on the limb in front of her. "Look." She bent forward and pointed but didn't say anything else.

Landon's lips curled into a smile, but it was only temporary. In fact, the sight of the name scrawled into the tree appeared to make him angry. "That was a long time ago."

"Yes." Julia sighed. "But I remember it as if it were yesterday. Don't you?"

Landon was silent as his gaze remained on the bark of the tree. He seemed to be replaying the day in his mind. "As I recall, you were upset with my mother and ran away. Not exactly a pleasant memory, I should think."

"But you found me, and tried to cheer me up by carving my name here." She traced the letters, which, for the most part, were unrecognizable, with her finger. "You said it would henceforth be Julia's tree."

"Did it work?"

She gazed at him, her brows creased with confusion.

"Did it cheer you up?"

"Of course." Julia nodded. "You always cheered me up..." Her voice trailed off as her thoughts wandered, and her eyes clouded over with images from the past. How vividly she remembered it all after so many years—clearly, intensely, as if it were happening again before her eyes.

"Especially *that* day...when you promised—"

Julia felt Landon's body grow tense beside her, so she didn't finish the sentence. But the memory had come crawling back from the place where she had buried it, and was replaying itself as she spoke. While painful to re-live, the recollection helped cleanse her soul of things best let go.

"You were so kind, putting up with me always tagging along." Julia rested her head against the bark again. "There was a time when I truly believed you'd wait for me to grow up." She smiled. "I actually thought I could catch up to you."

When she opened her eyes, Landon's gaze rested on her thoughtfully. He did not confirm he remembered the promise he'd made when she was young—but neither did he deny it. A long, brittle silence ensued, interrupted by a low roll of thunder from the west.

Julia glanced at the sky and saw a mass of black clouds moving toward them. She hadn't noticed that the wind had picked up, until she felt the hair that had loosened from her braid blowing about her face.

"We'd better get going, or we're bound to get wet."

Julia shrugged. "It will just be a shower. I don't care."

"We can beat it." Landon descended the tree and mounted his horse, which was grazing nearby. "Hop on."

Julia eyed him and his outstretched hand warily. "That wouldn't be very ladylike."

"And that's what I always liked about you, Julia Dandridge." He leaned over and plucked her from her perch with one strong arm. She had no choice but to hold on tightly as he kicked his horse into a gallop.

A light pattering of rain soon began—just a few drops here and there—the kind that is a precursor to a cloudburst.

But Julia remembered the wind most of all…and her cheek pressed against Landon's strong back…and her arms wrapped tightly around his waist, holding on for dear life.

Chapter 17

L andon reined his cantering horse to a sliding stop in the stable yard just as the clouds let loose. Torrents of rain spilled down in a massive curtain that seemed to reach from Heaven to the earth.

In a flash, he'd thrown his leg over the saddle, dismounted, and pulled Julia down from the horse, but they were both still wet by the time they ducked under the small overhang of the barn. With a gentle touch, he maneuvered her closer to the building to protect her from the water splashing off the tin roof.

Julia squeezed the moisture from her single braid and laughed. "We almost made it."

When Landon didn't respond, she looked up at him, standing so close she could feel his chest expanding against hers with each breath. He was smiling, and for a moment, it was if no time had passed at all—as if nothing stood between them. He took a strand of hair that had come loose from her braid and studied it intently.

"You used to wear your hair in pigtails." His gaze lifted to meet hers. "Do you remember?"

Julia swallowed hard, too surprised for a moment to speak. The sudden intimacy and the question shocked her—not because he was impulsive in taking the privilege, but because he'd remembered such a thing in the first place and felt inclined to share it with her. She gloried briefly in the shared moment.

"Of course. I remember every moment of the time I spent at Welbourne." She bit her bottom lip without knowing it. "With you."

Landon dropped the tendril and became all business. "Yet I have changed considerably in your eyes since then." He studied her as she stood silently, and for the first time, she thought she heard a hint of regret in his voice.

"Not irreversibly," she murmured.

Landon's eyebrows rose, and Julia thought she saw a glint of gladness—or perhaps relief—on his face. But when she took a second look, the bored, detached expression had returned, making it clear she had imagined any sign of consideration from the man.

The door behind them suddenly opened, and two stable hands came out to collect his horse. "It's dry in here, suh."

Landon stepped into the barn and listened to the rain pelting the roof. "We may as well stay here until it passes. No sense in getting drenched on the way to the house."

Julia took a deep breath. "There's no place I'd rather be." Her wet skirt dragged on the stone floor, but she took no notice. The sweet scent of hay, and the sound of pampered horses munching contently in their stalls made the barn seem warm and inviting. Julia began walking down the aisle, looking at each horse, as a feeling of familiarity and camaraderie sent a surge of happiness through her.

"I had started to believe you were more at ease in a parlor than a barn."

Julia stopped and turned toward Landon. Something in his voice sounded strange. Unfamiliar. "You, of all people, should know better than that."

"That is why I ask." He eyed her noncommittally. "The Julia of the past would not know how to pour tea."

She tried to divine what he was thinking by gazing deep into his eyes, but she found no answers there. "Is that so remarkable a feat?"

"I suppose not." He started walking again, but paused to pat the nose of a horse that bobbed its head in greeting. "Except, if memory serves, you would be more inclined to bait a hook than undertake such domestic endeavors."

Julia laughed, trying to lighten the mood. "In case you haven't noticed, I have grown up some since then."

Landon's eyes narrowed and he grew more pensive. Though his lips remained silent on the subject, his expression seemed to convey the opinion that he had indeed noticed.

Julia felt a distinct, natural connection to him, yet the war and its secrets kept her at a distance. His conspicuous coolness troubled her, but this equally dangerous warmth was perhaps even more disquieting. "May I ask you something, Landon?"

He turned around at her suddenly serious tone. "Of course."

"Have things changed so much between us?"

A look of pain crossed Landon's face, but he mastered it. "I don't know what you mean." He stared at nothing as he spoke, making it clear he knew exactly what she meant.

Julia's heart hammered foolishly. "I thought that we…I mean, I wish that…"

Landon spoke quickly, still staring straight ahead. "You wish for me to speak the truth?"

"Of course."

He turned his piercing, liquid black eyes toward her. "Manners should prevent me from doing so, but if you insist, I shall be without manners."

"I don't understand. What do you mean?"

"Although news is slow to reach us here at Welbourne, we are, nonetheless, not so isolated that we are entirely unaware of events outside our immediate surroundings."

"What has that to do with me?" A tremor of discomfort began to crawl up Julia's spine.

"One has only to read the society pages to see your name mentioned." His brow creased with obvious irritation. "*Prominently*, I might add—and in the highest political circles."

Julia remained stoically still, suffering an agony of contradicting emotions. She felt a flush of surprise—but not guilt—suffuse her face, and hoped it did not confirm the truth of his suspicions. A few long moments passed as Landon treated her to the most prolonged stare she'd ever been forced to endure.

"I answered your question, and now you have nothing to say?"

"I did not know the statement required a response." Julia's heart pounded in her ears and then sank at the sight of his suspicious stare. "I lived with my aunt and uncle in Washington and, as you are aware, he is a well-known businessman and highly respected in the community."

Landon tilted his head and raised his brows in such a way that forced her to continue. His attitude remained so tense and unfriendly, Julia had to work hard to keep her voice from shaking. "Therefore, of course, I was required to be present at social functions."

Whether Landon accepted her answer or not, she could not tell. Nor could she discern if the expression on his face was disappointment or pity. He turned toward the door. "I don't hear the rain on the roof anymore."

"Landon?"

He stopped. "At your service, miss."

Julia smiled at the answer he had always given her as a child, one that always made her feel grown up and proud. She wasn't certain if it had slipped out because of habit, or if he was trying to make up for his frostiness. She nervously cleared her throat as she prepared to ask him the question that had been foremost on her mind. "Landon, have you heard from Gideon?"

"Your brother?"

Julia looked down and nodded. "Yes. I'm very worried about him."

Landon turned to a groom standing nearby, and gave him low-voiced commands. As the sound of footsteps on the stone faded away, he finally responded. "I have no news on that account."

"But...do you know...I mean—" Julia shook her head as she tried to form a coherent sentence. She blinked to restrain the tears welling in her eyes. "I just wish I knew where he is. If he's safe."

Something haunted Julia, warning her that the brother she loved was alive but in desperate peril. She could not wipe away from her memory the way he had looked the last time they'd chanced to meet in the deep darkness of night. The change in him had been drastic. The worn, tired look about his eyes and mouth, the solemnness of his face, and the gloom in his voice. He had seemed so withdrawn and remote—irritable and surly even— as if a forbidding shadow stood between them.

"I should think, in this case, no news is good news." Landon studied her as he spoke, and his face darkened with an unreadable emotion. His words, at least, had some note of reassurance in them—even if his tone did not. "If you have heard nothing, it is likely he is busy in the field."

"But he has not made contact with me for months. It is so unlike him."

"Perhaps he does not like the company you keep, either." The words were blurted out so coldly and bluntly that it knocked Julia off guard.

She felt impaled by Landon's intense, condemning glare as he regarded her with an expression of accusation and distrust.

Julia looked away. The spell had been broken. The tangible bond between them torn. They were no longer living in the past. The present had caught up with them once again.

Chapter 18

The men who were sprawled about the room watched their leader scan the newspaper article. They had expected to see raw anger, a surge of rage, unparalleled fury. But they were mistaken. His eyes crinkled with merriment, and his mouth turned up into a rarely seen smile.

"Have you seen this?" He raised his head and gazed at them as he lifted his coffee cup to his lips.

They nodded hesitantly, not sure how to react.

The man leaned back in his chair and read from the paper with mirthful eyes: *"General Carlyle, whose neglected bed barely knows him now, has a plan to summarily eradicate the Lion."*

Recognizing the mood of their leader as a jovial one, some of the men chuckled briefly, but everyone grew silent when he continued.

"Far from being the bold, fearless leader he is purported to be, the Lion and his men are, in reality, a herd of cowardly sheep, striking only upon the weakest and most fragile among us."

Without moving his head this time, their leader studied each man in the room with a slight smile, and then continued reading.

"General Carlyle's actions upon the battlefield have heretofore been irrefutably heroic. His valor, audacity, and gallantry forever worthy of praise. And now, with unsparing hand and unyielding fury, he pledges to destroy this band of miscreants and all who provide them aid."

"Looks like the Yanks are still smarting from our last exploit," one of the men said. "I'm beginning to feel sorry for them."

"Riley did a commendable job of passing as the courier, and the slight changes Jenkins made to the dispatch did not raise any suspicions."

"Fooled them, all right—and all by changing a couple of words."

One of the men laughed. "Fooled them entirely. Instead of saying that the ford was 'heavily guarded, do not proceed,' they received the communication, 'the ford is lightly guarded, attack at once.'"

"And attack they did."

Another rare smile formed on the face of their leader as he recalled observing the rout from a nearby hill. The surprise had been complete. The Confederates were well prepared to meet the assault of the Union troops, who believed they would be facing a small defensive position.

Additional southern troops had then flanked the enemy lines, attacking from behind in successive and thunderous waves. Union forces were obliged to retreat as best they could or be annihilated. The few who managed to escape were quick to tell the tale of the horrific ordeal, and blame the chaotic disaster on the legendary Lion.

"Shall we take this bait, my men?" The words were spoken in a calm tone and with the penetrating eye of a man who knows no fear.

One of the men looked around at the others and then spoke. "What do *you* think?"

"Why, of course. General Carlyle is goading us. We must not let him down."

"But it appears to be a trap intended to draw us in. They will be prepared."

Their leader laughed. "Nevertheless, General Carlyle wishes to get some publicity, and I am inclined to give it to him." He relaxed his arms on the crude table in front of him, obviously deep in thought, and apparently oblivious to the light flurry of a late spring snow that could be seen through the window.

The merriment slowly left his eyes, as he seemed to reflect on the man they were discussing—and his own intention for revenge.

"Gather the men. We leave tonight."

***

The group of horsemen advanced single-file down the narrow, barely perceptible trail, their figures invisible beneath the canopy of trees. Even without the covering, the darkness was intense, requiring the riders to rely on their mounts to follow the horse in front of them—and on their leader to guide them to their destination.

It was late March, and a warm, drizzling rain had started to fall, creating a misty haze as it melted the light layer of snow at their feet. In the last mile or so, they had picked up their pace to make up for an earlier delay. For unknown reasons, the last half of the group had stood still, thinking the whole column had halted. The front of the line had gone a considerable distance before realizing their comrades were missing.

Now, they were all back together again—behind schedule but moving toward their objective. What their objective *was*, none but their leader knew. Yet his guidance in prior such enterprises had imparted a confidence that buoyed their spirits and spawned an inherent courage that boosted their nerve.

Most of these midnight riders believed they were going to make an attack on a Union picket post, or perhaps harass the rearguard of a Federal unit on the move. They had no clear idea of the force before them, but they were moving rapidly and quietly, obviously with the intent of effecting a surprise.

After crossing an icy stream and moving single-file through dense brush and trees, they reached an opening in the forest and halted within the shadows. Their leader gathered them into a small circle and calmly revealed that their present location was about four miles inside enemy lines. They had managed to squeeze between Union picket posts without raising the alarm.

The men sat quietly with their hands on their reins, but it was not hard to tell what they were thinking. They were twenty-four men—completely surrounded by thousands of hostiles. It took no great knowledge to understand the difficulties and dangers they now faced. Their safety lay in the utter audacity of the enterprise.

The news may have been surprising, but it was not unnerving. Certainly, this was not the first time these men had found themselves in such a situation. They were not shocked or intimidated in the least. Just a few weeks earlier, they had ridden to the very edge of Washington City and made off with almost an entire regiment of cavalry.

No feat of such bravado had ever been tried and, they assumed, would never be attempted again. Why indeed would anyone tempt fate after achieving such laurels as that? They remained emphatically behind their leader—even if they did not feel implicit confidence in their ability to execute the next task asked of them.

Most of the horsemen surmised that their mission entailed sneaking into the nearby cavalry camp, helping themselves to the finest stock, and riding back out as a way to humiliate or embarrass a certain Federal official. Their leader did not like bravado, and especially detested those who embellished their record or, in some cases, made it up from scratch. The type of officer who did that sort of thing always equipped himself with the best horses. This excursion into dangerous territory would likely be worth the peril in horseflesh.

But the men soon discovered their leader had much bigger game in mind.

With bits jingling, and saddles creaking, the group rode a short distance and then turned to the left. The men looked at each other with disbelief and astonishment as they trotted brazenly down the main street of the town of Fairview.

It was now two o'clock in the morning. Other than a few drowsy sentinels who barely looked up at the passing horsemen, all was quiet, wrapped in sleep. They encountered no resistance. Elicited no alarm.

The great coolness and courage on the part of the men could only be attributed to the trust they placed in their leader. They knew he would never guide them into a place from which he was not able to take them out again. He had long ago made them think they were invincible by his mere boldness and the example he set. The danger of this endeavor only added to the significance of the attempt, making the ultimate success exceptionally more satisfying.

Even though he possessed a fierce passion for the fight, their leader instinctively knew when to initiate combat and when to calmly await attack. He never showed weakness, even under the most protracted strain, and he presided over his men with intrepidness and skill even in the darkest storm of battle.

Yet still, they gazed around in awe at what they had accomplished. This town was an important stronghold for the Yankees, containing a large number of troops, officers, and supplies. It was, therefore, heavily fortified with picket posts and sentries positioned in tight intervals around the entire perimeter.

Somehow, their leader had found a gap and squeezed two dozen horsemen through the gauntlet. The man seemed to possess a consummate knowledge of the geography and resources of the theater of war, as well as an unerring faculty for finding the way by night or day through forest and field.

It didn't seem to matter to him that they would be numerically inferior and vastly outgunned if attacked. He relied on his men's spirit and prowess, which he knew was unsurpassed—and he counted on the Federal troops being poorly trained and gullible, which was becoming abundantly clear.

Despite the Yankees' lack of diligence and their failure to sound any alarm, the invading force did not blame them for this lapse in protection. They pitied them. In positioning and deploying their pickets, the Union officers had done what was reasonable. They'd prepared a defense to guard against any type of invasion that was probable.

This was not the least bit probable.

Chapter 19

When an alert sentinel at last called out and asked who they were, the answer was "Fifth New York Cavalry," a regiment posted there. The darkness of the night aided their deception, as it was impossible to tell from their appearance to which side they belonged. The guard questioned them no further.

Upon reaching the town's courthouse square, the leader separated the men into squads, assigning them specific duties to accomplish in a precise allotment of time. Some went to the stables to collect horses, others to the different houses where officers were quartered, and still others to cut the telegraph wires.

As for their leader, he took five of the men and motioned for them to follow him. Halting in front of a stately brick home, he dismounted, climbed the steps, and knocked loudly on the front door. Within a few moments, a head stuck out from an upper window and inquired who was there.

"Fifth New York Cavalry with a dispatch for General Carlyle," was the immediate response.

Footsteps were soon heard tripping down the stairs, and the door opened a minute later to reveal a man standing in nothing but his shirt and drawers. The leader of the small group seized him by the collar and whispered something in his ear that caused the man to recoil with fright and raise his hands in surrender—

proof of the terror the Federals attached to the Lion's name.

Some of the men then rushed up the stairway and into the house, while two stayed behind to guard the horses. Pushing open the first door they came to, one of the soldiers lit a match, and discovered the general fast asleep in bed.

A glance around the room revealed the reasons for his deep slumber. Uncorked champagne bottles lay helter-skelter on a table, and signs of revelry were evident everywhere. It appeared the general had been entertaining the ladies of the region in a style befitting a commanding officer.

Within the Union ranks, Carlyle was notorious for his boisterous, menacing, and intimidating persona. Yet, he was much more renowned for his ability to throw a party than for his fighting skills.

Despite the clamor of the men bursting through the door and their laughter at finding him snoring, the general did not wake. One of the rebels grabbed the blankets, and with one swift yank, stripped the bed of its covers.

Still, he slept.

Aggravated at the delay, the leader approached the bed where the general lay on his side, facing the far wall. He pulled up the sleeping man's nightshirt and gave him a loud smack. The effect was electric. The general sat straight up, and with an authoritative tone, inquired as to the reason for the offensive disturbance. "Who the devil are you, why the hell did you wake me, and what the blazes do you want?"

The leader, who wore his hat down low on his head and a black bandana tied around his face, replied calmly. "General Carlyle, have you heard of the Lion of the South?"

The general blinked wildly and heaved a great snort of excitement. "Of course! Have we caught him?" He looked up at the man standing over him, but obviously saw nothing but his eyes—and with the darkness, not even that.

Some of the men in the room snickered again.

"No. *He* has caught *you*. Get up."

The general gazed around now with a look of anger and disbelief. "This is folly. It cannot be. Where are my men?"

"Get dressed, General."

"Guard! Guard!" Carlyle's eyes were red and swollen, proving he was newly over, or perhaps *nearly* over, a drunken bout.

One of the Lion's men picked up a dirty sock on the floor and stuffed it into the general's open mouth. In order to deprive him of any hope of escape, Carlyle was then informed that Stuart's cavalry held the town, and General Jackson was close by with several thousand troops.

The now-subdued general hung his head, and the sock was removed. "If General Blackford is close by, take me to him. We were classmates at West Point."

Everyone in the room grew quiet, knowing their leader would be more inclined to take this man out and hang him from the nearest tree than allow him the honor of being taken to an old friend. His answer, therefore, surprised them.

"Certainly. But we are in a hurry."

The general insisted he be afforded the opportunity to dress, a wish that was granted warily considering the crucial element of time. When he was done and humbly emerged before his captors, more than one snickered at the sight of a uniform that appeared to have just been cleaned—or more than likely, never been near the smoke of battle.

With some nudging and prodding, they were soon on their way back to the square where all of the squads had collected. Here, they discovered a mere dozen and a half men had captured about three times their own numbers in prisoners, as well as dozens of horses and various materials of war.

Even though the numerical advantage of prisoners meant they could have overwhelmed the rebel force, the idea apparently did not occur to them. Perhaps they could not see who was who in the intense darkness, and did not think they could rally the troops. It seemed more likely, however, that their state of confusion and shock prevented them from thinking at all.

Ordered under threat of death to obey commands, the prisoners mounted horses, and the entire group rode out of town. The earlier delay had cost the group of rebels much time, making the journey to reach their own lines by daybreak an urgent one.

Most of the prisoners were trusted with their reins, but the sulking general was too great a prize to leave his fate to chance. His reins were in the hands of one of the young men of the group, and it was clear that only death would cause him to release them.

"You will profit from my misfortune, I suppose," the general commented as the man who wore the bandana upon his face strode past him to gather his horse. Carlyle spoke as if his capture and the resulting humiliation he would endure were no fault of his own.

The leader paused. "I do not know what *misfortune* you refer to—unless it was meeting my men."

This man who had goaded and harassed the Lion at every turn was a very special prize indeed. Yet the impudent Federal officer, in his usual cavalier and overconfident way, still believed he would come out the victor.

"You may be bold, but you are going to get caught," the general muttered to anyone who would listen. "You will never get away with this atrocity. My men will rally against such an outrage as this. You—"

"Be quiet, or I will hogtie and gag you." The young man holding the reins leaned in close and spoke in a low, threatening voice, so the general could understand the seriousness of the situation.

Apparently, General Carlyle expected at any moment to hear his own cavalry coming in hot pursuit, but as the town disappeared behind them, it became clear that his faith was for naught. The few soldiers who had escaped the Lion's grasp in the town had no interest in chasing this mysterious foe in the darkness—especially with no officers to lead them.

Still, there was cause for concern for the invaders. The sum of prisoners outnumbered the Lion's men by almost three times, and they had many miles to travel before reaching the safety of their own lines. Their intrepid leader slowed his horse and took his place at the rear of the flying column, seeking, as was his custom, the point nearest the enemy.

His hand was on his gun, and he frequently stopped to listen, expecting perhaps—as the general did—the Union troops to gather their wits and give chase. Yet no hostile form materialized. The silence, and the total absence of footsteps or gunfire, revealed a weakness in both leadership and discipline. A well-trained regiment would have given chase no matter the odds. No military organization with any dignity or respectability would permit the enemy to just ride away.

For many a mile, no sound disturbed the deep stillness of the night, except for the reverberation of a galloping horse crashing through the darkness every now and again. Even though the Lion had spaced his men out along the flank and sides of the large group, some of the prisoners were able to escape into the shadows.

Would *they* have the sense to rally the troops? Had they counted the actual numbers of the invading force and calculated their ability to overwhelm them? This group of stealthy horsemen could still be trapped between the outer picket line they had not yet reached, and the defenses of the town behind them. If the alarm was sounded, they were boxed in by two large—and angry—forces.

Upon reaching the pike, their leader spurred his horse forward, apparently believing they had put enough distance between them and the danger behind.

Now, the threat lay in front.

Chapter 20

A gleam of hazy light—only visible to those whose eyes anxiously searched for it—began to glimmer in the east, while the campfires of the enemy surrounding them still contrasted intensely with the darkness.

Now was not the time to breathe a sigh of relief, even though they felt safe from pursuit. The peril lay ahead. Sweet rest and safety were almost close enough to touch, yet the stream—heavily picketed by the enemy—lay between. Not only did they have to squeeze through another line of enemy posts with close to a hundred men and horses, they also had to avoid running into a roaming squad of their foe.

And another, perhaps even more sinister problem faced them. Daylight was near. The sun would not be an ally, and it might very well prove deadly. Their fate trembled in the balance.

All eyes turned to their leader. He rode confidently in front now, but frequently stopped to listen. He appeared watchful and circumspect, but continued to display calmness in the face of this new danger.

Still, the hearts of the men lurched and throbbed as the magnitude and significance of their exploit began to hit them. It was incredible that this rag-tag group of men had spent more than an hour in the town—raiding the headquarters and capturing a commanding general—without firing a single shot or having one fired at them.

They knew this escapade would have a substantial impact on the enemy, and would strike a more terrifying impression on the imagination of opposing troops than any battle could.

But they were not yet safe.

One look at the brightening sky made some believe their luck had run out. Had their leader gone too far this time? Pushed too hard? Were they to come so close to pulling off the perfect caper, only to be overtaken by the morning sun?

The beginning of a new day usually brought with it a sense of renewal and serenity. Today, it felt like a spear to the heart. The sun was not yet visible—the eastern sky merely promised that it was there waiting. But the glow from the approaching dawn was sufficient enough to reveal the outlines of trees and the long distance they still had to traverse.

The eyes of the men were fastened on their leader in keen expectancy and with unwavering trust, while he, silent and alone with his heavy responsibility, sat scanning the shifting circumstances of the field with a composed and penetrating gaze. To his men, he displayed a disposition of heroic calm, and gave no hint of the tremendous strain he was under. He had proven to them time and again that he was the same in victory and defeat—always unruffled, never corrupted by praise or success. They loved him like a brother and revered him as a commander.

Despite the odds, most of those in the small band continued to believe the mission they were on would be accomplished without loss of life—and if it wasn't, it had been worth the try. They moved more swiftly now, but with prudent regard, determined to be victorious or die in the attempt.

The slow but steady increase in light helped them move at a faster pace, yet made their travel more perilous. Minute by minute, the rich luster spread, casting its rose-colored shafts higher into the sky, creating enough clarity to spot the smoldering fire of a picket post by the road about fifty yards ahead. The entire group came to a sudden halt.

One man, their leader, galloped forward with pistol drawn, and discovered that the picket post had been abandoned. The officer in charge had no doubt concluded there was no danger, and with the rising sun, had returned to camp for some sleep. With no known enemy near or threatening, it seemed the logical thing to do.

With a wave of his hand, he moved them forward again—and at a rapid pace. If the Lion and his men did not make up for lost time, their only solution would be to lie in concealment until the darkness of another night rendered it safe to venture forth once more. With such a large group of prisoners, and the increasing number of patrols most likely on the prowl, that plan was swiftly discounted.

Man and horse moved forward, a hazy mist helping obscure their forms as they traversed an open field. Most of the riders kept their heads down so as not to dwell upon the view of cannon staring at them threateningly from not more than two hundred yards away. The deadly weapons were just outlines now, but the sparkling rays of dawn would soon reveal more clearly a spectacle they had no wish to see.

These men knew their leader had placed all his trust for the success of this mission on the darkness and the element of surprise. With both of those factors now lost, they had to rely on his ingenuity and fortitude—and pray for the best. They knew they were in reliable and dependable hands. The Lion's own courage and endurance had been abundantly proven any number of times, and no one who rode with him had occasion to doubt either.

But keeping the faith was no easy task, as the extreme measures General Carlyle had taken to protect the town became more distinct in the gray light of early dawn. All of the heights above them were crowned with a formidable array of guns, through which it seemed impossible for any force of mortals to pass—if one should be so rash as to try. The line of cannon stood like sentinels, seeming to eye with marked vigilance every being that intruded on their boundary.

And who was to say how many companies of infantry could be found behind those guns? In truth, that was not a worry for these men. The magnificent—yet horrible—array of cannon was quite enough to annihilate the entire group. Followers of the Lion would have to rely on their conviction that the Union sentinels would be too careless and cavalier to send a detachment to check and challenge them.

Nevertheless, it was beginning to appear that the affair was taking on the aspect of a problem—even for their leader. His black eyes measured the distance that separated them and the enemy's fortified position, and then searched the road in advance for a section of woods in which they could scatter. The landscape revealed no assistance in that respect.

The savage stare of that line of sullen, silent cannon seemed devoted to the piece of land upon which they rode. The last thing they wanted to hear was the low growl of thunder as those giant guns cleared their throats.

If the unexpected happened. If cavalry suddenly attacked in overwhelming force and without any warning, these men had two choices: Pray to God, which they would—or worry about staying alive—which they wouldn't. Courage and devotion had worked before against superior numbers. They relied upon these traits almost as if they were their most dependable weapons.

The difficulty, if not the impossibility, of this mission was beginning to become abundantly clear, as the men realized the enemy could rain hell upon them with the contingent of guns on the hill. The disparity of numbers, should the Lion's men be attacked, was fearful, but they would have no choice but to fight.

The loyalty, enthusiasm, and devotion of the men did not diminish, even with these risks, but some were beginning to wonder if the entire operation was one of which the Almighty did not approve.

Hope began to warm them, bringing courage along with it. Indeed, the heavens appeared to be in collusion with their plans when clouds rushed in to conceal the face of the sun just as it began to breach the horizon.

But as they drew closer to the enemy post, their worst fear took form. A sentinel in the parapet called for them to halt. Since they were coming from the direction of a Federal camp, he'd apparently assumed them to be a friendly patrol. Otherwise, he would never have allowed them to approach and get within shouting distance before challenging them.

To respond to the order was certain death—to ignore it, only probable demise. It was now do or die, and if the sentry raised the alarm, there was certainly enough weaponry to swallow the mighty Lion and his followers, whole. Their approach and arrival had been too unexpected to raise suspicion thus far, but they still had a few more miles to go.

Then another sentinel called for a halt, swiftly followed by a gunshot. Turning in their saddles, the Lion's men discovered that one of the captives had tried to run to the safety of his lines, and one of their group had shot at him. The shot missed, but in the dim light, the horse stumbled into a ditch, tossing the rider. A few men dismounted, helped the poor Yankee back into the saddle, and they were again on their way.

All of this was in full view of the sentry on the parapet, but since they were coming from the direction of Federal lines, he apparently assumed it was a body of Union cavalry playing around with a new recruit.

They heard nothing more from the guard, and soon put the fortified lines behind them. The exhalation of relief from the group of Confederates was noticeable, but the alleviation of mental and physical strain was short-lived. A new danger confronted them.

The rain from the last three days, combined with the melting snow, had caused the stream in front of them to swell. The current ran so swiftly that the body of water appeared impossible to cross.

Behind them, in full view, were the white tents of the enemy and the mouths of the cannon.

Their leader did not deliberate a moment, but plunged into the raging torrent and swam to the other side with his strong horse. He then rode hastily downstream to help those less fortunate get to safety. His eyes, his tone, and his manner, professed a confidence of success to his men that made them entirely unwilling to contemplate any fate other than victory.

***

The remainder of the ride back to safety was a wet and cold one, but at least they no longer risked capture or death. Daylight overtook them when they reached the top of a knoll just outside their own lines. With terrain perfectly suited for an observation post, they pulled their horses to a halt. There was a general feeling of relief and surprise as they scanned the road for miles.

Although their eyes were heavy from groping so long through the night, it was a welcoming sight they now beheld. The road was clear. No dust from an approaching cavalry squad could be seen. No sound of pounding hoof beats reached their ears.

They had accomplished the impossible. They had slid between the posts and snatched their prey from the very jaws of cannon, under the potent threat of death. The feat would no doubt depress the spirit of the Federal troops, and in the same degree, serve to increase and encourage the determination of those in the South.

The pride this triumph would awaken throughout the Confederacy was immeasurable. The confidence that it imparted in the Lion's men—and the terror it generated in his enemies—would be seen and felt for years to come.

At that moment, the red eye of the sun burst through a thin veil of clouds, shooting a brilliant shaft of light on the men, as if to reassure them that all was well.

Their leader was the only one who did not smile or show any sign of emotion. In fact, he gazed upon the rays of sun with a scowl, as if it were a personal affront to him. He stood there for some time, field glasses at his eyes, striving to find a pursuit that was not forthcoming. Although exhausted from the long night's tramp, his brain remained active, and his eyes alert.

After some time had passed and he felt assured all was well, he placed one of his most trusted men in charge of the prisoners and horses, and spurred his mount away to destinations unknown.

Chapter 21

The day had finally arrived for the horserace and grand ball. If the warm sun and clear sky were any indications, everyone was going to have an enjoyable time. The girls were so excited, they had risen before dawn and began dressing hours before it was necessary, resulting in altered decisions on the previous choices that had been made.

Now, gowns lay strewn throughout the room again, some hanging over chairs, others lying on the bed. Both girls had decided what they were going to wear to the afternoon gala, but the dress for the ball later needed more thorough deliberation.

"You gals had better eat something, or you won't be fit for dancing tonight." Aunt Mazie walked through the room, throwing the discarded gowns over her arm.

"Oh, yes." Sallie glanced over her shoulder at Julia. "I'm starving, aren't you?"

"Now that you mention it, yes—but I still want to fit into my gown."

Aunt Mazie shook her head. "You ain't nothin' but skin and bones. I'll make something so's you can dance all night."

As soon as she had left the room, Sallie began to chat again. "Today is going to be so much fun. Everyone for miles and miles will be there."

"I hope our gowns don't get too crumpled during the journey."

"Aunt Mazie knows how to pack them…as soon as we figure out which ones we're wearing, that is."

"I like the deep blue one the best. If you're not wearing it, may I?"

"Of course. You look better in it than I do," Sallie said, wistfully. "It's beautiful with your light hair."

"Now, which one for you?" Julia pointed to two that were lying on the bed. "I like that pale lavender one, and the rose-colored silk the best."

Sallie sighed. "Me, too. I can't decide which one."

"I guess you'll have to try them on one more time."

Both girls giggled.

"I can't wait to show you off at the ball." Sallie stood in front of a mirror, holding one of the gowns up in front of her while gazing at the reflection of Julia behind her.

"Show me off? To whom?"

"Everyone. Who knows? Maybe you'll find a husband, and then you can stay in the neighborhood forever."

"What about you?" Julia laughed. "You might find a husband and move away."

"No. Never. Anyway, Landon has already told me he has to approve of any match."

At the mention of Landon, the room grew quiet.

"I wish you wouldn't be so hard on him." Julia spoke while sitting in front of a mirror and brushing her hair.

"What are you talking about?" Sallie placed the gown on the bed and stood with her hands on her hips.

"You know. That he's home, not out…I don't know. Never mind."

"No. What do you mean?" Sallie's voice took on a touch of irritation.

"Forget I said anything."

"I'm not going to forget." Sallie stamped her foot. "Tell me."

Julia took a deep breath. "I just think he needs time to heal. He was very close to Sawyer and blames himself."

"Lots of people have lost loved ones." Sallie did not seem sympathetic.

"I just wish you wouldn't constantly allude to the fact he's not on the battlefield."

"Well, he's not. I love him dearly, but I'm not saying anything the whole neighborhood isn't saying."

"It seems so unlike Landon." Julia spoke as if to herself.

"I think that's why it bothers me so much," Sallie interjected. "I never dreamed Landon would turn into a…" She stopped mid-sentence, causing Julia to turn around.

Landon stood at the door.

"Mazie asked me to inform you ladies that your breakfast is ready." He turned and walked away without another word.

Neither girl knew how long he'd been standing there.

Chapter 22

Priscilla Barton stood in front of the looking glass, holding a gown in front of her and turning from side to side. "I think I like this one."

"Oh, yes, miss. That one looks very striking on you."

"Well, of course, they *all* looked good on me." She spun around and watched the graceful folds of the gown flow in the mirror. "But I think Landon will like this one."

"I'm certain of it, miss," her handmaid agreed.

"Very well. Pack it up and send for Bessie to do my hair."

Priscilla sat down and began brushing her red curls, trying to remove some of the waves. She wished for long, straight hair, but had to make do with what she had. Men seemed to like it curly anyway—so much so that she had no doubt she could have her choice of them.

Well, most of them anyway. The one man she really wanted had no need of her wealth, and was among the most eligible men in the region. Priscilla's position in society and her assets would be of no value to Landon Graham.

Then again, he was going through some hard times right now. That could work to her advantage.

Despite his known reluctance, Priscilla convinced herself that a relationship with Landon was not a farfetched idea. In fact, it made perfect sense. They'd spent much of their childhood together, been intimate friends—were practically betrothed, as far as she was concerned. Even Landon's mother had been an enthusiastic proponent of the union, and helped to get rid of the one thing that had always stood in Priscilla's way.

Julia Dandridge.

Why Landon had spent so much time with that child, Priscilla did not understand. Pity, most likely. Landon was a consummate Southern gentleman. Julia had no position in society—and would have none still if Landon's father had not welcomed her and her brother into the Graham household. It had been downright humiliating for Mrs. Graham—a cultured and sophisticated woman of high standing—to be made to endure Julia's homespun and uncivilized behavior in her home.

When the elder Mr. Graham was in good health, he had avowed the two children would remain as long as they wished. But when he became suddenly ill, Mrs. Graham took over the decisions.

After years of enduring the mortification, she'd penned a communication to Julia's aunt and uncle, demanding that they take possession of their kin. Arrangements were made and bags were packed. Little was explained to the orphaned children, and no notice was given. They were simply put into a carriage and sent away.

Landon had been infuriated—more so than Priscilla could have ever imagined. He'd broken off all communication with her and practically disowned his own mother. Then the war had come, and Landon had gone off to fight with no regard for Priscilla's future or her feelings.

With all the young men marching off to the battlefield, she'd known she could not wait any longer to find a husband. She had to accept a reasonable offer while there were still men left to make them.

Priscilla gazed over her shoulder at the painting of her late husband. He'd been a suitable match. Though much older, he had prevented her from becoming just another wealthy spinster—a status she had dreaded all her life.

The gamble had turned out to be a wise one. Her husband was dead and buried, and she was now a widow, with even more affluence than before. With the changed circumstances, perhaps Landon's big heart would open up and take pity on her. He was in his thirties, after all. Too old to remain unwed much longer. She had no doubt that his drinking—and the slight hitch in his reputation that it caused—would be swiftly forgotten by the region's genteel society.

Priscilla picked up a fan and swished it by her face as the maid brushed and tugged on her hair. The heat and color of emotion blossomed noticeably on her reflection as thoughts of Julia Dandridge flitted across her mind.

She leaned in close to the mirror, which caused the maid to pull her hair. "Ouch. Be careful," she shrieked as if it were the servant's fault.

Touching the fine lines around her eyes, she frowned, causing new creases to appear around her mouth. She was still appealing, she decided, but wasn't getting any younger. *You'd better make up your mind soon, Landon Graham.*

Priscilla had a way of getting what she wanted, and there was nothing she wanted more than Landon. Of course, it was no secret that she wasn't the only one dreaming of becoming his wife—a fact that made him all the more appealing.

Some women, no doubt, wanted him for his money. Others, for his striking good looks. And then there were those who were probably enthralled by those inconsequential characteristics that Landon possessed in abundance...Trifling things like integrity, decency, honor.

What Priscilla cared most about was freeing herself from the horrible moniker of *the Widow Barton*. The mere thought of it caused a shiver. Why, it was almost as bad as being called a spinster. The title conjured images of an old lady with gray hair, stooped over a cane. Priscilla intended to use this trip to change the designation. There would be no whispered gossip about *the Widow Barton*, if she could help it. The name *Mrs. Graham* sounded so much more distinguished and important.

Priscilla smiled at her reflection in the mirror as her thoughts returned to Landon. Everyone in the community knew he was going through a difficult time, grieving the loss of his brother. But none would dare hold it against him in the long run, and most appeared ready to accept it as only a temporary affliction. If given the chance, Priscilla knew she could improve his condition and make him forget about the war entirely.

She licked her lips in anticipation as she envisioned the evening. Her attraction to Landon and her desire for his devotion melded perfectly with her real reason for returning to the neighborhood. It wasn't something she could discuss with the inhabitants of this region, of course, but General Carlyle had requested that she attempt to discover the identity of the Lion.

Having been raised in this section of Virginia, she knew the strong loyalties of the local inhabitants. They would never aid someone who was trying to unmask their most renowned warrior. But she was one of them—or had been—and could mix and mingle with her old friends without raising any suspicion.

As soon as Carlyle had made the request, her sharp mind had calculated who could possibly possess such guarded and important information. One man stood out above all others—Landon Graham.

It was simple really. Landon knew everybody and everybody

knew him. As a result of his vast holdings and business dealings, it was quite possible—and perhaps probable—that he was acquainted with the mysterious villain who worked so hard to prolong the ghastly war.

Yet, if her attempt to wed Landon failed, there were other eligible bachelors who had found ways to avoid the battlefield. None of them could be regarded quite as handsome or wealthy as Landon, of course, but there was one who had caught her eye.

His name was Preston Moxley, a flamboyant merchant from Washington who possessed both wealth and standing—as well as a slightly cunning personality that Priscilla found enthralling.

Preston traveled in all of the most notable circles and was acquainted with politicians, businessmen, and socialites. A life with Preston would consist of attending the most fashionable dinner parties in the city and meeting its most distinguished citizens.

The thought of it tempted Priscilla to give up the challenging attempt to win over Landon. The lifestyle of living in Washington would be so much more exciting than residing in the boring countryside at Welbourne.

But when the green-eyed monster of jealousy raised its head, she batted her eyes flirtatiously at the mirror and smiled. She was not going to let Julia Dandridge have him, not without a fight. In Priscilla's opinion, that wild, unpretentious, untamed orphan had no right to a man of such stature as Landon Graham.

Priscilla drummed her fingers on the top of the vanity as she reflected on the reality of the future. If she could secure the identity of the Lion, Preston would be enamored…utterly captivated. She would be propelled into the lifestyle of entertainment and fashion she cherished.

A life with Landon, on the other hand, was shaping up to be insecure—or at least uncertain. Why, General Carlyle had told her just a few weeks ago that the demise of the Confederacy was certain. The Grahams stood on the cusp of losing all their land holdings and possibly their fortune. Their lives of elegance and splendor could disappear in the blink of an eye if the war ended as predicted.

A sly smile gazed back at Priscilla in the mirror. Those facts gave her the upper hand. Landon Graham could cooperate—or he could dismiss her at his own peril. If he knew who the Lion was, Priscilla would find out. She had only to persuade him to divulge the much-needed information—knowingly or not.

Chapter 23

Welbourne was alive with activity as the servants hurried to pack the carriage with the array of items the girls would need to go from their race-day attire to the formal ball gowns they would change into at the mayor's house.

Aunt Mazie had braided Julia's long, blond locks and coiled it into a loose bun, leaving a few tendrils down for a wispy, natural look. The style was more for comfort than elegance since they were going to the horserace first. Tonight, it would be curled and fixed in a manner that displayed refinement and sophistication.

"I swear, Julia. You're going to make all of the unmarried women of the region jealous." Both girls stood in the front parlor, but Sallie talked nervously and paced. "Where is Landon? I do hope he has not been drinking."

At that moment, Julia happened to look up and noticed Landon standing on the bottom stair, rigid, defiant, with one hand on the banister. He was handsomely dressed, aristocratic-looking; wearing polished riding boots and carrying a greatcoat negligently over one arm.

His appearance suggested the type of man who had not been compelled to work a day in his life—but his broad shoulders and overall physique told a different story. A vague, undefinable something about the way he carried himself projected the appearance of a strong will and irrefutable resolve. Yet there was also an overall weariness about him—as if the many hours he spent alone did not afford him sufficient time for sleep.

"Are you talking about me again, dear sister?" Landon did not make an attempt to conceal the irritation in his voice.

"Landon, at last." Sallie ignored the question and walked toward the door. "The carriage is ready. Hurry or we'll be late."

Landon's gaze came to rest on Julia, and his expression spoke volumes even in its silence. The compelling black eyes, the firm features, the confident set of his shoulders, could not conceal an inner pain. Yet with that perfect gallantry that characterized his every move, he stepped forward and opened the door for them.

"It bears mentioning that I intend to ensure my conduct is impeccable." He bowed courteously to his sister as she passed.

"Let us hope it is more so than your punctuality," Sallie quipped over her shoulder, as she hurriedly made her way to the waiting coach.

Julia glanced at Landon and ached at the hurt she saw reflected in his eyes. After a brief pause, during which he seemed to fight for self-control, he threw back his shoulders and waved her in front of him with a swing of his arm. "After you, my dear."

Trying to ignore the tension, Julia stepped outside onto the porch and took a deep breath. The day was clear and pleasant. A recent shower had laid down the dust and cooled the air, but the sun's bright presence promised that nothing more than a light cloak would be needed, even after dusk.

By the time Julia reached the carriage, Sallie had already climbed in with the help of a groom. Julia accepted Landon's help, and was surprised at the strength she felt when he took one of her hands in his, and placed the other on the small of her back. His touch was firm yet gentle, strong and supportive. His voice, his charm, his manners, produced a deluge of memories and torrent of feelings that caught Julia off guard. As she settled into her seat, she wondered if she would ever meet a man with a more disarming and appealing nature.

Landon leaned in as the girls smoothed out their gowns. "Everyone comfortable?" His approving gaze rested a little longer than necessary on Julia, but it was Sallie who spoke.

"Aren't you coming?"

"I'll sit on the box." That's all he said before closing the door.

Julia knew his action was not necessarily a sign that he was angry with his sister. It was more likely an indication that he preferred the conversation above to the one below. Indeed, Julia regretted she could not join him. Sallie had spread the flowing folds of her skirt across the red velvet seat on each side of her and was chattering merrily.

Julia loved her friend dearly—like a sister—but Sallie had lived a sheltered life. With no responsibilities other than keeping herself occupied, she had not experienced the war or its misery on a daily basis as Julia had. Of course, Sallie felt the sting of the blockade like everyone else, and was aware that brave men were fighting and dying.

But until the loss of Sawyer, it had apparently not been real to her. Now, she seemed intent on suppressing her feelings and refusing to recognize the depth of her grief.

Sitting stiffly erect, her hands folded in her lap, Julia only half listened to the one-sided conversation. She fixed her gaze on a shiny brass fitting, but her thoughts were on the man sitting a few feet—yet a world—away.

She wished she could talk to him again, alone, but knew the chances of that were slim. Landon was a complex man, difficult to know intimately, and unpredictable in every way. If he went off with his friends to the card room, as Sallie suggested he would, she had little hope of having the opportunity to converse with him.

When the coach grew dim, Julia's gaze drifted to the window to see what had caused the sudden shadows. A slight smile touched her lips as she recognized the landmark—the tunnel, as she called it. Stately oak trees lined both sides of the road, their branches linked in an embrace that appeared to have lasted centuries. The leafy foliage overhead blotted out the sun until they came out the other side, back into dazzling light.

Spring had awakened, and all of nature seemed to be smiling in happy response to the warmth of this glorious morning. Sunlight trickled through the oaks, dancing in slivers in front of them—a sort of liquid gold streaming through a cathedral of green. Above that rose a vast expanse of blue sky with only a puffy cloud here and there to break up the monotony. Serenading them on their journey were birds of every variety, singing and calling to one another with apparent jubilation.

"Julia? Are you there? I'm talking to you."

"Sorry." Julia turned back to Sallie. "Just reminiscing."

"Well, you sure are quiet. Aren't you excited about seeing everyone again?"

"Of course." Julia smoothed her gown. "I only hope they are excited about seeing me, as well."

"Why wouldn't they be?" Sallie shot her a sideways glance. "If you're referring to your time in Washington, I don't think any of them will see it the way Landon does."

Julia's head jerked over to Sallie. "And how does Landon see it?"

"Oh, forget it." Sallie waved her hand in the air. "You know how Landon is."

"But I saw you when you walked around the lake." Julia

touched Sallie's arm to get her attention. "You were talking about me, weren't you?"

Sallie bit her bottom lip as if trying to figure out how to get out of the situation she had put herself in. "Why must we talk about such things today? We're going to have so much fun!"

"He dislikes me, doesn't he?" Julia said gloomily, turning her head back to the window.

"I didn't say that, and you know that's not true." Sallie reached over and squeezed Julia's hand. "You are closer to Landon than anyone I know. He adores you. It's just that…that…" She leaned back and closed her eyes. "I don't know. The war. He's so different now. Sometimes, I don't even know if he likes *me*." She reached up and swiped her cheek. "See what you've done?"

"I'm sorry." Julia forced a smile and clasped her hands together on her lap. "No more gloomy talk."

"Yes. No more gloomy talk."

The carriage rounded a sharp curve, and Julia turned her head again to stare at the rich landscape spread before her. Everywhere she looked, no matter the direction, budding trees verged on bursting into their finest greenery. Fence rails were thick with honeysuckle vines, and the pink and white blossoms of fruit trees dotted a nearby orchard. The dogwoods were the most spectacular of all. Fluffy white blooms burdened each branch, giving the appearance of snow that had neglected to melt.

"We're almost there." Sallie clapped excitedly, her sadness apparently forgotten. With her eyes glued to the small window, she pointed out people she recognized, even from a distance. "There are the Gilberts and the Carters. Oh, look, there's Johnny Fulton. Isn't he the most handsome thing you ever saw?"

In spite of her dismal mood, Julia couldn't help but feel a twinge of excitement as they drove through a grove of trees. Children ran here and there among picnic tables piled high with food. Beyond the wooded lot lay an open field, where horse and buggies of all descriptions were arriving.

She felt Sallie reach over and squeeze her hand. "You'll have every eligible man in the region courting you, Julia. I have no doubt you'll soon forget all about Landon."

Julia continued staring out the window and did not answer or react. Sallie was wrong about that. There wasn't a man alive who could ever make her forget Landon Graham.

Chapter 24

The heavens conspired with the sun to create the perfect day for a horserace. A light breeze provided just enough relief from the bountiful rays to make the day enjoyable, and the grounds contained an abundance of trees for shade if the afternoon proved too warm.

Nothing could dim the spirits of the citizens who had gathered to forget about the war and all its tragedy for the day. The wealthiest and most powerful residents of the entire region were expected to be in attendance, as were the meekest and the most meager .

A grand tent on a hillside provided refreshment and chairs from which to view the race, but most of the people stood outside, talking, laughing, and gossiping with those whom they had not seen for many months, or perhaps even years.

Landon had disappeared shortly after their arrival, but Sallie had eagerly taken Julia's arm and re-introduced her to old friends. Some were surprised to see her and hugged her enthusiastically. Others, like Judson McGuire and Matthew Sweeney, were gracious and polite, but not overly welcoming.

But young or old, male or female, rich or poor, the news on everyone's lips was the latest incomprehensible escapade of the enigmatic Lion. Julia had heard the tale recited at least five times—in five different ways, but always with the same result. The

Lion had captured one of the most loathed generals in the Union army—stolen him from his very bed, some said—and then the Lion and his men had vanished like ghosts into the night.

At first, Julia had thought it too incredible to possibly be true. But Judson McGuire possessed a newspaper from the North confirming that some terrible misfortune had befallen one of their officers. The article lamented the general's loss, and protested quite fervently the discourteous and demeaning method of warfare that had caused the calamity.

Sallie leaned close to Julia, interrupting her thoughts. "Jud just told me Thomas Cunningham has arrived."

"Really? Where?" Julia turned and looked over her shoulder. "Let's go find him."

"No!" Sallie smoothed her dress, trying to look calm. "I need to fix my hair first."

"Your hair looks fine. I'm certain Thomas will think so." Julia took Sallie's hand to let her know she was teasing, but felt the palm in hers tremble. "What's wrong?"

"Nothing...well, it's just that I haven't seen him for so long and…"

Julia wrapped her arms around Sallie and gave her a hug. She knew Thomas had been corresponding with Sallie ever since he joined the army. He had risen swiftly through the ranks and was now a cavalry captain. After not seeing him for more than a year, it was understandable that Sallie would fear things had changed between them.

"Your hair does look fine, but go. I'll be right here when you get back."

Sallie hurried away, leaving Julia standing alone in the shade of a towering oak. She sighed as she listened to the low hum of conversation, laughter, and the loud greetings of old friends as they reunited with one another.

"If it isn't my old friend, Julia Dandridge."

Julia looked over her shoulder as a tall, impeccably dressed man approached from the shadows. He bowed and reached for her hand. "How very fortunate I am to find a familiar face." His words were deferential, but his keen, close-set eyes were not. They studied her. Scrutinized.

Rather than find a way to extract herself from the situation, Julia froze, too startled to react, her mind spinning with bewilderment. The next moment, the man had taken her hand and bent over it as if she were a queen. "How lovely it is to see you again."

"Mr. Moxley, what a wonderful surprise." Julia hoped her voice did not betray her, but she was more shaken than she cared to admit.

Born to one of the most powerful and prominent families in Washington, Preston Moxley projected a manner of self-importance and conceit. His grandfather and father were well-to-do merchants, a lineage that helped Preston move in the most influential circles of Washington. He considered himself a merchant, as well, but what he did to earn the title, no one really knew.

In fact, his reputation in that regard was not a positive one, nor was he known for being particularly forthright. Raised by doting parents, he'd never known a day of strife or turmoil in his twenty-eight years—other than that which he created himself by flirting too openly with other men's wives.

With dirty blond hair and an ever-present smile, he had a conniving and calculating look about him that could be misconstrued as thoughtful or reflective, depending on your point of view. With his round, scheming eyes, he appeared to be judging and condemning those whom he considered of a lower class than himself. Yet it was no secret in the circles in which he ran, that Preston

Moxley would be among the first to question a man's word of honor—and be the last to keep his own.

The unsavory reputation that followed him did not matter to most women. Preston was considered both handsome and rich, which made him highly sought after by those in search of a husband from the dwindling supply. He stood before her now, fixing his shirt cuffs and gazing around confidently, obviously proud of his good looks, and fully aware of the approving glances cast in his direction.

Julia considered him much too pale and delicate for her own tastes, although it was obvious that Preston believed he embodied all of the virtues of manhood. Impeccably dressed from head to toe, he stood now with his arms crossed, appearing insufferably impudent as he regarded Julia long and hard. Even his gaze was cavalier as he studied her, seemingly reading every thought.

She knew she should say something, but her thoughts were so scattered, she stood there rigid and silent.

"Your powers are quite deceptive." He wore a confident— some might call it cocky—expression on his face, and spoke with exaggerated arrogance.

"I'm sure I don't know what you mean." Julia adjusted her bonnet, feeling trapped and panicky.

"Well, the last time I saw you, I believe we were in Washington. How strange it is to find you *here*."

Before Julia could answer, he continued. "And for a moment, I was afraid you were going to ignore my greeting."

"My dear sir, how could I ignore an old friend of the family? You simply caught me by surprise." Julia's voice was light and frivolous as if the whole matter were inconsequential. In reality, she felt decidedly distressed, like a noose was settling around her neck. "But I can say the same thing about your presence here, can I not?"

He gave a haughty chuckle. "I am a businessman and must travel—even during this terrible conflict in which we are engaged." He paused and gazed around with a look of intense perplexity upon his face. "You, on the other hand…"

"Whatever do you mean?" Julia began to flutter her fan in front of her face. She was suddenly very warm, though the temperature was not. She wished to get away from this man whose eyes took such liberties.

"My meaning is clear." He gestured with his pale, feminine hand. "Among the enemy."

Julia forced a laugh. "I am here to reunite with old friends, not talk about the war. Now, if you'll excuse me…" She was too well schooled in courtly etiquette to outwardly show any signs of discomfort or uneasiness, so she curtsied politely and turned away.

Preston wrapped his long, slender fingers around her arm to stop her, and bowed slightly. A slow, purposeful smile spread across his face, but it held no humor, no warmth. "I meant no disrespect, of course."

Julia stiffened but forced a pleasant smile in an attempt to ease the tension that had formed. "So, what is it that brings you to Virginia, Mr. Moxley? I did not know your occupation brought you to this part of the country."

"Business, of course…" A smile peeked out from beneath his mustache, but it could scarcely be called genuine. "And this and that."

"I see."

"Now that I've run into you, perhaps I could compel you to help me." His devouring appraisal roamed freely. His eyes seemed to shine a light on her, exposing the secrets she kept from even her closest friends.

"Me?" Julia felt her voice catch, as if unseen fingers were closing around her throat. His words had sounded rehearsed, planned. Was this meeting by chance? Or design? She searched her mind for a reason. For any possible slip-ups she had made. "In what way could I possibly be of service to you?"

"Not to *me,* per se," he corrected himself as his mustache twitched, seemingly of its own accord. "To your country."

Julia felt the blood drain from her face. Did he know something? Warning spasms of alarm erupted within her.

"My confidence in your discretion induces me to ask you this favor." He inclined forward with a sudden change of manor. "Will you agree to do a service for your country?"

Julia laughed again, masking her inner turmoil with deceptive calmness. "That is hardly a question I can respond to with a yes or no. It depends upon the kind of service she—or *you*—request of me."

"Have you ever heard of the Lion of the South?"

"Heard of the Lion of the South?" Julia's voice sounded care-free and jovial again, as if she took comfort in just hearing his name. "Why, everyone I meet talks of nothing else. Bless me, if he isn't more popular than the weather."

Preston had not moved nor changed his expression while she chattered, nor did he attempt to interrupt her. He simply cleared his throat politely when she was done. "Since you have heard of him, you understand he is a man who has taken it upon himself to prolong the war, and is, therefore, the vilest enemy of every man and woman in our country."

Julia's heart began to thump in her ears, but she revealed no emotion to Preston. She acted indifferent and blithe. "Oh, dear, I'm not sure what to say about that. The country has many bitter enemies these days."

"But you are the daughter of a soldier of that country and

should be ready to help her in this time of chaos and peril."

"My, but you do have a way of twisting everything to your own interpretation." She wagged her fan more vehemently, more from nerves than the heat now. "My father devoted his life to the country, yes, and died when I was but a child. As for me, I can do nothing…"

"Perhaps you are mistaken." He took a step closer and lowered his voice, which caused a shiver of revulsion within her. "I have agreed to help discover the identities of those who take part in this League of the Lion. This cursed gang of outlaws has pledged to help convicted prisoners—traitors, mind you—escape the punishment which they deserve."

"It's my understanding that many of those imprisoned by the North are jailed illegally, and some have died as a result."

"Nonsense! Gossip! Speculation! Lies!" Preston pulled a silk handkerchief from his pocket and patted his forehead.

"I hope you take no offense if I share a contrary opinion." Julia talked in a low tone, but nodded and smiled at a passing couple as if the conversation were a light one. She secretly yearned for them to stop to talk, but they merely acknowledged her and moved on.

Preston too, watched the couple, and waited for them to walk some distance away. "Of course, I take no offense, but your opinion is a strange one."

The way he studied her as he spoke caused the flicker of apprehension coursing through Julia to surge into a flood, gnawing at her confidence and composure. She cleared her throat, and tried to explain her earlier comment. "We both know that politics has played a role in ensuring that prison exchanges are now a thing of the past. To penalize those accountable for wrongdoings, there appears to be a new policy of punishing the innocent. Many are the men who suffer and languish within prison walls."

"That is ridiculous, irrelevant, and immaterial." Preston placed his handkerchief back in his pocket, though the sweat continued to glisten on his forehead. "These people scorn principle. They reject the laws of a civilized society and repudiate all ideas except their own. They have ravaged this country and left behind nothing but a cursed trail of ruin!"

"In any event, it is none of my business, and certainly not my place to agree or disagree." Julia brushed an imaginary piece of lint off her gown, as if that was of greater significance than the topic of the conversation. "Are you planning to watch the race?"

Preston responded by moving closer and ignoring her attempt to change the subject. "These escapes are planned, organized, and effected by a band of rogue jackanapes, headed by a man whose common sense is as limited, as his identity is mysterious."

Julia listened to Preston without uttering a word. She wanted to look away, to *run* away, but under his steady scrutiny she could barely breathe, let alone think.

He continued despite her silence. "The government, thus far, has been unsuccessful in unmasking this most infuriating foe. All of the most determined efforts on the part of spies sent by my uncle have failed to discover who he is."

Julia's gaze jerked up to meet Preston's. She knew that his uncle was Charles Thorpe, chief detective for the government. "So *he* sent you?"

The man nodded. "I and many others are attempting to uncover the identities of all those who secretly work in the shadows to destroy our country. The others are seeking the minor players, while I intend to strike at the top."

"A profitable way to spend your time, I'm sure." Julia flashed him a look of disdain. It mattered little what his loyalties were—if he were truly a merchant or actually a spy. He was wealthy, well-bred, and unwed. He traveled at will in a country at war, and no one would dare question his authority to do so.

"I feel sure my uncle has been looking in the wrong places." Preston held out his hand and studied the large ring on his finger as he talked. "I believe this mysterious marauder is a young buck in Southern society. I want you to help me find him." He cleared his throat. "For your country, of course."

When Julia had first heard of the Lion's courageous band of men, who so bravely endured impossible situations against incredible odds, she could not help admiring them.

Now, as Preston spoke, her thoughts turned to the gallant and mysterious leader of the daring little group. He had stepped up and assumed a mantle of responsibility that was thrust upon him, certainly not sought out by him. Despite the increasing danger, he continued to risk his life daily—not for fame or power, but for the sake of his fellow man.

Julia stood motionless save for the lace of her gown rising and falling with her quick breathing. She no longer heard the noise from the other guests roaming the grounds. Her thoughts had wandered to the legendary hero as she tried to envision what he looked like. Regardless of his appearance, everything about him appealed to her. Strength. Bravery. Loyalty to the land of his birth. And above all, the anonymity which revealed—even more so than his courage—that he was a man of incredible virtue.

"It is no responsibility of mine to help you or your uncle with such a deed," she quipped. "Furthermore, I have no detective skills that I'm aware of, nor any I wish to acquire."

"Miss Dandridge, I merely need you to be observant and listen." Preston managed a look of injured innocence. "Certainly, you can agree that it is your duty."

"If I agreed with you, we'd both be wrong." Julia lifted her head a notch higher. "There is a long line of ancestors—including my father...not to mention my *own* honor—that stands between me and this thing you suggest."

"But you must." Preston's eyes rested on her with obvious disfavor and dismay. "For the sake of the country."

"You are talking nonsense." Julia began to turn away. "The Lion and his men are like the wind itself. Nobody knows from whence they come or whither or when they go. Why, I wouldn't have the slightest idea how—"

"I simply wish for you to assist in the return of peace by faithfully bearing your part in the burden of war." Preston's tone was gentle, but his eyes were not. "I must tell you again, it is your solemn duty."

"And I must tell *you* that I would never consent to do such an underhanded thing. In spite of his willingness to fight for principles unique to the South, the Lion is gallant and brave. In fact, I cannot help but extend to him the tribute of wonder and admiration—"

"Surely, his devotion and courage are worthy of a better motive." Preston again did not allow her to finish. He leaned down and stared into her eyes, his brows raised questioningly. "And surely *yours* are not in accord with those of this dastardly villain."

"The best of virtues can be committed to the worst of causes," Julia replied without a moment's hesitation. She could feel her cheeks growing red with emotion. "Let me be clear. Never, *ever* would I lend a hand to the treachery you propose."

"Even for the sake of your own reputation?" Angry eyes betrayed a temper the smiling mouth endeavored to suppress. Preston's entire manner suddenly became a shade less cordial.

Julia reacted by laughing. "My reputation? Oh, my. You must

jest." She began to turn away, barely succeeding in suppressing the urge to run. "If we're going to examine each other's character, perhaps we should start with yours."

Preston did not move, and his tone was grave and menacing. "I'm afraid your idea of humor is greatly askew if you believe my comment was made in jest."

Julia swung back to him. "What do you mean?"

"Shall we take a walk?" Preston took her by the arm and led her down a secluded garden path, giving her little opportunity to resist. "Allow me to put it to you this way…" He paused as if choosing his words carefully. "You are here among friends who reside in the very heart of the rebellion—"

"Yes. And I—"

"Patience, my lady." Preston continued on in a steady, unemotional tone. His expression was one of cold calculation. "And yet, in the not so distant past, you socialized with their enemies, mingled with the highest officials in their government, and were allied with the most prominent officers in their military."

Julia stamped a smile on her face as if his words had no effect. "All true. But my friends are well versed as to where I have resided and with whom I have come into contact."

They had stepped into an open area with a beautiful sculpture of a rearing horse spilling water into a pool below. A few other couples lingered about, some sitting on wrought iron benches, others walking through from different paths. Julia was aware of the shifting flecks of sunlight through the leaves, and the soft sound of water as it trickled from the overflowing fountain.

"But do they know of your close relationship to General Carlyle?"

"Close relationship?" Julia stopped walking and turned toward him. She tried to sound appalled rather than alarmed, but she felt a terror like she had never known before creep up her spine. "Why, that is absurd. What would make you say such a thing?"

His eyes stabbed her with mockery. "It may be absurd, but you are indeed acquainted with him. I'm certain any number of people have seen you together." Preston spoke slowly now as if watching the effect of his words. "If such gossip were to be whispered into the ear of Mrs. Dayton, it would no doubt spread faster than a wildfire on a windy day."

He had taken unerring aim. Julia bit her lip to hide the fact that the arrow had struck a nerve. "I have met him only once and that was briefly," she finally said, recalling the recent gathering at which they had both been in attendance.

But as she studied Preston's expression, it was plain to see that facts and truths were not the object of his scandalous revelation. It was clear he would lace his reprehensible rumor with shameful accusations and disgraceful innuendos. What would Sallie and Landon think if they believed she was romantically—or even just socially—linked to the man solely responsible for their brother's death? They would never forgive her. *Never.*

She should have known something was amiss when her aunt had insisted she attend a private gala at the general's headquarters. It had seemed strange—yet innocent enough at the time. Her aunt often attended such gatherings, and it was not unusual for Julia to accompany her. Now, it was becoming clear, there had been a more complex reason behind the invitation.

Preston appeared to be reading her thoughts. A muscle in his cheek twitched with anticipation as he observed her trying to maintain—or regain—her self-control. "In a region where respect isn't awarded lightly, and friends aren't made easily, I fear such news would forfeit all claims of respectability and regard you now enjoy in Virginia."

His hostile expression held Julia as motionless as a gun to the head.

"Nevertheless, I can defend myself." She knew her face was likely flushed with a mixture of anger and anxiety, but she was able to keep her voice from shaking. "I will not do your dirty work for you at any cost to my reputation."

"Temper, temper, Miss Dandridge." He gazed around, grinning with diabolical malice as if to see if anyone were paying attention. "I hope I have done nothing to offend you."

"Aside from your insolence and arrogance, no." Without another word, Julia turned and walked toward the house, trying not to run as she felt Preston's eyes boring into her.

"I do not believe that is your last word, Miss Dandridge. I will see you again."

"Perhaps you will see me again." Julia spoke over her shoulder without stopping. "But I assure you, that *is* my last word."

Had Julia taken the time to turn around, she would have seen that Preston's expression was not dismayed, nor did he show the slightest sign of being hindered from achieving his objective.

On the contrary, his face revealed a menacing smile that appeared reassured—even pleased.

Chapter 25

The tavern appeared to be closed, if one were to judge by the curtains pulled tightly on the windows. But the saloon inside was already raucous even at this very early hour in the afternoon. Spindly chairs and rickety tables sat scattered about the large room, while the majority of the clientele hung onto the bar.

Only one table, sitting in the far corner of the space, was occupied. Two men, seemingly oblivious to the boisterous talk around them, sat in the dimly lit dining area with their hats pulled low over their faces.

"The exploit with General Carlyle is the talk of the town," one said, raising his mug in a simulated toast, though he instinctively talked in a low voice.

"As well it should be," his companion answered. "It was magnificent."

"And you had no problems?"

"An early delay that caused us to run behind schedule." The young man brought his own mug to his lips. "The sun was sprinting into the sky by the time we were clear of the town. I have never seen it rise so fast."

Both men laughed as if barely escaping with one's life was considered great fun.

"It *was* very dangerous."

The younger of the two men nodded. "Yes. Enough to make it interesting, I'd say."

"And the Lion is well?"

"Oh, yes. He led the entire venture—just like the time he rode right up to the pickets at the Chain Bridge. Wouldn't let any other man take the chance."

"I believe he has nine lives. His boldness is incredible."

"That is what carries him through."

They were both quiet for a moment. "Strange that he's so pleasant to deal with—"

"Unless you are fighting against him," the other finished the sentence.

Both men shook their heads in amazement, and then the younger one tilted forward. "He wants you and Warren in Leesburg on the first of next month."

"That is next Tuesday," he responded thoughtfully. "What dangerous task is he proposing now?"

"I believe he has his sights set on Washington City."

"Washington? What folly is that? It is surrounded. Heavily fortified inside and out."

"Exactly to the Lion's liking, no doubt. The pompous Yankees would never expect such a thing."

"Yes, they never learn, and we never forget." The man exhaled soundly. "It would definitely be rare sport to get in without a scrape, and to get out at all, I'd wager."

"It will challenge even the ingenuity of our leader," the other agreed. "I hope I receive orders to take part in the mission."

The older man tipped back slightly and kicked out his feet. "What is his objective?"

"I think he means to hit Old Capitol Prison. A number of his friends are held there."

"And he means to rescue them?" Despite his age and experience, the man looked up with disbelieving eyes.

"I believe that is his intention. It would be an incredible feat."

"It will be accomplished, too," he said before taking another gulp of his drink, "if it is possible for flesh and blood to do it." He wiped his mouth with his shirtsleeve. "Have you any specific orders for me?"

"Yes. It appears that a man named Thorpe, a detective who works for the government, has sent some troublemaker to uncover the identity of our leader."

The two men leaned closer to each other over the table, as the one continued to speak in whispered tones.

"He has brought a whole army of spies with him, and until the chief figures out who they are, he thinks we should meet as seldom as possible." He moved even closer, and talked even lower. "And on no account shall we talk to *him* in public places, at least for a time. When he wants to speak to us, he will work out a way to let us know."

The two of them continued talking in muted tones, mere shadows in the dim light, while the other side of the room was loud and unruly. The younger man took an envelope from his pocket and withdrew a paper, which he unfolded and laid on the table to catch a bit of light from a small candle.

With head touching head as they leaned over the table to read the note, the two men lost track of everything else that surrounded them. Little did they know that a figure had skulked over from the bar with noiseless movements. Closer and closer he crept to the them, as another stealthy figure also made his way toward their table.

"You are to read this note, commit the instructions to memory, then destroy the paper."

As the young man began to place the empty envelope back in his pocket, a tiny slip of paper fluttered out and fell onto the table.

"What's that?"

"I don't know."

"It dropped from the envelope. Perhaps it was with the other communication."

"I don't think so. I don't remember it being there." He picked up the paper and studied it. "Perhaps it is from the Lion."

Both stooped to try and decipher the few words that had been hastily scrawled, when a slight noise suddenly attracted their attention. They turned their heads, but it was an instant too late. Each received a stunning blow between the eyes, which threw them violently to the floor. Within the short span of a few seconds, they were both seized and pinioned.

"Search their pockets."

They were blindfolded, and a man who did not speak took possession of all their papers.

He scanned one or two of the letters and noted the tiny scrap of paper. But it was another letter, personally signed, that seemed to give him the greatest satisfaction.

A most significant find, he thought. *Yes, Preston Moxley will be happy indeed.*

Chapter 26

Many hours had passed since her unfortunate encounter with Preston Moxley, but Julia was still not at ease. That was, until the races began.

Sitting excitedly in the front row of chairs, she examined the horses closely as they paraded in front of the crowd, intent on choosing her favorite. She recognized many of the riders and had heard about many of the horses, since they were all from the region.

"Julia, Thomas and I are going to take a walk."

Julia gazed up at Sallie before shifting her gaze to the tall man standing beside her. He looked striking in his uniform, and wore a beaming smile that added a boyishness to his martial appearance.

"You may come with us if you wish," Thomas offered politely, though it was clear he wanted—and expected—her to decline.

"No, thank you. The races are about to start."

Sallie bent down and spoke in a low voice. "Are you really interested in watching?"

"Of course, I am." She motioned Sallie with her hand. "Go on. Have a lovely time."

"Very well. We'll be back soon."

Thomas nodded politely and then placed his hand on Sallie's back as he guided her away from the crowd.

Julia blocked out the low, buzzing sound of conversation

around her and concentrated on the first race. She stood and clapped when it was over, even though the horse she had chosen had lost by a head. The excitement of the bystanders and the pride exuded by the owners of each mount were contagious.

An overall sensation of exuberance at this pleasurable diversion seemed to radiate throughout the grounds, and lift the spirits of everyone in attendance.

As soon as she sat back down to wait for another set of horses and riders to parade in front of the chairs, someone leaned in close from behind her and spoke quietly in her ear. "A word with you, miss?"

Julia turned quickly in alarm. "Mr. Moxley, you frightened me. Please, I am trying to enjoy the race." She tried to appear indifferent and unconcerned, as though she had no recollection of a previous conversation that might be considered unfinished.

"This is my only opportunity." He took a seat close behind her so he could whisper in her ear without disturbing others.

"Perhaps we can talk at the ball tonight when I am not otherwise engaged." Julia had no intention of talking to him at all, but was hoping she could at least postpone the event.

"Now is quite sufficient," he said with condescending politeness.

"Since when did manners cease to be a virtue?" Julia fiddled with the lace on the sleeve of her dress as she stared straight ahead. "Today started out so very pleasant—"

"The horses are not yet on the field. I do not intend to take up much of your time."

"Very well, but make it quick," she snapped as though her heart wasn't racing with fear. "And I will thank you to keep politics out of it."

"My dear lady, that is impossible." His tone and his words were as sinister as they were subtle. "Everything we do, every thought we have these days, relates to politics."

"Not here." Julia had to clench her teeth to keep them from chattering. She wasn't sure if it was because she was angry or frightened. She was utterly alone in this place, even while residing among friends. None of them knew the service she had performed the last fourteen months.

Did *this* man? He'd appeared as if from thin air. From another life. Another world. If she had been in a parlor in Washington, she would have flirted and been demure. But here, she was caught completely off guard. There were spies everywhere—she knew so better than anyone. No one could be trusted. She'd been anxious to leave the city for just that reason; had felt a silent noose tightening around her.

Julia assumed Preston accepted her reason for being here—to visit old friends. But did he *believe* her? Or did he have reason to question her true allegiance?

"I have something of great consequence to say. I should think you'd be interested in listening to me."

Julia instinctively shivered. Moxley talked gently, yet there was something in his attitude that created a strange sensation, like bullets not yet fired. "My goodness. That sounded like a threat."

"No." He paused as if to torture her, and indeed, she sat without breathing, waiting for him to continue.

Finally, she could take his silence no more. "Say your piece and be gone. Please. I am here to enjoy the horserace."

"My dear, has no one ever told you that a sharp tongue can cut your own throat?"

Not a muscle moved in Julia's face. She pretended to concentrate on the horses parading in front her, yet she could not focus. "Please, you must leave."

She tried to ignore the feel of his breath on her neck, but

when he did not move or speak, she grew impatient again. "Well?"

The ensuing silence came across as dreadfully loud and sinister to Julia's way of thinking. She concentrated on breathing slowly as she waited nervously for him to respond—but he was in no hurry. He seemed content to bait her, watch her suffer, as a spider waits for its victim to weaken before making its deadly move.

"Well?" he responded indifferently, forcing her to respond.

"If you have something of importance you wish to share, what is it?"

"It is news that I think will interest you very much, but perhaps we should start at the beginning."

Although Julia wasn't looking at him, every nerve was strained to hear what Preston had to say.

"Earlier this day, I asked for your help, thinking I could rely on you. Despite your supposed loyalty to the government in charge, you gave me your answer." She could feel his intense, probing eyes upon her and heard him inhale deeply. "Since then, some new information about the mysterious organization we discussed has come into my possession."

"I do not see what that has to do with me," Julia said irritably, her hands clenched in her lap.

"I have obtained a paper which reveals another traitorous scheme for the escape of prisoners by that devious, conniving Lion. But I only have some of the pieces. You must help me gather the rest."

Julia merely shrugged her shoulders and spoke gaily, "Haven't I already told you that I do not care about your plots or about the mysterious Lion?"

"A little patience, I implore you."

"Please, the horses are lining up. The race is getting ready to start. You must—"

"Two gentlemen…spies…were detained recently, and their papers seized."

In a moment, Julia guessed the danger. "Papers?" The very thought struck her with nameless terror, yet she refused to show this man any alarm. "Heavens, why should I care about such things?" Her fan came up.

"These documents contain certain names and movements. Perhaps enough to halt their next operation—but not enough to stop them completely."

"So in other words," Julia responded in a jovial, impertinent tone, "you still don't know the identity of the Lion, and you are back where you were before."

"Except for one thing." Preston paused as if wishing to extract every nerve. "There was another letter…written by your brother."

Julia attempted to suppress the jolt that ran through her, but wasn't sure of her success. "And?" She tried to appear calm, even as her very breath escaped her. "So? What is your point?"

"The letter shows Gideon Dandridge to not only be a sympathizer of the enemies of the United States but also a helper—if not a *member*—of the League of the Lion. It mentions in great detail a person who was later rescued by the evil-doer himself."

The match had been lit. The consequences were momentous. Julia would remember it as a span of time suspended, a moment without thought or sound. All along, she had been expecting it. Somehow, deep down inside, she had known it.

Her brother Gideon would never stand by if he could help in any way. That was the reason for his long estrangement. He had probably been closer to her than she'd guessed. It was quite possible he'd been living in Washington, pretending to be a citizen while spying for the Lion.

Julia's mind raced with these and a thousand other thoughts, but she refused to show Preston how his news affected her. She straightened her shoulders, trying to appear unconcerned...dismissive even.

Yet she could not deny that the facts weighed heavily upon her. A letter of Gideon's was in enemy hands. Worse yet, this foe was calculating and shrewd. Preston would use that document for purposes of his own, purposes that boded ill for her dear brother. All this Julia understood, yet she continued to smile.

She turned to Preston, looking him squarely in the face. "My brother Gideon in league with the Lion?" She covered her mouth with her fan to smother a feigned laugh. "Dear, sir. I'm afraid this tale is too imaginative for even the most sensational novel."

"Let me make my point clear," he said with unruffled calm. "I must assure you, your brother is compromised beyond the slightest chance of exoneration. His arrest is imminent."

Julia had never expected news such as this, yet somehow she did not flinch. She accepted that Preston was telling the truth, because he was too innately evil, too intent on keeping his influence and power, to create falsehoods.

If Gideon were indeed in Washington and suspected of working with the Lion, he would not be treated as a prisoner of war—a fate that would be uncomfortable, but at least not deadly. No, he would be treated as a spy. And with the hatred for the Lion of the South running rampant, he would no doubt be hanged as an example to others.

The sound of applause emanating from the makeshift grandstand came to Julia in muted tones that made her dizzy. Riders waved joyfully to the crowd as they paraded by, but she did not see them. Meanwhile, Preston seemed to take great pleasure in her anguish and speechless distress.

"Mr. Moxley," she replied at last in a low voice and with none of the boldness she had conveyed earlier. "I wish to make sure I understand what you are saying."

"I would like that very much, as well." His eyes glowed with sarcasm. "From the first moment I met you, I could see you were a lady of rare intellect."

And I could see you were a man of doubtful worth. Julia dared not say the words aloud. Instead, she lifted her chin and spoke softly, as if she were in church. "It is my understanding that you are anxious to discover the identity of the Lion, is that so?"

"That is correct." Preston's eyes gleamed unnaturally. "Of course, I am not the only one who wishes to reveal and punish the nation's most vile enemy."

"Most honored protector, you mean." Julia heard a slight huff of impatience and hurriedly spoke again, not wanting to push the man to a point at which he would no longer negotiate. "And you wish me to meddle in the business of my dear friends who have been so kind as to welcome me back to Virginia. I must perform this loathsome deed in exchange for the safety of my brother."

"Such ugly words you use to describe our little arrangement, my dear lady." Preston's tone conveyed that he'd taken offense. "I'm asking you to provide a service in the name of the United States. I don't believe that offering this valuable assistance to your country could be considered meddling."

"Where I come from, that is what it is called," Julia said irritably before turning to meet his gaze. "Have I laid out your purpose correctly? Is this your intent?"

"My *intent* is to find the Lion. That goal will be accomplished with your help, and, as a result, your dear brother will escape the hangman's noose."

"I see." Her tone was a mixture of anger and sadness. "One

would think there are evils enough in the world without men such as you endeavoring to increase them."

"Please, Miss Dandridge, you wound me." Preston inclined forward and spoke dramatically. "Such a dreadful thing to say. I am not without sentiment."

"Yes, it is a soul and morality you lack."

"I beg your pardon." His voice was no longer calm or particularly friendly. "You must help me stop this foe. By prolonging the war, the Lion has doubled both the calamity and the expense of it. What I ask of you is not only a personal service, but a national obligation. You can do your part by providing this minor assistance."

"And what exactly is it that you request of me?"

"As I revealed, we have found a communication. I want you to watch and listen for me tonight." He handed her a slip of paper, which she held up and read.

Remember the need for secrecy, but if you wish to speak to me, I shall be at the ball.

"What does it mean?"

"Isn't it clear? See the wax stamp here in the corner...A lion with wings."

"The Lion of the South? He will be at the ball tonight?"

"That is how I interpret it," Preston said unemotionally. "Those in league with him will have the opportunity to talk to him tonight. Now you see how simple it all is?"

Julia stared sullenly straight ahead, no longer interested in the horses that were just then coming down the final stretch. "You hold me tightly by the throat with one hand, and release me with the other. You may find it simple. I do not."

"I offer you a chance to save your brother from the consequences of aiding and abetting the enemy."

Julia's face softened and her voice was almost a whisper.

"Gideon is the only being left in the world who loves me. Why must you be so cruel?"

Her words and tone had no effect on Preston's attitude. "Go to the ball. Watch and listen. No one will suspect you. You can tell me if you hear a chance word or whisper. Find out who the Lion is, and I pledge to you the safety of your brother."

Julia knew this man would not make an empty threat. She turned slightly again so she could see his face. "And if I pledge to do this thing, you will give me the letter?"

"If your assistance results in the unmasking of the Lion, I will give you the letter...tomorrow."

"But," she said with a hint of despair in her tear-choked voice, "You do not trust me to do so now?"

He smiled cruelly and only answered by saying, "It is not a matter of trust, my dear. It is a matter of identifying the Lion."

"Even if I were willing, I feel powerless to help you." Julia saw only the faintest movement of his left brow at her statement. She could not decipher if the reaction was caused by scorn or skepticism.

"Your brother's life is at stake. I believe you will find a way."

Julia shuddered, knowing he would show no mercy. Preston held all of the power. The life of her brother was in his hands. If she did not help him reach his goal, he would make sure Gideon paid the price...with his life. She had always been strong and in command of her own fate. Now, she was a captive to it.

"Surely, this is not too much to ask of a patriot such as you." He leaned in close again. "What are you afraid of, my dear?"

The sounds of the horses and the crowd seemed to reach Julia in muted tones. She sat rigid, staring straight ahead as if in a trance. "I'm afraid of being persuaded to attempt that which I cannot accomplish."

Preston laughed. "If you have any regard for your country, concern for yourself, or love for your brother, banish those thoughts from your mind."

Julia swallowed hard, an action she could not prevent, and knew Preston had likely noticed. Her mind wandered from her brother, whose life was in danger, to the other man who this awful scheme would affect. The Lion was the last person she wished to hurt by agreeing to this horrible scheme. Oh, how she yearned for someone she could turn to, someone who could provide comfort—or at least advice.

Her thoughts turned to Landon Graham. He had plenty of muscle, if not desire and pluck. Surely, if she could get him to stop drinking, his martial skills and energy could help save Gideon from the vengeful hands of evil—without endangering the life of the virtuous leader who dared all for his beloved country.

"Heed my words. They are not spoken in jest." Preston moved in close again and whispered in a voice that was low and threatening. "*Either. Or.*"

Julia did not turn around, but she whimpered softly, choked by indecision.

Suddenly, someone cleared his throat from behind Moxley.

"Err…the race has concluded. I imagined you wished for an escort to that blasted ball. But, excuse me. Perhaps I interrupted."

It was Landon, standing there with a half-shy, mostly-drunk smile, and looking exceedingly drowsy. As he extended his hand toward Preston, who had risen at the intrusion, he stumbled forward slightly.

Julia sighed as her last hope vanished. Without looking at Landon, she began to walk toward the line of carriages. "Yes. I am ready to go." She did not say anything else, but knew that her silence most likely gave Preston supreme satisfaction.

Chapter 27

"Oh, that was fun, but I'm so glad it's over." Sallie sat in the carriage fanning herself, while Julia stared sullenly out the window. "I can't wait to change into something more elegant and dance the entire night away. Can you?"

Julia did not answer. Landon had chosen to ride on the box with the driver again, leaving the two girls alone. She wished she could share Sallie's childlike enthusiasm, but a cloak of despair hung over her. Rolling hills, beautiful homes, and some of the best horseflesh in the country could be seen in every direction. Yet all she saw before her was her brother's contagious smile and his warm, gentle eyes.

"Why are you so quiet?" Sallie inclined toward her when she did not answer immediately and enthusiastically. "Didn't you enjoy seeing everyone again?"

"Of course." Julia forced a smile. "I'm just tired."

"Tired? The fun has not yet begun!" Sallie sounded aghast. "Anyway, Mayor Chanceford has put rooms aside so that we may rest and get dressed before the festivities. You will have time to take a short nap if you wish."

Julia wanted the night to be over, but she could not confide that to Sallie. She put a smile on her face so her friend would not see her distress. "I'm sure I will feel better after a short respite from the heat and excitement."

"Of course, you will." Sallie's attention turned to the window. "Oh, look. We have arrived."

Julia gazed out and saw carriages and horses everywhere, as well as dozens of well-dressed groomsmen hurrying to assist those waiting along the large, circular drive. Most of the horses would be unhitched and stabled since the majority of the revelers would be spending the entire night.

There would obviously be plenty of room. The mansion, which stood upon the brow of a sloping hill, was magnificent. Massive oak trees, planted generations earlier, graced each side of the long drive. As they pulled closer, Julia spotted a large table filled with punchbowls and food on the veranda—a welcoming sight to the weary travelers disgorging from every means of conveyance imaginable.

William Chanceford II—the mayor himself—stood on the front steps, waving his arms and welcoming each attendee, while his wife moved about from one group to another, spending time with each as if they were intimate friends. The mayor was a prime example of an old Virginia gentleman: kind, generous, and full of hospitality and warmth. He was a notable figure, who had been born into a family of good social position, and held that position still.

Everyone knew that this gala would be one worth attending. The region had practically been in mourning for a year, and this would perhaps be the only bright spot for another year to come. Mirth and laughter would be as abundant as the food-lavished tables. Everybody who was anybody had contrived to be in attendance—to forget the war and enjoy the festivities.

Landon helped both women out of the carriage and escorted them up the steps, where the mayor greeted them enthusiastically. "Ah, the Grahams have arrived. How wonderful of you to grace our home with your presence."

"We would not miss it for the whole wide world," Sallie said. "This is Julia Dandridge. Perhaps you remember her?"

The mayor looked confused for a moment, and Julia saw him glance hurriedly at Landon before returning his attention to her. "Of course. Of course. Welcome, Miss Dandridge. Very nice to see you again."

As another group of arrivals came up the stairs, Landon ushered the girls into the house, where a servant waited to show them to their room. Before they parted ways, Landon stood uncomfortably in the hall. "Do you ladies need anything?"

"No. Julia is going to lie down. Once our things are brought up, we can begin to get dressed."

Landon's attentive gaze rested upon Julia for a long moment, but he made no comment about her health or wellbeing. "Very well."

After he'd turned and disappeared, the two stepped into their quarters. It was spacious and tastefully appointed with a large four-poster bed over which hung a three-tiered chandelier. Two ornately carved mahogany chairs sat on each side of a small table that was graced with a vase of lovely spring flowers.

Damask curtains on the floor-to-ceiling windows were pulled back to expose the view of the wide, stone terrace and the lush garden below. Beyond that stood a stylish arched gate that welcomed guests to a path through manicured avenues of colorful blooms.

Not only did their clothes arrive shortly thereafter, but so did a tray of sweetened biscuits and sponge cakes, along with two glasses of Madeira wine. This would not be anything like the amateur theatricals, charades, and contribution parties where everybody was supposed to bring something to put toward the refreshments. The mayor had spared no effort to make sure there was more than enough of everything to go around.

No, this was going to be a night to remember. The mayor's intent was to host an event that would be talked about for years—and perhaps decades—to come.

Julia laid on the bed, staring at the ceiling, wishing there was some way she could excuse herself from the upcoming festivities without creating alarm or suspicion.

"You don't look like you're sleeping." Sallie took a bite of a biscuit. "Eat something."

"You can have mine. I'm not hungry."

"Not hungry? I'm famished! We've not eaten since breakfast. What is bothering you?"

"Nothing. Just thinking." Julia remained quiet a moment.

Sallie stopped chewing. "About Landon?"

"No. Why?" Julia's eyes flew open. "Did he say something to you?"

"No. Of course, not. He has barely spoken to me all day."

Julia tried to keep the disappointment out of her voice. "He hasn't spoken to me either."

Sallie remained quiet a moment but then shrugged. "So? I told you how things have changed." She took another bite of her biscuit. "Especially you. You were just a little girl back then."

"I suppose."

A loud, shrill laugh from outside interrupted the conversation.

Julia sat straight up in bed. "Is that Priscilla?"

Sallie ran to the window. "It must be. No one else screeches like that."

Julia joined her and leaned out to get a better look. Indeed, no one could imitate that mirthless, bitter, contemptuous cackle that struck one's nerves like a jarring chord. Worse yet, the irritable woman had the habit of laughing at anything and nothing with equal fervor.

"She's the wealthy widow Barton now," Sallie said. "Probably looking for a new husband."

Julia studied the redhead as she departed the carriage. A number of men waited to assist her up the steps, and more stood at the top to greet her. Julia blinked when she noticed Landon in the crowd.

"Landon knew she was coming, didn't he?"

Sallie turned away. "How would I know?"

Julia's heart seemed to stop beating. She'd found it surprising that Landon, known for his reclusiveness even before the war, would so easily agree to escort his sister and her friend to these festivities. Perhaps he'd been in correspondence with the widow, and knew she would be attending.

Priscilla had always been highly sought after and well-endowed, but why men pursued her, Julia could not understand. She was conceited and controlling, and despite the wealth she'd inherited as an only child, was consumed with the notion of increasing her fortune.

The marriage that had left her an affluent widow was no doubt just a stepping-stone to a bigger catch. Julia sat down hard on the bed and stared straight ahead, lost in brooding silence. It took little acquaintance with Priscilla's reputation to know she would preserve neither dignity nor character in her methods to obtain a suitable match.

"What's wrong with you?" Sallie walked toward her.

"Oh, nothing." She attempted a smile.

"You aren't jealous, are you?"

Julia's gaze flicked up to Sallie's. "Of course, not."

"I know you and Landon were close, but you can't really

blame him for wanting to settle down with a wife."

"Is that why he's here? Looking for a spouse?" Julia felt the blood drain from her face.

"How would I know?" Sallie glanced out the window again and then studied Julia. "You look like you don't feel well."

"I feel fine," Julia replied with a certain amount of forced cheerfulness.

Sallie turned and rang a bell for a servant. "I know she is the first one at the bottom of your list for Landon, but you will forget all about Priscilla when the music starts. No doubt, you'll have every eligible man in the region on your dance card. Now, let's get dressed."

It occurred to Julia that there was only one eligible man whom she would be pleased to have on her dance card, and the odds of that happening were far from good. Priscilla would likely monopolize Landon's every free moment, a situation of which Landon did not seem to disapprove.

Even though she was no longer in the mood for gaiety, Julia complied with Sallie's suggestion and began to dress for the affair. But she dreaded the long night ahead of her, and feared the consequences it might bring.

Chapter 28

It seemed nothing had been spared to make this the largest and most elaborate event in the region. Even though it was still early, lanterns burned brightly, and an orchestra played lively strains as new arrivals continuously flooded into the home.

The ballroom itself was magnificent in both size and grandeur. The floor appeared as smooth and shiny as a mirror, and the pillars and the overhanging gallery were wrapped in festive array. Spring flowers of every variety perfumed the air, their colorful blooms cascading over the rims of dozens of large vases set pleasingly around the room. The curving staircase that ascended to the balcony walkway gave the impression of stateliness and splendor, but there was an overall feeling of cordiality and warmth in the room.

Well-dressed women, and men clad in military finery, strolled throughout the house and in the gardens, displaying a sense of old-fashioned grace. There seemed to be a total absence of pretense as neighbors greeted neighbors, and old friends reunited.

In a setting such as this, hardships were lightened, perhaps because sorrows shared were easier to bear. Many in attendance were living with unspeakable grief, yet they made an attempt to cast the sadness away for the sake of a night of happiness and unity with their neighbors.

On a small landing facing the bottom of the fine stairway, the distinguished host continued to receive and greet his guests. Prominent men and refined women filed past him, exchanging elaborate bows and curtsies before dispersing to the ballroom, reception hall, and parlors beyond. Many wandered through the dining area where tables were ladened with every delicacy that could please the eye and satisfy the appetite.

Not far from the host stood Preston Moxley, observing each entrance with silent interest, taking quiet survey of the arriving throng. His dull, insipid eyes glanced toward the door every time a newcomer entered.

Seeming to know he would not be the most welcome of guests, he stood somewhat isolated. A few men had taken the time to shake his hand, but most ignored him altogether. He acted supremely indifferent to the snubs, and actually appeared to scorn those in attendance as if they were of a class beneath him.

A group of woman whispered nearby, not endeavoring to hide their obvious approval of his looks, but he ignored them. Preston was not here to gain friends—female or otherwise. He had come for one purpose and one purpose only. He firmly believed that these rebels were enemies of the country, and he would not care if every one of them was eradicated.

The discussion among the women soon changed, and the chattering rose to such a level that Preston was able to catch snippets of conversation. It seemed they were all enamored with the romantic persona of the mysterious Lion, and believed him to be a superior being in every way.

The conversation aroused a surge of anger in Preston. This enigma of evil had made fools out of good men like his uncle, Detective Thorpe, and his friend, General Carlyle. Preston had sworn to his uncle that he would discover the identity of the meddlesome man, and then…

Preston drew a deep breath of satisfaction at the very thought of seeing the traitor's neck falling on the rope, and the cheers that would erupt from those in attendance.

Suddenly, there was a great stir on the curving staircase, and all conversation stopped. A grim smile rose on Preston's lips as the figure of Julia Dandridge descended the steps with her friend, Sallie Graham.

There was no denying that they both looked beautiful, making their entrance with a confidence that commanded attention. But Julia Dandridge displayed extraordinary allure as she floated gracefully down the stairs. Her blue gown seemed to suit her willowy, regal figure to perfection, and the hum of many whispered comments attested to that fact.

A score of gallant men fluttered like moths on the bottom landing, attracted to the dazzling beauty like a flame. Many more admiring eyes followed her movements from afar.

The mayor and his wife greeted the two guests with much fanfare, handing each a glass of refreshment and toasting to their health. "Thank you for attending, my dear ladies."

"Why, how could we miss it?" Sallie laughed as she lifted her glass. "Don't we owe the honor of this great celebration to our protector, the Lion of the South?"

"Hush," the mayor said quickly and breathlessly.

At that moment, Preston Moxley walked confidently by, wearing the assurance of aristocratic superiority, whether anyone else thought it due him or not. He stopped and addressed the mayor. "Please," he said, as if in direct response to the challenge. "Do not check the young lady's display of gratitude. The name of that mysterious character is well known to me—and everyone in the country, I do believe."

"And perhaps *you* know more about our legendary hero than *we* do." The mayor followed his statement with a boisterous laugh, though it was clear he did not trust the young man who had more or less invited himself to the festivities. "If perchance you know who he is, the ladies are waiting to hear his name. You would make yourself popular among them if you were to gratify their curiosity."

Preston's lips curled into something that could hardly be called a smile. "Ah, but rumor has it that *you*, sir, are in a better position to give that account than anyone." He looked at the mayor with eyes that were little more than slits, and then turned his gaze to Julia, who watched with a stoic and unemotional expression.

The mayor did not flinch but spoke with wonderful charisma and dignity. "It is not often that an occasion offers me the opportunity to speak of a man whose deeds of valor have earned such praise and celebration as the Lion has done." He turned to the women standing in a small group and bowed. "I'm sorry, ladies. As his identity remains elusive, it appears you will have to be content with using your imaginations."

"Imaginations are not necessary to know that he is like a knight of old," Julia said, her eyes shining fearlessly. "Like Lancelot himself, he follows the dictates of his conscience to defend honor and liberty, and help his fellowman."

"Yet it is so strange that he will not reveal his identity, save to his faithful followers." A woman with silver hair and sparkling jewels about her neck spoke in a loud, clarion voice. "We do not know if he is tall or short, fair or dark, handsome or not. We only know that he is the boldest among bold, the most gallant and chivalrous gentleman ever to walk the Earth."

"Oh, but he *must* be handsome," a young lady interjected, her cheeks glowing. "I've heard he has muscles of steel and that his energy is quite supernatural."

A general murmuring of agreement and a nodding of heads rippled through the crowd. It seemed not a single tongue remained silent. The mere mention of the Lion and the image he inspired had everyone wishing to interject.

"They say he is from this very region," another stated. "I don't doubt it is so."

Others shrugged as if that were a well-accepted point. The military profession was deemed one of the most virtuous pursuits that could claim the devotion of a Southern man. They joined the ranks whole-heartedly and gave to the cause all they had—which, in many cases, meant their very lives. Their dedication to their country and their commitment to principles, stood as testimony to the deep understanding of the sacrifice involved.

As for the population of the local region, it was occupied almost entirely in agricultural pursuits. These men were therefore familiar with life in the open air, and were accustomed to hunting, physical exertion, and exposure—conditions of life that naturally fostered a martial spirit. Without a doubt, the boys of this region were superior to most. Their capacity for endurance was marvelous, their riding skills unparalleled, and their marksmanship matchless. They were first-rate soldiers—the pride of their homeland and the joy of their homes.

"I have no doubt whatsoever that the gallant Lion is a Virginian," a stylishly dressed man said, raising his glass. "Hear, hear to the Lion."

Preston stood quietly, not disputing the words spoken, even though he recognized them as insults and unjustifiable affronts. He did not like to be treated with disrespect, especially by those for whom he had such little regard. But this moment would pass. He would have his day.

His gaze swept the room, taking in the sight of the bright, cheery faces, their eyes all aglow with stubborn, invincible pride.

He detested these people, including the mayor, who was suspected of being in league with the Lion. As for the beautiful woman who stood proudly erect with unflinching blue eyes, he need not worry about her. Her defiance was a mask. She was entirely under his control.

A loud, jolly drunken chortle broke the sudden silence that had fallen across the room. "And we poor men," came the booming voice of Landon Graham, "have to be content with standing by while all the beautiful women in the region chatter about a mere myth. Such abominations have fallen upon us with this damned war."

His words came slowly, slurred, in no way matching the astuteness or intensity of his eyes. He lifted a glass to his lips and took a slight step forward as if that action had knocked him off balance.

Everyone laughed as the hostility in the room was instantly was relieved. But there was also whispering about the eldest Graham son, who appeared a little unsteady already, and the night was still young.

Some whispered that it was the death of his brother that caused this fall from grace. Landon had changed noticeably, and many would say, intensely, since that day he had ridden away with his brother in '61 to lead a regiment of local recruits. Rumor had it that he shunned company almost entirely now, and spent most of his time locked away.

But it would be difficult to miss that there was something going on beneath that mass of wavy black hair. His eyes still pierced, even if the old astuteness and reliability were gone. And he still demonstrated that air of inborn civility peculiar to Southern gentleman, a manner that his wealth and position emphasized.

Strangers to the region might have thought that the extensive gossip and whispering in the background would disturb Landon Graham. But those who were acquainted with him, knew he had never been the type to care much about public comment.

Nevertheless, it was anybody's guess whether tonight's lack of offense at the flapping of tongues was due to his unexcitable and imperturbable personality—or the amount of alcohol he had seemingly already imbibed.

Chapter 29

As the crowd broke up and dispersed into adjoining rooms, Sallie sighed and looked around. "Just imagine. The very man may be right here among us."

All the ladies present stood up a little straighter and gazed around longingly. Silver candelabras, polished to a shine, glowed and reflected in the mirrors and off the crystal chandeliers, creating a romantic and mysterious scene.

"I think he is tall, dark, and handsome…with the very devil in his eyes," one of the women replied dreamily.

"And yet he is probably just the opposite," another laughed. "Short and frumpy, a farmer's son, no doubt. Trying to make his mark in another way."

"No matter his looks, he is a noble man," Sallie spoke, as if she were defending him. "And yet, his identity is known only to those who have pledged a silent oath of allegiance."

"I've heard he has a string of spies and soldiers, sworn to utmost secrecy. Valor and complete confidentiality are the only requirements to serve with him."

"But those who work under him know nothing of the others. If one is caught, they cannot deceive him by naming their compatriots—because they do not know them."

"Yes, I have heard that, as well. A rather brilliant plan."

"I wonder if the Lion himself knows who some of the men

are…or if they know who he is."

"The Lion." Someone laughed. "It's as if we know him and are calling him by his given name. Why should we call him by such a label?"

"I believe it's because he possesses the heart of a lion," one of the women answered.

"And nerve enough to match, I'll warrant," another added.

Sallie spoke up then, her gaze focused dreamily on the flickering flames of a candle. "It is the symbol he has chosen to hide his identity so that he may better succeed in accomplishing the gallant tasks he has set himself to do." She sighed as if picturing the heroic knight. "There is no better or braver soldier in all the world. Merely for love of country and his fellowman, he accepts the daily peril of death."

"Soldier?" A man stepped forward. "Methinks the Lion is more hunter than soldier." He followed his statement with a loud laugh.

"Indeed," another said. "And a confident gamesman at that— out stalking prey he is certain to take."

"Have you heard the latest poem that has been circulating?" The mayor's wife elbowed her way to the center of the group.

"No. Tell us, how does it go?"

She cleared her throat and spoke dramatically, emphasizing each word as a circle of bodies formed around her.

"He strikes them here. He strikes them there.
He seems to strike most everywhere.
Some say he's real. Others say he's not.
Three cheers for the Lion, may he never be caught."

Everyone cheered and repeated the lines with much jubilation and delight. Julia shook her head, incredulous as she listened to the chatter. It seemed absurd that this man, who was quite conceivably well-born and rich, should run the terrible risks he did for nothing more than honor.

The Lion must indeed be a great leader to make every man in his little band follow him so enthusiastically and with such passionate devotion. Surely, respect and love for a commander were the only forces powerful enough to raise men to this heroic level.

"His daring is proverbial," a woman walking by chimed in.

"His power of endurance inexhaustible," another added.

"And his sagacity in divining the purposes and movement of the enemy is almost prophetic."

Julia listened, but her attention had turned to the far end of the room where Landon had disappeared with some of the local men, no doubt to a room with a gaming table, according to what Sallie had disclosed.

As someone took her hand, she felt a surge of relief that she could focus on the moves for a quadrille rather than the heavy thoughts controlling her mind. But the relief turned instantly to distress when she glanced up and recognized the debonair smile of Preston Moxley. She had the urge to flee, and almost did so, but a tight grip on her wrist prevented her from bolting.

"I do hope you are having a good time, Miss Dandridge."

Julia was angry, agitated, and shaken, but she pretended to be at ease. "Mr. Moxley, how perplexing to see you so soon after our last encounter."

"You must pardon me as I have need to get straight the point." He bowed to her and then turned to face one of the other couples and bowed again, as the dance required.

"Have you seen or heard anything as yet?" He led Julia through the first steps, after which they switched partners. When they met up once again, Julia's teeth were clenched. "Of course not."

Again they switched partners, and again they met but for a few seconds. "I will simply remind you to be alert."

The dance continued with Julia dreading their next encounter. When their hands again touched, her fingers twitched with revulsion so visibly that Preston noticed. "My dear lady, do not be so prickly. We are merely doing business. I do not wish to be your friend."

At their next meeting, Julia expressed four words. "Your wish is granted."

They spoke no more. She stamped a smile on her face that was as painful as it was feigned, and passed the rest of the dance in complete silence. Preston, too, wore a smile, but it was a sly, malicious one that gave the impression he was hiding a secret.

When the music ended, Julia had the urge to run for the door, but a strange sensation caused her to remain on the dance floor. She scanned the room, seeking the reason for her hesitation—and it was soon found.

Landon Graham stood alone on the other side of the room, leaning against a doorway in a lazy pose, silently observing the scene. For a moment, he ignored Julia as if looking for someone else, but she sensed that he knew exactly where she was. His expression appeared irritated, impatient; his eyes as dark and impenetrable as she had ever seen them.

When the music began again, Landon advanced toward her, displaying a calm, quiet dignity that kept Julia's eyes riveted upon him. She didn't wish to converse with him here, yet neither could she force herself to turn away. Even in a crowd, his presence was compelling. His bearing, his comportment, his striking features, radiated a magnetic allure that captivated.

But that long, purposeful stride and those bold, unflinching eyes told Julia that this dance was not merely for pleasure.

"This is a waltz, I believe?" A gentleman standing at Julia's side repeated his question and seemed to be waiting for her to take his hand. Through the ringing in her ears and the sound of the music, she could barely make out his words.

Her gaze remained fastened on Landon, and her body felt precariously off balance. She was torn between memories of him and the current situation, making her want to welcome him and rebuff him at the same time. Yes, she had wished to speak with him tonight, but she now feared the encounter.

"Shall we dance?" is all he said when he reached her. It was posed as a question, but the firm grasp informed her he was not interested in waiting for an answer, nor was he seeking permission from the gentleman beside her who had already claimed the privilege.

Julia imagined she saw something flicker in Landon's eyes when his hand settled lightly on her waist. She had little time to wonder if he was thinking of days long past. Her feet barely touched the floor as he swept her masterfully across the room—as if there were no one else in attendance. Landon Graham danced as he did everything: efficiently, politely, and with an air of distinction and grace.

"You have improved since last we waltzed." He expressed the words matter-of-factly, as if he were simply making conversation, but the eyes gazing down at her were tender.

"I had a good teacher in my youth." Julia answered impulsively as she tried to control her emotions in that first dizzying moment when she was back in his arms. He made her feel small and fragile, yet she was exhilarated by the great strength that encircled her. Every nerve in her body tingled at the closeness, but a chilly feeling followed in its wake.

It was unforgivable of him to whisk her away like this. Of all of the impolite, impertinent, and presumptuous things to do. The feelings surging through her, the memories, were too alarming and too thrilling to contemplate. She turned her head away from him, determined that he should not see how the firmness—and the gentleness—of his hand affected her.

"I had little hope of seeing you this evening." Julia stared out over his shoulder as she fought the vitality he exuded. "I thought you would spend the night in the card room." Her eyes darted to his.

Landon let the comment pass with nothing more than a cool stare that told her his mind was somewhere else. After a few minutes of silence between them, it became clear where his thoughts had roamed.

"You are acquainted with the merchant from Washington, I see." His black eyes rested on her casually, but she detected a hint of wariness in his words.

His impenetrable expression caused Julia to study him more closely. He had a way of staring vacantly while taking everything in. Perhaps he was not as intoxicated as she'd expected him to be. Was the expression on his face curiosity? Or suspicion?

The statement might have been an innocent attempt to make conversation—or a deliberate effort to extract information. Julia struggled to decipher its meaning. Did it imply anything? Everything? Nothing?

Her mind roamed like an untied horse, refusing to cooperate. As Landon waited in silent expectation for her reply, Julia decided to steer the conversation in another direction. She knew it would be difficult to fool him with a direct reply, especially when he made her so insecure and shaky.

"You saw me speaking with him at the races, as well," she said somewhat coldly, "yet you did not question our association then."

"I was trying to be polite."

"And now?"

"I'm asking politely."

Swallowing hard, Julia focused her attention on a dazzling chandelier overhead. It was difficult to keep her eyes from staring at the face enshrined in her memory as someone with whom she could share complete confidence. Oh, how she wished she could. "I know him only slightly."

"I see." Other than a hint of exasperation in his tone, the reaction to her reply was up to its usual code of indifference. But she could feel the barely controlled strength and emotion coiled within his body—and she sensed that his manner had altered into suspicion.

Julia hoped he could not feel her erratic pulse. The man who so often appeared wobbly and weak, felt steady and graceful beneath her touch; his steps were agile and smooth. And despite his apparent effort to remain withdrawn, his strong features and vibrant, black eyes yet held a hint of sensuality that no amount of remoteness could mask.

Julia's mind wandered to the forest and fields of Welbourne where they had so often escaped together on early morning rides. She could almost smell the sweet pine, envision the morning frost still glittering on the hedgerows—and see the tall, graceful horseman beckoning her to catch up.

She stole a glance at him as he gazed out over her head, and tried to penetrate the deliberate secrecy of his eyes. They appeared intensely observant, even though they didn't seem to be looking at anything.

The soft radiance of candlelight reflected in the mirrors revealed his clearly chiseled features and a mass of wavy, black hair. He was a devastatingly handsome man, and despite his drinking

problem, was still very much in demand, if one were to judge by
the number of women staring in his direction.

And why not? Dressed as he was in his stylish attire, his entire
bearing displayed strength and sophistication. Yet there was an air
of isolation and loneliness in his manner that gave the impression
he was hurting.

Julia struggled to draw breath as he whirled her effortlessly
around the room, but he did not seem to notice. What was he
thinking, she wondered. Of times long ago when they were innocent youths and enjoyed each other's company?

Or something more ominous?

Julia wished she could talk to him as she used to do, share
every thought and feeling. But an invisible wall kept her from
revealing the painful secrets she longed to disclose about her time
in Washington. She had to be content with soaking in the comfort
of his nearness for these few brief moments.

The music continued, but the silence between them widened
into a wall of separation. Did he feel what she did? Were memories of their dancing lessons and the laughter that followed in the
library at Welbourne playing before his eyes, as well?

Julia stole another quick glance. His jaw was set, and his eyes,
accentuated with long, dark lashes, stared out expressionlessly.
She could not tell what he was thinking, and she dared not ask.

Although she was accustomed to silence when in his presence, tonight it strained her nerves and aroused her imagination.
That calm, composed reserve she remembered so well had not
changed. His inner thoughts were still well sealed. The privacy he
treasured was secure.

The music slowed, the song ended, and couples moved away
from the dance floor. Before they parted, Landon's hand closed
unexpectedly over Julia's, creating a sensation of familiar, com-

fortable warmth that sent her emotions reeling.

He said nothing as he bent down to study her with a look that held her captive no less than a rope pulled tightly would. As his gaze traveled over her face, he seemed to be searching her inner thoughts. She tried to do the same to him, but perceived only the tortured dullness of distrust and disappointment in his dark expression.

When he withdrew and turned to leave, Julia felt the strength and vitality of him slip away from her, as if the bolt of energy that had run between them was severed. He did not speak before striding back to the room from which loud conversations now emanated, but Julia was almost certain she had felt his hand tremble.

***

At ten o'clock, all of the grand rooms in the house were filled with guests, as were the verandas and gardens beyond. The largest room had been set apart for dancing, and the dainty strains of music were a nice accompaniment to the loud chatter and merry laughter of all in attendance.

The mayor's wife was taking a break from her hostess duties by sitting near the orchestra. She smiled and tapped her foot to the lively strains, while watching the couples on the dance floor whirl by her in unrestrained jubilation.

Julia stood in a group of old acquaintances when she heard a loud, raucous laugh coming from the room into which Landon had disappeared. She felt her cheeks flush when she recognized the outburst of Priscilla, and peered over the shoulder of the man conversing with her. Julia did not hear a word he spoke.

Priscilla stood in the doorway, erect, defiant, one hand holding onto Landon, the other grasping an empty glass. She must have been looking for Julia because she stood there now, beaming, the very personification of self-assured pride and arrogance. Julia met the redhead's gaze quite boldly, though the effort caused her to feel nauseous and shaky. Priscilla smiled smugly but tottered a bit, giving the impression she was drinking in her close connection to Landon—as well as everything else in sight.

Taking a deep breath, Julia tried not to let the spectacle affect her, but the room had started to churn and spin. The dancing flames of the candles that had seemed so very fashionable as they shimmered and reflected in the ornate mirrors around the grand room, now resembled a giant mass of chaotic confusion.

Julia stole one more glance before turning away, knowing she had just witnessed her last chance for a reconciliation with Landon. Priscilla had changed her position and now leaned intimately and securely in the crook of Landon's arm. She wore a proud, possessive look upon her face that proclaimed, "He's mine."

Meanwhile, the orchestra sounded dreadfully out of tune, and the voice of the gentleman trying to regain Julia's attention grew more muffled and indistinct. Julia nodded her head and smiled with no regard for the conversation in which she was supposedly a part.

"I don't believe you've heard a word I've said." The man's voice finally broke through her reverie.

"Oh, I'm sorry. I confess my thoughts were elsewhere for a moment. It's very hard to concentrate in the midst of all this commotion."

"Perhaps I should procure some refreshment?"

Julia pretended that would solve all her problems, even though all she wanted to do was run out the door and go back to Welbourne. "Yes, that would be lovely. I am a bit warm and thirsty. You're so kind."

When the man turned away to carry out her wishes, Julia's gaze unintentionally strayed to Landon. His compelling black eyes seemed riveted upon Priscilla. He was dashing as always, but the way he rested against the redhead made him appear a little worse for wear.

Julia gulped back her jealousy and despair. She was relieved when the music and the corresponding commotion stopped, and the mayor stepped forward to make an announcement. "Eat, my good friends. And drink a toast to the Lion, whose fame has spread throughout all the South and beyond. May the Almighty continue to bless him with the courage he so brazenly exhibits, and the safety he so nobly deserves."

"Trust in Fate," another's voice rang out, "and believe in the Lion to preserve our liberty and protect our homeland."

"Hear. Hear. To the Lion," echoed throughout the house.

***

Priscilla had ignored the glances of the other men in the smoke-filled room when she made her way toward Landon. She knew this was an area off-limits to women. Propriety would dictate she wait for him to step out, but time was of the essence. The only brief appearance he'd made was to dance with her nemesis, Julia Dandridge.

The hour was growing late. She had to make a move, or the entire evening would be lost.

Landon was leaning against a fireplace mantel, staring vacantly toward the door, but he didn't seem to notice Priscilla's approach. "Landon," she said, "won't you come away and take a walk with me?"

The boldness of the question in this room full of men was sanctioned by neither policy nor respectability, but Priscilla didn't care. She was a widow in high standing. Surely, the gossip that followed would be tempered by her status and position.

Landon's absorbed gaze shifted to her when she spoke, but for a long moment, she didn't think he was going to respond. At last, he held out his arm, which she hurriedly grasped before he could change his mind.

Priscilla laughed loudly as they made their way toward the door, as much from nervousness and excitement as from the gaping expressions on the faces of some of the other men in the room.

"I've missed you, Landon." Priscilla flicked her green eyes up at him and squeezed his arm when they stepped through the doorway. She instinctively scanned the ballroom, and studied the blue-eyed woman whose attention she seemed to have caught. Priscilla relaxed slightly and leaned into Landon a little more, as her determination to succeed in her mission intensified.

"I was sorry to hear about your husband," is all Landon said.

"Yes, well, life goes on."

"So I hear."

Priscilla laughed again, this time purely from nervousness. Landon's voice sounded cold and unfriendly. What had he heard?

"Well, I see no need to agonize about it. I can't bring him back." She skillfully stepped into the crook of his arm. "Shall we walk?"

"This is far enough."

He leaned into her a little as he talked, but Priscilla had the feeling it had more to do with balance than desire.

"What brings you back to Glennville?"

"Seeing old friends." She gazed up at him and batted her eyes. "Dear...old...friends."

"So, you're just visiting?" He lifted a drink from a tray as an elegantly clad servant walked by.

"That depends."

"On what?" He lifted the glass to his lips and stared at her over the top.

"On how the visit goes."

"I see." He took a sip of the drink and seemed to relax a little. "I thought perhaps you were like the others here—searching for the elusive Lion of the South."

Priscilla jerked her head back in response. "Why? What do you know of him?" She tried to relax and regain her composure. "I mean, of course, everyone is interested in discovering his identity. I am not immune from curiosity."

She emptied the glass of wine she had been drinking. "Does that mean you know something?"

"If I did, it would not be something I could share—certainly not here, anyway."

"Take me back to Welbourne with you." Priscilla snuggled up close and increased the pressure on his arm, taking his words as a proposition. "Perhaps I can provide an incentive."

Landon ignored the comment. "Look around." He swung his glass out toward the ballroom, causing some of the fluid to slosh over the edge. "Who do you think it is?"

Priscilla glanced around the vast room and then back to Landon, who was studying her intently, as if trying to read her mind and motivations. "It is impossible to guess."

"Then I suppose his identity shall remain a mystery." He emptied his glass, bowed politely, and returned to the card room.

Chapter 30

Here and there, dotted among the distinctly Southern beauties, stood men who had been to war and returned. The effects of the conflict could be seen in their eyes, or confirmed by a lost limb or their obvious scars. Even some of the women stared idly into space, their thoughts far away with a husband, brother, or son—maybe still in danger or with a fate unknown.

After a great swishing of silken skirts, much whispering, and a general stir of curiosity among the attendees, Julia sat down, wishing the night would end. She suffered intensely, yet she smiled and chatted, hiding the torment as best she could.

Inside, Julia felt like someone condemned to death, with a noose already settled upon her neck. Her nerves, which had been in a state of painful tension ever since she saw Preston, had become even more strained in the brief time she had spent in Landon's company. The hope that she might be able to confide in her old friend had vanished as quickly as it had come.

Julia was aware that her heart was not the only one that bore a weight of ceaseless, gnawing pain, yet she could not help but lament her own situation. With Landon's utter change of disposition and his complete shift of character, she was alone and helpless.

The feeling of desperation and despair caused a wave of anger to wash over her. She had thought she could rely upon

Landon for moral support—if not physical assistance—in this heart-rending crisis, yet every response from him was contemptuously cold and uncaring.

Julia weighed her choices, and at last convinced herself that future events were in God's hands, not her own. Yet that did not change the fact that Preston would show no mercy. He had set a price upon her brother's head and left it for her to pay—or not—as she so chose.

As her gaze swept the jovial crowd around her, Julia began to wonder which of these honorable men could be the mysterious Lion. Who was the man who controlled the reins of such miraculous plots and held the fate of so many lives in his hands? If only she could find him before the Federals did, she could warn him of the treacherous plot against him. Perhaps then, he would help her save Gideon.

It seemed impossible that he could be right here, somewhere in this room. For months, tales of his ingenious schemes had spread far and wide. Julia had never given a thought about who he might be—the need for anonymity was obvious. She had been glad just to know such a man existed. But now, she longed to identify him, not so she could give in to Preston's demands, but for her own sake.

She studied everyone—the young, the old, aristocratic, and poor—and tried to decide which one conveyed the boldness, the intellect, the courage, required to lead a group of high-born Virginian gentleman on such dangerous and perilous missions.

Whoever the Lion was, Julia could not help but admire him. War had cast its shadow across the land he loved, and his strong will and intrepid resolve had risen to meet it. She believed the Lion was a distinguished and honorable man who embraced Southern values and principles, and would defend the sacred soil of Virginia with his life.

After studying the schoolmaster, Jud McGuire, for a moment, she ruled him out. He was much too lighthearted and friendly. Her gaze shifted to Thomas Cunningham. He appeared courageous enough in his uniform of gray and his captain's rank. But that easy-going smile and relaxed attitude as he talked quietly with Sallie made him appear incapable of such feats.

As she reconsidered the possible involvement of Jud, she watched him stroll toward a small corridor somewhat isolated from the festivities. There, he paused and rested against a small column with his arms crossed as if trying to look relaxed.

Julia abandoned the attentive cavalier who had gone to find her a drink and skirted the crowd, drawing nearer to where Jud stood. Why she had this sudden urge to spy on him, she did not even know. Compelled by something other than thought, she paused behind a large vase of flowers and held her breath. Someone else, a man on crutches, brushed against Jud and then continued on his way.

Julia kept her eyes on Jud as he disappeared through a door, all the while nonchalantly nodding her head and smiling at those who addressed her. It seemed that the ball, with its sounds of music and laughter, its displays of colorful gowns and flickering candles, no longer existed. Julia's mind was consumed with only the memories of her dear brother and his protecting arms. Nothing else mattered. All else was forgotten.

Gideon was in deadly peril. And it might be within her power to save him. Slipping into the room where she'd seen Jud disappear, she discovered him leaning in close to a candelabra to read a piece of paper he held in his hands.

Holding her breath, Julia crept in close behind him, her slippered feet making barely a sound on the luxurious woolen rug.

When he looked around and saw her, she uttered a groan and passed the back of her hand across her forehead. "Oh, Jud, how glad I am to see you. I feel faint."

She tottered toward him, causing him to crumple the note in his hand to support her.

"You don't feel well? Let me find Landon to take you home."

"No. No. I think just a chair will do."

He guided her to a chair, and Julia sank into it, closing her eyes. "Don't worry. I feel better already. It was just the heat of the ballroom."

Julia wasn't sure what to do next. But with her eyes closed, she saw the image of Gideon's face. He seemed to be looking at her while the ghastly gallows loomed behind.

The sound of laughter and conversation in the glittering ballroom beyond contrasted with the sudden silence in the room she occupied. Jud stood awkwardly in front of her with the paper still in his hand, not uttering a word.

"Oh, how fortunate, a fan." Julia took the paper before he had time to react, and began to wave it in front of her face. "Thank you so much. I feel so silly to have frightened you, but I am better now."

Jud's face turned ashen, his full attention remained on the note in Julia's hand. Unsure of her next move, Julia fanned the paper even more frantically, causing one of the candles in the candelabra to extinguish.

"Oh, dear, look what I've done."

Jud stood perfectly motionless, seemingly holding his breath, his face pale with angst and fear.

"Perhaps you should relight the candle. It's quite gloomy in here."

Jud nodded mechanically and turned toward the table. In that split second, Julia brought the note to her eyes and scanned the missive. As soon as she sensed the candle flare back to life, she began fanning again. "I do feel so much better. Thank you, Jud."

The poor man had not yet uttered a word. His eyes remained wide with anxiety.

"I suppose you want this back." Julia talked with perfect composure now. "From the look on your face, I fear it is very important to you. A love letter perhaps? From Lena Jennings?"

Jud didn't say anything one way or the other. He continued to stare at the paper in her outstretched hand.

"I am certain she would be mortified if she thought anyone else had seen it." Julia arose from the chair with regal grace, and Jud anxiously retrieved the paper. "Thank you so much for tending to me. It most certainly must have been the heat and exertion from dancing."

"Shall I summon Landon for you?" His voice cracked slightly.

"No. I feel so much better." Julia turned to exit the room. "Thank you for your kind assistance, Jud."

As she walked out of the room and passed by an ornately carved clock in the hallway, Julia wished she could move the hands so this night would be over. She had very little time to make up her mind between two horrible choices. Either keep the knowledge she'd gained to herself, leaving her brother to a dreadful fate. Or willfully betray a man whose life was devoted to his fellowman. These were the stark, undeniable facts.

Either. Or.

Preston's ultimatum echoed in her ears. He had made it sound so easy.

Either save her brother and send a brave man to the gallows, or hand the same fate to her dear sibling, whom she loved and cherished.

It all seemed too horrible. Gideon, who was as noble and brave as anyone she'd ever met, would never suspect such treachery. Gideon, who loved her as only a brother could, would never have paused to risk his life to save her. Yet here she was, hesitating to save him from certain death.

Julia put her face in her hands as her brother's image appeared before her once again. His eyes were pleading, seeming to say, "I was your protector. Now you have the chance to save me."

Could she choose the life of a stranger and send her brother to certain death?

All these conflicting thoughts raced through her mind, while, with a smile upon her lips, she strolled about, feeling like an actress upon a stage. Somehow, she glided through the graceful moves of a dance, her composure and poise a mere act.

She could allow no one to see the dreadful struggle raging within her heart. She had to hide the effects of the torturous decision she must make. By sheer force of will, Julia displayed a calm and dignified deportment, even though her mind and body were in chaos.

Julia tried to evade Preston, hoping she could avoid making the ghastly decision. Yet she could almost feel his keen, hawkish eyes upon her, and knew he would never let her get away. Now, only half an hour remained before the destinies of two brave men would be pitted against one another. One a dearly beloved brother, and the other, an unknown hero.

She prayed that something would occur to shift this terrible burden of responsibility from her weak shoulders. Her eyes darted to the clock as it counted down the minutes, leaving her to feel breathless and out of control.

Chapter 31

After a short break by the musicians, the dancing had resumed—at least by the younger set. It was well after midnight, and many of the older couples were gathering their things and saying farewell or good night.

Julia stood off to the side, scanning the large room, her nerves stretched taut as she thought of her terrible ordeal. A light tap on her shoulder caused a sudden tremor in her chest.

"There you are. I've found you at last."

Julia flinched and turned, only to find Sallie standing behind her, bright-cheeked and smiling as if it were the happiest day of her life. She was being held securely around the waist by Thomas Cunningham, who wore an equally cheerful expression upon his face.

"Wasn't it a delightful party?" Sallie asked. "I've barely seen you all night."

"Yes, of course." Julia forced a smile. "But it's getting late—"

Sallie closed her eyes and shook her head emphatically, causing her curls to bounce. "I don't want this night to end."

"Nevertheless, I am tired." Julia hoped Sallie would offer to find Landon so they could return to Welbourne, and she could put this terrible ordeal behind her. Unlike Sallie, there was nothing she wanted more than for this night to end.

"Mayor Chanceford and his wife have requested that Sallie spend the night and eat breakfast with them in the morning."

"Yes," Sallie said. "Mrs. Chanceford wants to show me her paintings."

Julia looked from one blissful face to the other. She knew Mrs. Chanceford and Sallie shared a love for art—but it appeared there was more to Sallie's desire to stay than paintings. "Very well. I'll tell Landon when I see him."

"That would be wonderful."

Sallie seemed relieved that Julia would be the one to tell her brother that she wouldn't be returning to Welbourne until the next morning.

Julia took a deep breath and let it out slowly as the couple walked away. She didn't wish to dance, but she wanted to stay occupied to avoid Preston. When her gaze accidentally met his from across the crowded room, she knew he had divined her thoughts. There would be no evading him, no escaping his revolting scheme.

Torn though she was, Julia made a decision, and resigned herself to follow through with it. She must save Gideon at any cost. He was her brother, had been mother, father, and friend to her. To think of Gideon dying a traitor's death at the end of a rope was too horrible to conceive.

As for the stranger, the hero…well, fate must decide his destiny. Julia would exchange her brother's life for his, yet she would pray that the Lion could extricate himself from the trap. The daring warrior had baffled an army of spies for more than a year. Certainly, he could evade Preston and his evil minions.

Julia thought of all this while nodding absently in conversation with a man who seemed to think she was interested in the conversation. When she observed Preston standing nearby, her heart sank with a feeling of dread. "Will you do me a favor?" she asked the stranger.

"Of course. I am entirely at your service."

"Will you see if Landon Graham is still in the card room? And if he is, will you tell him that it is very late and I would be glad to go home soon."

The gentleman prepared to obey instantly. "But I do not like to leave such a beautiful young lady alone."

"Don't worry. I will be quite safe and undisturbed here. But I do hope to get home before daybreak."

Julia had not seen Landon since he disappeared with Priscilla. The dread of having to speak with Preston was overshadowed by the despair of having lost touch with the one person she thought might help her.

As expected, the moment the gallant young man departed on his errand, Preston slipped in next to her. "You have information for me, I hope."

An icy chill swept down Julia's spine. *Oh, Gideon. Will you ever know the terrible sacrifice I have made for your sake?*

For a few long moments, she issued neither denial nor confirmation in either her look or word. But then, with a deliberately casual movement, she turned to face him. "Probably nothing important." She stared straight ahead, not daring to meet his eyes.

"What is it?" He leaned forward impatiently.

"I found a piece of paper—"

"Did you see its contents?" He licked his lips anxiously, not allowing her to finish.

She nodded and continued in the same calm, mechanical tone of voice. "In the corner of the paper, there was a red wax seal with the impression of a winged lion. Above it, I had time to read but two lines."

"And what were those lines?"

Julia's throat seemed to contract. For an instant, she felt as if she could not speak the words, knowing full well that by repeating them, she might send a brave man to his death.

"It said: I leave tomorrow for Washington. If you need to speak to me, I will be in the library at precisely one."

"It is lucky that you were able to read a bit of the note." Preston's brow creased with feigned concern. "It might have been bad for your brother had you not."

Julia's pulse beat rapidly at the coldness of his tone and the threat conveyed.

Preston didn't seem to notice. He turned to the clock and smiled.

"What are you going to do?" Julia's lips were so numb she could scarcely form words. Oh, this cruel war. What had it made her do? An abhorrent thing? Or one that was necessary? It seemed to her that it was both, in equal measure, but that thought did little to console her.

"What are you going to do?" she repeated when he did not answer.

"I guess you could say, 'it all depends.'" His eyes shone with a look of amused contempt.

"On what?"

"On the person I find in the library at one."

"You will see the Lion, of course. But you do not know who he is."

"No. But I shall…soon."

"He may have been warned." Julia silently prayed that he had.

"I don't think so. Whoever is there when the clock strikes one will be the Lion. According to information I have received, a group of his men are departing tomorrow for Washington City itself. And of those, one shall most certainly be the man I discover in the library."

"And?"

"I shall also leave tomorrow. The papers I have in my possession make it clear the irksome Lion wishes to outdo himself and rescue some traitors from the very bowels of our capital.

"And Gideon?"

Preston's lips twitched up into a condescending smile. "I have given you my word, my dear. As soon as the Lion and I start for Washington, I will send you the letter by special courier. Moreover, I pledge to you that as soon as the Lion is in my possession, Gideon will be released unharmed. I do not see how I can be more accommodating."

"Would that you could be as deficient in self-esteem as you are in mercy," Julia murmured, staring into the distance.

Other than the smug expression he wore, Preston did not reply. He simply bowed deeply, ignoring the pain on Julia's face, and sauntered from the room.

Julia put her face in her hands. The deed was done. She thought she would feel a sense of relief, having saved her brother from a terrible death—but it was remorse that gripped her now. Remorse and a misery so intense, she feared she might be unable to bear it.

***

When Preston reached the library, he found it to be one of the few rooms in the house that was vacant and quiet. Chairs were turned toward each other in groups from earlier conversations, and one or two lay overturned, demonstrating that it had been well occupied by the partygoers earlier in the evening.

Even the candles had burned down and barely flickered in their holders, making the room appear gloomy and cold. Preston stood still and listened, but there was nothing to hear but the gentle hum of distant talk from other rooms in the house. He was glad the room empty. It would make his job of identifying the

Lion that much easier.

As he stared idly at his surroundings, Preston tried to envision what the man would look like. He felt a shiver of excitement at the thought that he would soon be face to face with the legendary character who had so successfully concealed his identity—and who had so triumphantly rained down terror upon his foes.

The mere mention of the Lion's name was enough to rouse a superstitious shudder among those in the North, and Preston felt a tremor creep up his own spine as he looked back at the door where the hero would soon appear.

If she has played me for a fool, her brother will suffer the extreme penalty.

As he continued to decide on his best course of action, Preston became aware of the gentle, repetitious exhalations of someone on the far side of the room. The cadence of the breaths indicated it was a person who had succumbed to a full stomach—and perhaps too much wine.

Preston listened for a moment longer, just to make certain the peaceful napper would not interfere with his trap. Convinced the man was indeed deep in dream-filled sleep, Preston sat down in a dark corner and waited for his mysterious adversary to make his appearance.

Chapter 32

Julia sat alone, her mind conjuring the vision of what was happening in the library at the fateful hour of one. She envisaged the mysterious leader's entrance and tried to imagine what he would do.

She wished she were there to witness it all, but as the minutes ticked by, and Preston did not reappear, she feared that something had happened. Had his plans somehow been spoiled? Or was the Lion, even now, trying to break free from his trap?

"My lady, you must have thought me very remiss." The voice struck her like a hammer on an exposed nerve. "I had a great deal of difficulty delivering your communication."

Julia had forgotten all about her message to Landon, even though more than half an hour had passed. Her thoughts were only with her brother.

"I found him at last and gave him your message. He is giving orders for the carriage to be brought up now."

"Thank you." When he did not depart, Julia feared he would start up another conversation. "Will you forgive me? I am tired, and would like to be alone."

"I would be happy to assist you to the porch," he replied courteously. "It is cool outside, and you look like you could use some air."

"I am only tired," Julia repeated wearily as she allowed him to take her arm. Once outside, the man pulled aside a chair for her. Julia sank into it as slowly and gracefully as she could, but her legs were trembling and seemed unable to support her any longer.

"I suppose Landon was at the gaming tables." She said the words to herself, speculating that Landon might not be in any shape to assist her back to Welbourne. It would also explain why it took so long for the young man to return.

The gentleman heard her and responded. "No, miss. He was in the library. Fast asleep. It took me more than one shake to wake him."

"In the library?" she asked the question mechanically.

"Yes, ma'am. Sleeping it off, I would say."

"Was there anyone else there?"

"That merchant…Moxley, I believe his name is. He was slumbering, as well. It's right quiet in there. After such a long day, I wouldn't mind taking a nap myself."

Julia's heart leaped. Did that mean Preston had failed in his plan? Given Landon's presence, did the Lion chose another way to communicate with his men? A heartbeat later, she realized that would mean *she* had failed.

What would that mean for her brother? Had the Lion proved elusive once more? She would get no kindness, pity, or mercy from Preston. He had told her: either…or. Nothing less would satisfy him. He would no doubt think she willfully misled him.

Julia could not bear the thought that the plan may have been botched.

The horses had not yet come around, but she caught a glimpse of Preston standing at the door with a mysterious look on his face. She could not tell if he was amused or puzzled. When his eyes met hers, they became strangely mocking.

She stood and thanked the gentleman who had escorted her to the chair. "I feel so much better now that I am out in the air. Thank you. There is someone I should bid adieu."

He looked at her questioningly, bowed, and departed.

"Did you find the Lion?" she asked Preston when he moved to stand beside her on the dimly lit porch.

"The Lion?" His questioning tone was full of bored amusement, as if he enjoyed toying with her.

"Please," Julia said through clenched teeth. "I have done all that you've asked. Torture me no more."

"Compose yourself, miss." His thin lips curled upward into a smile. "As for any visitors to the library, I saw no one but a slumbering Landon Graham."

"Then you failed?"

"Perhaps." He tilted his head and studied her closely.

"But what of Gideon? You have hung the Sword of Damocles above him, and I fear the thread will snap."

"I remember my promise. The day I set out for Washington on the trail of the Lion, Gideon's letter will be in your hands."

"Which means that a brave man's blood will be on my hands." She failed to suppress a shudder.

"His blood or that of your brother," Preston said in a voice so full of malice it bordered on disrespect. "You must certainly pray that the Lion starts his trip soon."

"I have only one prayer." She stared out into the darkness.

"That is?" Preston moved closer.

"That Satan, your master, retrieves you from your earthly bonds."

Her words seemed to amuse him. "You flatter me."

Julia studied him, trying to read his thoughts, but they were thoroughly masked. Not a muscle betrayed whether she should fear what would happen next, or have faith.

"Give me some hope," she begged in a whispered voice. "Please. This is torture to me."

"Pray to Heaven that the thread does not snap," was all he said.

Chapter 33

A young groomsman sat on the seat of the Graham carriage holding the reins of four beautifully matched horses. Landon appeared, looking sleepy and a bit tipsy, yet his physique spoke of power and latent strength.

As he opened the door of the carriage, he looked up at the servant. "Where is Spencer?"

"He was called away, suh. He said you would understand."

Landon nodded. "Very well. You need not come along. I'll drive the ladies home."

The servant seemed happy to give up the seat—or perhaps knew of Landon's preferences and anticipated the request.

As the man tied off the horses, Landon held out his hand for Julia and gazed around. "I thought Sallie was with you."

"No. The mayor insisted she spend the night." Julia hesitated a moment. "And she was not yet ready to depart."

Landon's expression changed momentarily to a wistful one, but then he shrugged. "Very well. I'll send my coach back in the morning."

Again, he attempted to help her in.

"May I sit out in the open with you? Like the old days?" The question was asked spontaneously, with no deliberation and little thought.

Landon studied her a moment, his square jaw tensing visibly.

"At your service, miss." He held out his hand and helped her up the step.

Within a few minutes, the magnificent coach, drawn by four of the finest thoroughbreds in Virginia, drove off with Landon Graham on the box holding the reins, and Julia beside him, wrapped in an elegant cloak.

A fifteen-mile drive on a spring night after so much anguish and strain was something Julia welcomed. The darkness on each side of the road was intense, but a moon of magnificent brightness hung above. As clouds flitted across its face in a heavenly game of chase, the countryside plunged into darkness, only to erupt into brilliant light when the night star was once more exposed.

***

Julia knew from her younger days that Landon could be an enthusiastic coachman by sunlight, moonlight, or no light. The team of splendid horses from his stable were eager and fresh, judging from the tight grip he kept on the reins as the carriage bounced and swayed along the winding drive.

Indeed, the house and all its revelers were soon far behind, leaving Julia to delight in the few hours of solitude the journey would provide. The soft night air fanned her cheeks and helped her thoughts to wander. She knew Landon would speak little, if at all, and preferred that to the incessant chatter she had endured at the ball.

Out into the starlit night they went, the gentle clopping of the horses' hooves becoming a gentle, soothing rhythm. A mild breeze blew Julia's hair about her face and sent the back of Landon's greatcoat billowing behind him.

These nightly drives after balls and suppers had been a source of unending delight to Julia while growing up. There was no greater thrill than sitting beside Landon as he drove a set of spirited horses along the lonely, moonlit paths. He would travel for hours without making more than a casual comment about the weather, or remark on the superior condition of his horses, yet she cherished the moments in his company.

Tonight he appeared exceptionally preoccupied, and seemed therefore unaware of the speed they traveled. The coach flew along the road, over hill and dale, sometimes beside the river, other times not. As usual, he did not speak, but stared straight out in front of him, the leather seeming to rest quite loosely in his tanned hands. Perhaps it was because they were far out in the country that he allowed the horses to choose their pace. Or perhaps he was so consumed with his thoughts that he forgot to hold them in check.

Inhaling deeply, Julia delighted in the fragrant scents of spring that floated on the gentle breeze. At times, the moon glowed brightly enough to sufficiently light the countryside on both sides of the road. But just as often, it strove vainly to struggle through a thick bank of clouds.

Julia could see the river in all its majesty winding in and out beside them during most of the ride, but there were long stretches where she could only hear it. Even when they plunged into dark tunnels created by the embracing limbs of trees overhead, Julia knew where they were by the sound of rushing water or the silence of still pools.

The closer they got to Welbourne, the faster the horses rushed along. Julia could not suppress a smile as the speed, combined with the breeze, blew her hair into wild disarray. But when she glanced at Landon, she saw no evidence of good humor, nor any sign that he was enjoying her company or the stimulating ride. His pained, somber expression caused her to recall what his life had been like before he spent his idle time in card and smoking rooms. Before the war.

Julia suddenly felt intense sympathy for him, and the way his life's story had played out. Landon had been a good and noble man before the sudden and tragic loss of his brother had altered his path. Hadn't she learned, just tonight, how quickly fate can change and dictate one's destiny?

Without warning and all at once, the terrible reality of her own actions came crashing down on her. Julia hastily choked back a sob as she thought again of the consequences that could result from her alliance with Preston.

Had she done what was right? She closed her eyes and reflected on the question. She had chosen the life of her dear brother over that of a stranger. How could she have done otherwise?

Yet the stranger she may have unmasked was no ordinary man. He was a fearless warrior who selflessly risked his life for the good of the country at large. He was a man, who, in the span of his lifetime, might save hundreds, if not thousands of lives.

Julia's gaze dropped to her hands and then shifted to the ones that were expertly holding the reins. She quickly turned her attention from the power and strength they conveyed, to the scenery and the fresh night air. As the moon popped out once again, it created long shadows that made the trees appear as giant sentinels. And when it subsequently disappeared, all was dark again, save the fireflies hanging in the trees like thousands of sparkling ornaments.

Julia stared toward the south and tried to pierce the distance to the battlefields where courageous countrymen were defending the sacred soil with their blood. Then her thoughts turned again to her dear brother, and she almost wept aloud.

"Our own beautiful country." Landon spoke softly as if divining her thoughts.

That low voice fell soothingly on Julia's ears, but she looked up, surprised he had spoken. "Yes. Who could have dreamed of the events that have befallen us?"

He didn't respond to that, but she saw his calloused hands tighten on the reins, hands that in olden days had been gentle and comforting, yet strong enough to control the wildest horse.

Julia reached out and touched his arm, feeling the need to question him on the topic that his own sister had feared to breach. "I know Fate has not been kind to you, Landon, but now is not the time for Virginia's sons to turn their backs on her." The words escaped her lips involuntarily, for no sooner had she uttered them than she bit her lip, wishing they could be recalled.

He looked down at her, and even with only starlight illuminating them, the inky blackness of his eyes sparked like lightning. He gave the reins a swift snap, which sent the horses into a faster gait. "I am acquainted, to some degree, with the obligations that rest upon me as a soldier. I did my part."

"Landon, you were highly regarded as an officer." Julia could tell he was hurting by the way he kept his gazed fixed on the pike. "By all accounts, a successful one."

"No amount of success or victories can repair the loss of my brother." She heard a catch in his voice halfway through the statement, but he finished the sentence bravely. "A better friend, a bolder soldier, has never died for his country."

"But, Landon, what of your reputation?" Julia's voice was hushed, barely a whisper, because she was so astounded by his words. "Character is much more easily kept than recovered."

A look of strange wistfulness crept into his eyes, but it was swiftly erased, replaced by an expression of indifference. "That is for others to judge."

"I'm sorry." The rush of the wandering wind caused Julia to

pull her cloak around her, although she was not chilled. "I did not mean to reopen an aching wound."

Landon remained silent for a moment, but his body was tense, as if he were fighting an unseen battle within himself. "Such lofty virtues you possess," he finally said, with no emotion in his tone. "A little drink here and there is far less dangerous and painful than leading men into battle."

Julia had no response to that. She became buried in her own thoughts again, and apparently, so did Landon. It was with a sense of disappointment that Julia looked up to see the two large stone columns that marked the boundary of the property come into view. Within mere moments, Landon had turned the excited bays onto the road that led to Welbourne.

When approached from this direction, and especially in bright moonlight, the house resembled a palace. The white walls looked eminently picturesque against the night, and the lake in the distance, sparkling in the starlight, appeared poetic and peaceful.

With barely a decrease in speed, Landon guided the four bays up the drive, and then brought them to a standstill in front of the entrance hall. Within moments, a handful of grooms emerged from the barn.

Landon jumped down hastily and helped Julia alight. He grasped her waist and lifted her effortlessly from the carriage, setting her down in front of him. With her face just inches from his, Julia found herself breathless. What had happened between them so many years ago seemed like a vague dream to her. But when he touched her with those strong hands, when she felt his gentle fingers reach out and wrap around hers, the dream became a vivid memory.

She looked up at him reverently, hoping to see that he felt it, too, but something in his face forbade conversation.

"I'm sure someone is waiting inside to help you." He released her and bowed—and with not so much as a glance in her direction, walked away with the grooms who'd come to greet them.

His callous, emotionless, imperturbable attitude infuriated Julia. Too wide awake to think of sleep, she turned away from the door and walked around to the back of the house, gazing dreamily at the landscape of starlight and shadow.

Before her stretched the gardens, and up from the trellises came the scent of honeysuckle. Above her lay a magical domain of stars upon velvet blackness. Everything seemed at peace in comparison to the tumultuous emotions racing through her. She could hear the soothing lap of water on the banks of the lake, and the occasional soft and ghostlike calls of an owl in the trees beyond.

The night's calm was temporarily broken by the horses' prancing hooves on the cobblestones as they were led away to the stables. Then all grew quiet once again.

Chapter 34

J ulia sighed broodingly at her gloomy thoughts. Never had she felt so empty, so void of hope or courage. With one last deep breath of exasperation, she turned away from the vista of the river and headed toward the house. She knew it was late, but doubted sleep would come in her current state of agitation.

Just as she reached the edge of the tree line, she heard footsteps upon the brick walkway that meandered through the garden to the river. Searching the darkness, she watched Landon's figure emerge from the shadows.

He must have wandered down to the water's edge after handing the horses over to the grooms. Perhaps he too had wished for a few peaceful moments to clear his head, relax, and enjoy the quiet solitude of nature.

As if reluctant to return to the house, Landon paused a moment and stared up at the night sky. With his handsome face tilted toward the moon, he appeared like a mythical creature, not anything of flesh and bone. Julia's gaze drifted down to the open greatcoat that lay stretched across his broad shoulders. He stood perfectly still, his hands buried in the deep pockets of his stylish breeches, as he had so often done in his youth when pondering a problem.

Apparently, he did not notice her. But she thought she heard a long sigh escape him before he continued his trek to the house.

"Landon," she said when he reached the terrace.

He turned as if startled, and searched for the source of the voice. "At your service, miss," he said when he saw her, though he did not bother to hide the irritation from his voice at the interruption.

"It is such a beautiful night, Landon. Will you walk in the garden with me like we used to do?" She tilted her head toward the winding paths, lit only by the moon and stars.

When he did not move or speak, she added with disappointment evident in her voice, "Or is such a suggestion distasteful to you?"

"I have no doubt you'll find your walk more enjoyable without my company."

Julia noticed that his reply in no way answered her question—but his face did. It was as cold and unmoving as marble.

He turned to leave.

"No. Please. Just one minute." Julia drew a little closer and cleared her throat. They were alone at last. There were things she needed to say to him, things long ago folded away in her heart's deepest places that she needed to release. In all of her time here, not once had either eluded to the subject that occupied both their minds. Now was the time to do so.

Then, perhaps, she could leave Welbourne with a clear mind, and divest herself of this terrible weight.

"This tension…this estrangement that has arisen between us. Tell me, Landon. Is it of my making?"

He turned toward her and spoke in an emotionless voice. "You must pardon me there. An estrangement would require a close association, and my memory of any such a relationship— other than as children—escapes me."

He looked her straight in the eyes, a gaze that she returned.

"Escapes you, Landon?" Julia ignored the ringing in her ears.

"Then I am the only one who lies awake at night recalling every moment that we spent in each other's company?"

Julia stood motionless in the moonlight, expectant, her candid blue eyes never flinching from his. She'd gone as far as a discreet woman might, and much further than her modest upbringing would approve. The next move was his to make.

Landon seemed in no hurry to respond. He stood for a moment, looking agitated and stern, his stoic reserve seeming to hold him motionless and at a distance. Even had her back been turned, Julia knew she would have felt the intentness with which he regarded her.

"You bade me to linger, Julia," he responded at last. "It is late. I hope that it was not merely to discuss tender recollections of the past."

His voice was hostile and harsh. His stance before her stiff and unwelcoming. The defiant side of Julia urged her to return his indifference with indifference. Her pride, her dignity, bade her to sweep past him without another word, and return to Washington at first light. What they had shared together, no one but the two of them knew—but he could not deny it.

Yet something told her to stay and try again. Although she had little prospect of prevailing over his cast iron composure, she raised her chin, and assumed all the poise she could muster. "Landon, please. Just a short walk to forget about the turmoil and chaos of the present? Surely, it would not hurt to dwell a little in the past on such a night, to return to a time when we were young and carefree."

He bent his tall figure into a partial bow. "You must pardon me. The current state of affairs does not allow me to accompany you there."

Once more, he attempted to depart, and again she called him back.

"Landon."

"Yes, Miss Dandridge?" he spoke into the night, not bothering to turn around this time, but she could feel his leashed resentment and ire.

"Is it possible that such a bond as ours can die? I thought the deep affection we once shared would survive any adversity. Is there nothing left of that warm regard?"

As she spoke to him, his tall figure straightened still more. His shoulders moved in rhythm with his breaths, which were coming faster now, yet more shallow.

"As I recollect, we were children then." He turned his head, and a look of relentless obstinacy crept into his dark eyes. "At least *you* were. I fear you've spent too much time building a fairy-tale around the past, cultivating a dream that has no foundation in reality. Welbourne is not a castle, and I am not your prince."

Julia let out her breath in hopeless exasperation and bowed her head. "I do not understand you."

"Truly? Yet, I am a simple man. Easy to understand." Resentment and hostility dripped from his words. "Perhaps I should ask a question of you. Is it your desire to go back to the enchanting days of old so that you may have the pleasure of deserting me again?"

"Landon, I never deserted you...I—" Julia was silenced by his dark, strained expression.

"Yes, I have heard the tale," he retorted, sounding bored and impatient. "My mother arranged for you to be taken away while I was absent on business." He turned more fully toward her. "Yet that does not explain the years that have passed since."

The moon had disappeared behind a bank of clouds, so the two of them were mere outlines in the dim light. Not so much as a single star was visible, and the windows in the house were all dark. Landon stared out into the night, as if the endless black void in the distance held the secrets to their painful past.

"You hold me responsible for a situation I could not prevent. I was taken from this house with little regard for my wishes or welfare—and suffered intensely as a result." A tone of tenderness and sorrow crept into Julia's voice. "I told you what happened. The entire truth of the matter."

"Yes. Indeed you did. But not until after it had been described to me by others." His lips were tightly compressed, giving him a look of anguished torment.

"And you trusted *their* word. You believed them when they told you it was *my* idea. You asked for no proof. You accepted it with no question." Julia's voice quivered only slightly, though her entire body trembled. "You thought I desired to deceive you, that I ought to have reached out to you. Yet, had you attempted to communicate with me, I would have told you that none of it was true. Heaven knows, I had no say in the entire affair."

"And you did not contact me to explain it because?" He raised his voice for the first time, and there was savagery in it.

Julia exhaled in exasperation. "Anger sealed my lips. Pride." She placed her fingers on her temples and paused, trying to regain some composure. "I thought it was you who wanted me away from Welbourne. Your mother—and Priscilla—told me as much. I was hurt, distressed that you had sent me away. My silence on the subject was not the cold-blooded act that you infer. It was not done with deliberate malice."

She looked imploringly at him, but he offered no comment, no words of sympathy. His eyes never flinched from their stern, set gaze. And even now, as Julia struggled to swallow the tears that choked her, he waited, emotionless and still. His handsome face looked strained, etched with a deep pain that was apparently a part of him now.

"It is my understanding that you were informed within weeks of your departure that I had no knowledge of it." The effort to maintain his self-control was clearly a severe one. His voice cracked with emotion—though it was obvious that he was trying to appear indifferent.

"Yes." Julia raised her anxious blue eyes to his darkening ones. "Yes, I was told it was your mother's doing. Yet the fact remained that you believed it had been my decision. You, whom I thought knew me so well, believed that I, at sixteen, could make the decision to flee from the happiest life I'd ever known, from the only man I could ever—"

She stopped and turned away, not wishing to risk a longer sentence—and intensely aware she had already disclosed too much. Yet she could not wipe the vision from her mind of that moment in time so long ago, when she had watched him depart for a trip of short duration, never imagining it might be the last time she would see him.

There had been spectacular moonlight that night, and she recalled in vivid detail the figure of Landon standing on the wide porch of Welbourne, saying his farewells as he swung his magnificent cape around his shoulders and prepared to leave. It did not require a powerful imagination to remember him thus, the noblest-looking mortal she had ever seen.

As he had swept off his hat for a final adieu, he'd bent down and touched his lips upon the top of her head in a brotherly kiss. "Don't forget me, Julia." He'd said it kindly, yet jokingly, knowing he'd be gone but a few days. Her gaze never left him as he strode down the quiet lane in the moonlight to gather his horse, the dust rising from beneath his high boots, leaving a trail that hung in the air long after he'd disappeared from view.

But it was the kiss before that one—the one in the parlor with no light but that of a single candle, no sound but that of their own breathing—that materialized before Julia now. The memory of it, the passion of it, the sensation of being held against his strong body, almost dropped her to her knees. She had idolized this man throughout her childhood and loved him with every ounce of her being at the threshold of womanhood. They had understood each other perfectly, as no one else ever could. She'd thought they always would.

Yet now here he was, always grave, always looking as if he bore the weight of the world upon his shoulders. Tonight, he'd been invariably courteous and pleasant, but something still lurked behind a wall of sadness and secrets. His attitude showed little interest *in* her, and no concern *for* her.

Everything had changed. Even her own heart, which had once beat so wildly when near him, could now barely push the blood through her veins.

"I'll admit, it's a little difficult," Landon said after a moment of silence between them, "to remember events as you seem to recall them. If my memory serves, I traveled to Washington City at the start of the war—secretly, and at great risk to my own reputation—to implore you to leave. I recall that you offered me no explanation then and demanded that I leave you there."

Julia struggled to remain standing, to breathe. Torn between conflicting emotions, she forced herself to suppress what she must conceal from him—no matter the agony and anguish it caused her. "I wished to test your faith in me." Her lip trembled as she murmured. "And it did not bear the test."

Landon's breath escaped violently, and his hands curled into fists. Julia watched the carefully placed neutral expression on his face give way to one of anger.

"*I* did not bear the test?" His voice shook with emotion. "In all this time since your return to Welbourne, I have never *asked* you for an explanation because I have been waiting for you to *provide* one." His accusing gaze was riveted on her, his piercing eyes flashing with a mixture of resentment and disappointment. "Even after you mysteriously reappeared here, I was willing to listen. In fact, I gave you ample opportunity to explain your position any number of times, all of which you soundly rejected, refused, or ignored."

Anguish like she'd never known before rose in Julia's throat as she began to speak, but Landon stopped her by lifting his hand. "Had you spoken, I would have accepted your account and believed it unconditionally. You may defend your behavior if you wish, but don't try to justify it."

Julia studied the man before her. He no longer displayed a cold, impassive deportment. Rather, his voice quivered with an intensity of passion that indicated he was making every effort to maintain control. His dark eyes sparked with emotion, and his jaw was sternly set, as if his will alone held surging anger in check.

When amused, Landon's eyes were wells of enchantment and allure. But when they appeared black, as they did now, a powerful tempest was brewing. Julia studied his expression and wished she was mistaken. That instead of hating her, this man who stood before her might indeed still have feelings for her. Her fingers ached to reach over and touch him, to feel the strength of his arm, and soothe his distrust of her. Yet his look was so galvanizing and intense, it sent a tremor of fear through her.

Pride had kept them apart. Pride and the war…a war that had taken all she had to give and asked for more. A war that had created secrets that even now she must not reveal. Yet just the nearness of Landon gave her comfort that all could be made right again. The only happiness life could ever hold for her would be knowing that this man respected and cherished her.

"You are familiar with the stubbornness of my character," she acknowledged sadly. "I knew I was wrong and regretted it. But now I have returned to find you so changed, always wearing that mask of disinterest and indifference, as if you no longer have feelings for me."

She stood so close to him now that her gown brushed against his leg. He stared at her lashes, laden with the sparkle of teardrops, and closed his eyes to shut out the vision of her face—apparently not trusting himself to remain unyielding to her magical allure.

"It is no mask," he replied icily. "As for your walk, I'm afraid your sweet memories will have to suffice. Good night."

"Landon," she cried out impulsively as he turned. "Wait. Please, listen to me. I wished to speak to you because...because I am in terrible trouble...I have need of your help."

"I am at your service." His voice sounded bored, not supportive, as he stared straight ahead. It was not to be expected that he would be greatly moved by her request, but his unemotional tone still inflicted pain.

"How callous you are. It's as if you wish to apply poison as the cure for a wound."

"Julia, it is late," he said, still not bothering to face her. "How may I help you?"

"Landon, Gideon is in terrible danger. I felt it before. I know it now."

"Why? Have you heard something?" He turned now, and even bent down slightly to study her eyes. But whether that action was from concern, or merely to read the sincerity in her gaze, she could not tell.

Julia took a ragged breath, then plunged on carelessly. "A letter of his has fallen into the hands of a spy. Tomorrow, if not already, he will be arrested. After that, the rope, unless…unless… oh, it is horrible."

The tears Julia had thus far held to a trickle, began to surge. "It is all so dreadful. And you do not understand. And don't care. No one does…I am all alone."

"Again, I ask, Julia, how may I help you?"

At the sound of his heartless, impassive tone, tears streamed more freely. All her struggles and the awful uncertainty of Gideon's fate overwhelmed her. Julia put her face in her hands and sobbed bitterly.

"Heavens, Julia, will you dry your tears? I never could bear to see a woman cry."

Landon's voice sounded forced, as if what he really wished to do was stretch out his arms and comfort her. Instead, his hands were clenched by his sides. "The hour is late," he said indifferently, though gently. "Will you not look at me and tell me in what way I may serve you?"

Julia lifted her tear-stained face to him. "Can you do something to help Gideon? You have so much influence. So many acquaintances."

His gaze seemed to rest on her throat, where she could feel her pulse pounding. "Perhaps you should seek the influence of your friend, the merchant," he said, lifting his eyes. "Surely, he has more contacts in Washington than I do." His tone, which always seemed to be maintaining a balance between civility and savagery, took her off guard.

"Have you no mercy?" Julia's voice was whispered and hoarse. "I cannot ask him…I wish I dared tell you, but…but he has put a price on my brother's head which…"

Julia felt helpless. Powerless. Hopeless. She wished she had the courage to tell him everything…all she had done that night to protect her brother. How Preston Moxley had used her love for Gideon to control her. How he had manipulated her for his own purposes.

If the dear Landon of old stood before her now, she would have. But no, she dared not give way to the impulse. There was nothing to gain and too much to lose. She could not risk making another confession to him. He might not understand her predicament. He might not sympathize with her struggles and temptation.

No, Landon was the type of man with a high sense of character. The contempt he would feel for the deed she had done, however unwittingly...however unwillingly...would extinguish any affection he had left for her. He despised timidity and cowardice, and valued honesty and honor above all earthly virtues.

Acknowledging his reaction with a defiant lift of her chin, Julia tried to hide the hot mix of defeat and bitter disappointment. She took a deep breath, forcing herself to stifle the sense of injustice she felt at having to face her strife alone.

Deep down, she knew this was not the only thing she had to bear in silence. She had been tempted to confess everything any number of times, but duty had sealed her lips. Duty—and her fierce pride, which was too deeply rooted to be eradicated now.

No one—not even Landon—could know that she had stayed in Washington City only as a means to help the Confederate cause. Sworn to secrecy and determined to do her small part, Julia would never reveal that fact. She couldn't.

At the very beginning of the war, her services had been requested, and she'd fulfilled that appeal by pretending to be something she was not. How could she refuse? With her aunt and uncle's close ties to the government, Julia was perfectly suited to perform the duty. As a young lady from a reputable family, she'd become fully accepted into the elite society of Washington. No one questioned her allegiance. No one doubted her loyalty.

Any information she obtained through the careless lips of officers or politicians had been conveyed to a predetermined location. The reports were then gathered by someone she did not know and delivered to someone she had never met. It was an elaborate scheme in which she played only a small part.

Cutting her ties to Landon and the others in her past had been a great sacrifice, but the valuable results made the cost worthwhile. Operating with little oversight, Julia had socialized with senior officers, flattering them with her charm, and listening attentively while they poured out their fresh army lore. She had a quick and thorough grasp of detail when it came to a map or a document, and her memory was like a vault.

Once she had gained their trust, her job had not been a difficult one. Officers talked with much bravado and little hesitation in her presence, each trying to outdo the other in the intelligence they shared. In the beginning, she had only acquired small tidbits. But in time, her understanding had increased and the details of her information had become more specific. She knew which military units were poorly drilled, what troops were inadequately armed, and whose forces were least prepared to fight.

Within a year, she had so thoroughly gained the Yankees' confidence that she had been welcomed with great ceremony to their camps, and regularly accepted offers to be guests at their dinner tables. It took little coaxing to get them to reveal their deployments, their movements, and sometimes, their battle plans. She had even been a guest of the much-reviled General Carlyle once, and been invited to ride with him to oversee the disposition of his troops.

Julia knew there were other agents in the city, but all who were involved in the intricate network were kept in ignorance of the identity of the others.

She focused her gaze on Landon and studied his grave face. She believed in his unquestionable loyalty, but knew it would do no good to explain why she had remained in Washington. She'd detested every minute spent in the company of her adversaries, yet she knew it had been a valuable endeavor. Contributing to the war effort had been her honor. But she'd taken no pleasure in the loneliness or the deceit.

"Why did you come back here?" His tone was accusatory again. "And why now?"

Julia looked down. Oh, how she wanted to speak, to tell him all, to relieve her mind of this great burden. She had left because of a new level of tension in Washington, and feared she was being watched—perhaps even trailed. She was aware of a campaign to discover the identity of the Lion, and did not wish to be caught up in the trap.

Her unexpected meeting with Sallie had worked as intended, giving her an alibi to get out of the city. But when General Carlyle had caught wind of her intentions, he'd asked for her help discovering the identity of the Lion. She'd intended to do just that—though not to tell the Federals. She wished only to warn the intrepid hero of the larger plot. Whoever he was, she would tell him to be ever watchful and trust no one.

When she glanced up at Landon, he seemed to be studying her, trying to decipher what she was thinking.

"Is there something you wish to tell me?" His voice sounded hopeful...and doubtful.

"No." Julia looked away, forcing herself to withhold the secret of her bargain with Preston, lest she betray her brother to a fate worse than that which he already faced. "Only that I worry for Gideon's life."

"I pledge to you, Gideon shall be safe." His voice was calm

and confident, the Landon of old. But he could not possibly understand the depth of her despair, or the extreme peril of the
situation. Her brother's life was at stake, and he acted as if she'd
told him it might rain.

"Now have I your permission to go?" His tone was kinder
now, and his expression had softened.

"If you will accept my gratitude." Julia drew close to him
again, blinking away the teardrops that remained, and trying to
clear the mist that clouded her eyes.

"It is too soon for that, surely. I have done nothing as yet."
The cold mask descended. "In any event, the hour is late, and you
must be fatigued. Good night."

The words were kind enough, but the contempt in his tone
was enough to shatter her. Julia took a step back and bowed her
head. "I can hardly believe you are the same young man who
carved my name in a tree and promised me—"

"Perhaps the man is the same, and it is you who has changed."

The heavy lashes that shadowed her eyes flew up. Silence,
other than the sound of breathing, reigned for what seemed an
eternity, as the tension between them sparked and flared. Julia
swallowed hard and met his accusing stare without flinching. "If
you think so, you do not know me."

For mere seconds that seemed like hours, their gazes held.
Julia searched for a flicker of sentiment in his eyes—but if it was
there at all, it had been swiftly replaced with the detached, emotionless look he routinely wore. He revealed no willingness to
compromise, and displayed no compassion or concern.

She had always found the innate calm that Landon conveyed,
alluring and mesmerizing. Tonight, she found it infuriating. They
had been as close as any two friends could be until she had been
forced to stay away. He'd made it clear that he was anxious to for-

get the one, and never forgive the other.

Julia could no longer stand the tension and resentful silence. A wave of nausea passed over her that kept her from continuing the conversation, or even lingering any longer. She accepted that the strong, impassable barrier between them could not be breached. Without another word, she picked up her skirt and moved toward the house.

Landon stepped aside and bent his tall figure in a ceremonious bow, his expression making it clear he was relieved to be released from the conversation. He did not speak in the tense silence that followed, and neither did she. The only sound was the rustling of her long gown as it swept across the dried leaves on the terrace steps and grazed the large column at the top of the porch.

Upon reaching the massive doors, Julia paused once again to look at him. Her heart twitched involuntarily when she saw that he had not changed his mind as she'd dared hope he would. He was not standing there with his arms stretched out to her, an apology on his lips.

No, he had not moved. He seemed to be looking in her direction, yet his thoughts appeared to be somewhere else. His hands, curled into fists, were down at his sides. It was clear that the reconciliation she had longed for, was not to be.

Hot tears surged again, but she would not let him see them. She had begged for encouragement—or at least forgiveness—and received neither. Her stubborn pride and defiance raised their bitter heads again, as a swelling surge of anger overtook her. She would not ask again. Ever.

Turning abruptly, she ran through the door and up to her room, the elegant gown billowing behind her in her haste.

Had she turned back and looked once more upon the starlit

garden, she would have seen that Landon's strong will had given way at last. Overwhelmed by his own emotions and his despair, he had turned away with heaving shoulders and stalked back into the shadows to conceal his torment.

Chapter 35

W hen Julia reached her room, she found her maid dozing in a chair.

"Why, it's late, miss," the woman said in a groggy voice, upon awakening. "You must be tired."

"Yes. It is late, but I don't feel sleepy." Julia pulled the string of her cloak and let it slide from her shoulders. "I'm sorry that you waited up for me. You may go to bed."

"But…"

"Don't argue. Help me with my gown and be gone."

The servant was only too glad to obey. She helped remove Julia's gorgeous ball ensemble and dressed her in a soft, loose nightgown with a matching robe.

"Goodnight, Miss Julia."

When the maid was gone, Julia moved to window and pushed aside the curtains. Far away to the east, she knew the rising sun would soon begin to throw its first pink rays. Already she imagined she could see the faintest glow. When her gaze fell upon the deserted terrace below, she turned away, determined not to replay the events that had unfolded.

Julia placed one hand on her forehead and began to pace, as if that would stop the images that assailed her. When that action failed to calm her tightly strung nerves, she pulled a chair to the window and sat. Her heart still pulsed at too fast a pace to consider retiring. Her mind still raced too recklessly to consider sleep. Thoughts, memories, and misgivings tumbled through her brain…Things she might have said to Landon. Things she *should* have said.

But no, she could not think of such matters. The war had come, and with it came changes. Those in the field who'd given their lifeblood, and those at home who'd lost precious kin, had made much more of a sacrifice than she had.

Her love for Landon was alive—and so was he. She must take solace in that. How many families would give anything to have their loved ones returned to this world—even if it meant being estranged?

Julia's thoughts turned briefly to her brother. Poor Gideon was in desperate peril, yet the pain in her heart had nothing to do with him. It was Landon for whom she now grieved. It was Landon who controlled every thought and emotion. Despite his disinterest in her, his callousness toward her, she cared for him… deeply. No matter the difference in age, no matter his downfall from grace, she could never stop her feelings for him.

Yet when his dark eyes appeared before her—cold, uncaring, unyielding—she forced herself to change the direction of her thoughts. She had to leave Welbourne. She was not welcome here. She must pack at first light, and convince Spencer to take her to the outskirts of the city. Then she would find Gideon, and use all within her power to gain his release.

As the minutes slipped by, Julia's weary body began to relax. Despite visions of war, and dark foreboding thoughts that she could not shake, her head drooped down into a fitful slumber.

***

Julia knew she hadn't slept long, because the sun had still not breached the horizon. As she rubbed her neck, she listened to the joyful chirping of a few early-rising birds, and realized their jubilant songs must have awakened her.

Or was it something else? Hearing the sound of low conversation, she peered through the window and watched Landon receive a communication from a rider she did not know. He often received business correspondence at all hours of the day and night, but Julia was surprised that he was still fully dressed.

Moments later, the courier rode away, and shortly thereafter came the steady tread of Landon's boots as he paced in the parlor below her. She listened intently as silence replaced the tapping, followed by heavy footsteps coming swiftly up the stairs. She knew it was Landon. No one else moved with such strong, purposeful strides.

Julia sat silently, listening, waiting. Presently, she heard him in the hallway. Did he pause at her doorway and almost knock? Or perhaps listen to see if she were sleeping? She had steeled her heart against him, yet in spite of herself, she wished he would come in—and was correspondingly disappointed when he did not.

As rapidly as they had started, his footsteps echoed in a hasty retreat to his quarters. The next sound was that of his door, closing quietly behind him.

Knowing she'd be unable to rest, Julia stood stiffly and stretched. How she longed to sleep. Or to hear from Gideon. Or to know what Preston was doing at this very moment. The dreadful unknown was killing her. And this constant nagging in the back of her mind refused to be stilled. Something was wrong.

Still clad in her nightgown, and with her hair loosely braided to the side, Julia opened her door and padded down the stairs to the parlor where Landon had stood.

She too, paced for a moment in restless misery, thinking disturbing thoughts, wishing impossible things, until her attention was drawn to the curling edges of a piece of paper in the ashes of the fireplace. The fire had long since burned out, but the coals were still hot. Sticking her hand into the smoky enclosure, she pulled it out by the corner and instantly recognized the handwriting.

It was her own.

Chapter 36

Julia sank down into a chair as she frantically attempted to pull her scattered thoughts together. No. It was ridiculous. She was dreaming. Her nerves were so overwrought, she was conjuring up absurd mysteries and plots.

As soon as one thought whizzed across her mind, another followed. She put her hand to her head to stop the dizzying array, yet the harder she fought to ignore the truth, the more it persisted.

Then, the reality struck her like a thunderbolt. She had scribbled this communication during the horserace in the early afternoon, before summoning a servant from the mayor's household to personally deliver it. She'd provided the exact location where she left all of her correspondence, hoping against hope that one of the other operatives would check it.

The neglected stonewall on the outer edge of Washington was often used as a place to rest. Only a few knew of the small outcropping of rocks close by that offered a hidden shelf to keep messages out of the weather, and securely hidden from prying eyes.

She had taken this action out of desperation and fear. Julia had no way of knowing if the servant could be trusted, or if the note would get into the right hands. But she'd had no one else to turn to. She'd had to try, hoping somehow it would get to the Lion and that his outstretched wings would be willing to protect her and her dear brother.

The realization of why Landon would be in possession of this sacred communication was dredged from a place beyond logic or meaning. The letter was written to but one person, an individual she had never met and whose true identity she did not know.

Shock, followed by searing happiness, and then a jolting bolt of dismay, hit Julia in quick succession. With her thoughts scattered, the awful horror of what she had done traveled quite slowly from her subconscious to her active mind.

Preston had told her nothing about what he had seen in the library, but now she remembered the pleased, triumphant expression he had worn. Had he discovered something, after all? She became sick with terror and clutched her breast, tearing at her nightgown as if it were strangling her.

Still not believing what her mind was telling her, Julia walked as if in a trance toward the serving board. Reaching for the dark-colored decanter she'd so often seen Landon hold, she removed the top, mechanically poured some into a glass, and lifted it to her lips. The bitterness of the concoction made her grimace, but it was not alcohol. It was only made to look that way.

As the distressing realization washed over her, it became impossible to steady her throbbing pulse. Looking back, Julia recalled that Landon never used this bottle when pouring a glass for someone else. "Oh, no," he would say, if they asked to drink what he was having. "Only the best for you."

Her mind had refused to recognize the significance of his actions, but now the truth of the matter hit her with an overpowering force. The consequences were devastating.

Oh, how could she have been so blind?

As she paced, holding her hands to her head, Julia put it all together. The part he had played. The sacrifice he had made. The myth he had created at the expense of his own reputation. All this, for the honor of saving lives and protecting his homeland.

The memory of their last meeting came rushing back to Julia She had withheld secrets from Landon, and he had withheld secrets from her. And now, her childhood companion was the only man in the world who could save her dear brother. But, oh, what had she done?

Julia squeezed her temples and tried to control her breath, which now came to her in gasps. Perhaps Landon had meant to tell her everything. Perhaps he knew her role in all of this, and had wished—and been waiting—for her to trust him enough to divulge the truth. Or quite possibly, he did not know anything at all, and truly believed she would one day betray him.

She sank into a chair, staring at nothing. The guise of a drunken recluse had been a good one, and concealed well the man's true genius. No wonder Detective Thorpe's spies had been unable to identify the legendary hero, whose reckless daring and resourceful ingenuity had brought new life to a war-ravaged land. The most elite soldiers and the most fastidious spies had been completely confounded by the ruse of a solitary and foolish drunkard.

But why had *she* not seen it? She, who knew Landon so well? She, who had worshipped him as a child for the honorable qualities he possessed...Courage. Compassion. Integrity. Loyalty.

Julia felt a surge of desperate hope mixed with intolerable dread. Had Preston guessed the secret? By telling Preston what she had seen on the piece of paper, had she betrayed Landon and sent him to certain death?

Please! Lord in heaven, no! Fate could not be so cruel. Pain and fear stabbed Julia's heart so violently that she placed her hand there to stem the throbbing nerves. Reacting without thinking now, she rushed from the room, up the stairs, and down the corridor to Landon's apartment, where she banged her fist on the door.

She needed to tell him what she had only just come to understand. Whether he would forgive her or despise her, she did not know—but the admission could not wait. His life depended on her urgent action.

Her life depended on stopping the merciless plot she had helped place in motion.

When no one answered, Julia knocked again, louder. Hearing whispered movements within, she tested the latch and pushed her way through.

For a few moments, Julia just stood there, leaning against the doorway, breathless, startled and unnerved. She could not quite comprehend what she was seeing, so she made no attempt at speech.

Two people were in the room. One entered an exclamation of appeal, the other of warning, and both instinctively glanced at the floor.

"You can't come in here, Miss Julia," Aunt Mazie said, looking up.

"Where is Landon?" Julia's eyes scanned the room, her heart throbbing so violently it roared in her ears.

"He's not here, as you can see." Spencer spoke while awkwardly dragging a rug forward with his foot.

Julia detected the movement but continued to study the apartment. "He must be here. I heard him enter an hour ago."

"No, Miss Julia." Aunt Mazie stepped forward and took her by the arm, trying to impel her back to the door. "You're tired and hearing things. He's not retired for the night yet."

"But I definitely heard—"

"Well, maybe he was here...for just a bit," Spencer interjected, throwing a hesitant glance toward Aunt Mazie. "But then he had business to attend to. You must have been busy and not heard him leave again."

"No, I…" Julia shook her head, not understanding. "Business? At this time of day? Where?"

"I don't know, miss. He only said that it was unexpected and urgent."

Julia allowed herself to be led back to the doorway, but when she turned once more, she noticed that Spencer was standing directly on the rug he had been repositioning with his foot, and had a strange look of relief on his face.

"What are you hiding?" Julia lunged to the braided oval and dropped to her knees. Lifting the edge, she discovered a hinged door in the flooring. "Where does it go?" She clawed at the hair that covered her eyes, as she stared with accusing eyes at Spencer.

Aunt Mazie and Spencer glanced at each other, and then stared at the door as if they had never seen it before. Since no one ever entered Landon's room uninvited, they had apparently not been concerned about covering the secret door until they'd heard Julia's knock.

"Tell me!" Julia demanded in a loud and forceful tone.

At last, Mazie answered in a low, whispered voice. "To the stables, miss."

Julia ran to the window and leaned out, thinking she might hear galloping hooves. But no, he'd probably left an hour ago— shortly after she'd heard him enter. She had not been in time to hear him riding away, but she felt the silence of his absence in the deepest marrow of her bones. Nothing seemed real now. Nothing except horrible, speechless pain.

She turned to Spencer. "Listen to me. Prepare Landon's coach and the four freshest horses in the stable, at once."

"Oh, no, Miss Julia. Mr. Landon would not allow it."

"Spencer!" Her voice was high-pitched, almost hysterical. "It is useless to argue and dangerous to delay. Landon is in grave peril. You must help!"

The man hesitated no more, and ran for the door. "Right away, Miss Julia."

Chapter 37

The agonizing minutes that followed were among the worst Julia had ever been forced to endure. No wonder Landon was so suspicious of her and wanted her gone. He thought she was a spy—or at least that she could not be trusted.

And indeed, perhaps she could not. By trying to save Gideon, she had compromised Landon—the Lion of the South! She must try to get word to him.

The full brilliance of the morning sun splashed through the window, but the day was still young. Julia knew she could make it to the outskirts of Washington in a few hours, and procure a pass from an officer at one of the outposts to get back into the city.

That was as far as her plans went. She had no idea what Landon had arranged, or why he was headed there. The only thing she knew, the only thought that consumed her, was that she had to stop him.

A tear slid down her cheek as she thought again about her terrible deed. Preston knew—or at least suspected—that Landon was the Lion. And thanks to her, he was most likely hot on his trail.

Julia ran to her room to change, all the while thinking of the dreadful affair she had taken part in. It had been a trap—and she had helped set it. Now, the Lion—Landon—was in danger of being caught.

Oh, what have I done?

After hastily changing her light gown for a dark traveling costume, Julia started down the stairs. Just as she reached the foyer, a groom came rushing up the porch. He carried a sealed letter in his hand, which he extended to Julia as she opened the door.

"What is this?"

"It came by courier, miss," replied the groom.

Julia took the letter mechanically and turned it over with trembling fingers.

"Who sent it?" She did not look up, but continued to stare at the official-looking missive.

"The courier said his orders were to deliver this to you. That is all."

Julia tore open the envelope. Her breath escaped her after just a glance, because her instincts had told her what it contained. It was a letter written by her brother to one of the prisoners rescued by the Lion. It revealed no secrets, yet the tenor of the correspondence was such that it could be used to implicate Gideon.

Panic like she'd never known before welled in Julia's throat. Preston had kept his word. He had sent her the compromising letter, which meant he was on the track of the Lion. But there was another document, smaller in size, behind the letter from her brother. Written in a scrawled hand, it read:

> *I regret to inform you that your brother has been arrested, and has, in an unfortunate turn of events, fallen into the hands of General Patrick Carlyle, who was recently exchanged and returned to duty. His fate is therefore extremely dire, and completely out of my control.*
>
> *— Preston Moxley*

Julia's senses reeled. She felt sweaty and cold and didn't know which way to turn. Gideon. Imprisoned! And in the hands of a man who was out for blood.

And then there was Landon, who had started for Washington, utterly unconscious of the fact that Julia had placed his most relentless enemy directly on his heels. He had set out early that morning. Provided he could get across the Potomac and through the lines, Landon would no doubt be in Washington quite soon.

Once there, he would meet with his men. With Preston's resources fixed upon his every movement, Landon would not only be endangering his own life, but those who were planning to help him carry out whatever his enterprising scheme entailed.

Julia did not know where to start, but she knew she must warn Landon. The odds against him were too great to contemplate—and the peril even greater. If she failed to get to Landon in time, he would perish, and so would her brother. Such an outcome was too distressing to ponder.

When she tried to imagine going back to a life without Landon, the pain in her heart was instant and bottomless. She would not fail to warn him. She *could* not. Her eyes glowed with a new determination when she thought of seeing him again. If only she could be in time to stop this dreadful plot.

Ignoring any thoughts of danger to herself, Julia set her mind on the task at hand. Her mind was in motion, her brow creased in concentration. Already, her plans were forming.

With no reluctance or hesitation, she calmly walked out of the house to wait for the coach. Julia's heart heaved when she thought about her involvement in this terrible calamity, but she would not allow herself to dwell upon it. She had unwittingly put a plan into motion that could cost the lives of the country's bravest men. For that awful offence alone, she would never forgive herself.

Julia tried to think of someone who could help her. Sweeney perhaps? Or Jud McGuire? She discounted the names as soon as she thought of them. They, too, were likely on their way to Washington. They, too, might be ensnared in this trap.

Now she understood Landon's assertion that he would prefer physical torment to the pain of losing Sawyer. This was an agony too deep to comprehend, a misery that threatened to undo her.

Despite his reluctance to assist, Spencer brought the horses around to the front of the house in record time. Instead of getting into the carriage, Julia climbed up onto the bench next to Spencer, and they were off.

Since the secret was now known, she insisted Spencer tell her all. She smiled with amusement when he recounted to her some of the more daring escapes the brave Lion had contrived, all the while portraying himself as a lost, drunken soul.

Julia's heart swelled with love and pride at the stories of Landon's courage, his ingenuity, and his resourcefulness. She laughed at some of the accounts, and conversely broke into tears when the tales became too harrowing.

When they drew within a few miles of the Federal outpost, Spencer pulled the eager horses to a halt, and helped Julia into the coach. "Time to act like a proper lady agin, Miss Julia." He winked at her before closing the door.

As soon as Julia felt the carriage move, she rested back in the seat and closed her eyes. She hadn't slept for a full day, but she was not tired. She just needed to concentrate. In a very short time, she would need every ounce of her strength and wit to deceive the sentries.

She hoped her eyes did not reveal her fatigue—or her fear. She would need to outsmart the officer at the first outpost they reached in order to receive a pass into Washington. No doubt, they were on high alert with the news that the Lion would be coming through the lines.

She closed her eyes again and prayed.

Chapter 38

Gentleman Carlyle paced beside an overflowing desk, his face red with rage, sweat dripping from his forehead. The audacity. The callousness. The very brutality of his capture continued to replay in his mind. His reputation would never recover. His future career as a powerful politician had come to an end before it had even begun. He had been subjected to every vile and abhorrent ridicule known to mankind!

And now demoted—well, he *was* still a general—but assigned to a desk job in an office the size of a closet.

Oh, yes, he'd been treated with utmost courtesy by the Confederates once he'd been left in the company of his friend, but that did not lessen the severity of his ordeal. He'd been forced to spend a night in that dastardly Libby Prison before reasonable accommodations in a private house were obtained.

Then he'd had to wait for an official exchange—and now, here he was in this miserable little office in Washington, his valiant reputation sullied beyond repair by that intolerable Lion.

Carlyle held his hand out in front of him and squeezed his fingers together, imagining the Lion's neck in his grasp. *I will get you yet.*

A knock at the door interrupted his musings, but they did not stop his state of agitation and rage. "What is it?" he bellowed. "For what trifle do you interrupt?"

"A dispatch for you, sir." The aide talked through the closed door, fearful of entering.

"Bring it in."

The man came in, handed over the dispatch, and immediately left, apparently afraid it contained more bad news for the general.

But it obviously did not. As soon as the general ripped it open and began to peruse its contents, a smile tugged on the corner of his mouth, and a chuckle of amusement burst forth.

Well, well. A man named Gideon Dandridge is being held in the Old Capitol Prison, suspected of being in league with the Lion. Perhaps things are not so bad, after all.

The general called for his aide again, and when the man entered hesitatingly, he merely said, "Tell the men to build scaffolding."

"Scaffolding, sir?"

"Yes, scaffolding."

"For what purpose, sir?"

"To hang a man."

The aide took a step back. "And what man is that, pray tell?"

"Gideon Dandridge has been placed in my custody."

"And for what charge shall he hang?"

"Why, aiding the Lion, of course."

"And the evidence against him?"

The general threw his hands in the air. "Has not the whole countryside been warned that if any were captured and believed to be rendering aid to the Lion, their lives would be forfeit?"

"But surely you don't intend to hang a man without proof of his crimes." Even as he spoke the words, the aide seemed to understand that obtaining justice under General Carlyle was something beyond his expectations. It required but slight insight into the man's character to realize that anyone who had the misfortune of falling into the clutches of his power was doomed. And it took even less knowledge of the man's record to come to the determination that General Carlyle should be removed from his place of authority as fast as honor and justice would permit.

Had Carlyle been a fair and impartial man, Gideon Dandridge would have no reason to fear an investigation. But under Carlyle, and others like him who thought of nothing but their own power, any pretense of a trial would not be fair. Every effort would be made to induce the prisoner to implicate himself and others— even strangers, whose names were heard for the first time.

"But, sir, are you saying you are sure he will hang?"

"What else?" The general shrugged, as if surprised to be questioned. "George Washington hanged Andre, did he not?"

"With all due respect, as I remember, there was something else."

The general turned and stared at him with narrowed eyes. "And what is that *something else?*"

"He was *tried* as a spy."

"Pure nonsense! An utter waste of time to try and prove a self-evident situation." Carlyle flailed his hands in the air. "No case could be clearer. The time for being fair has passed. We must rely more heavily on intuition than justice."

The aide cleared his throat and spoke hesitantly. "Sir, yours is a name known far and wide, while mine is known only as your loyal subordinate. I would not, therefore, assume for one moment to question your judgment in this most important matter."

Carlyle sat down at his desk with a grunt, obviously disarmed by the flattery. The subtle tribute to his greatness was more than he could withstand. "But you have something to say," he said with a dignified wave of his hand. "Proceed. Despite your low rank, I shall be glad to hear your counsel."

"Sir, I would ask that you defer this man's execution until another day—until there is proof of a crime—and more importantly, a trial."

The general stood and banged his fist on the desk in one movement. "And be attacked by the Lion in the meantime? And have this man rescued right from under my nose?"

His face turned red with emotion, and his chest puffed out with bombastic pride. "Thank you for your opinion, but delays are dangerous." He stood and paced as he talked. "Business has been conducted far too long without flexing our muscle and proving who is boss. The nation demands...*demands,* I tell you, that we take the bull by the horns and crush these people to Earth." He slapped his fist into his open hand. "I conceive it to be my bound duty to make an immediate and telling example of this case and I have so decided."

As the general plopped irritably back into his chair, the aide tried once again to reason with him. "So, you intend to kill him?"

"Probably," the general replied with unaffected calmness. Then his eyes zeroed in on the young man questioning him. "I don't understand your reluctance, sir, to enforce the law and punish those who abuse it. Where do you stand?"

"I don't stand for murder." The aide mumbled the words while staring at the floor.

The general apparently did not hear him. He pointed to the door. "This is no time for trifling. We must crush them. Eliminate them when possible. That is the best policy, if not a military necessity." He stabbed his finger toward the young man. "Furthermore, you are obligated to carry out my orders, which are urgent and imperative."

The private stood silently, his hands curled into fists. Seeming to understand that arguing would be futile, he saluted and turned to the door.

Carlyle smiled and made a mental note to someday repay Detective Thorpe's nephew for the favor he had done in placing such a prize into his hands. He would not let this opportunity pass him by without using it to the fullest extent to restore his reputation—and destroy the Lion.

Chapter 39

When Julia arrived at the first outpost, she was relieved to discover that she was acquainted with the officer in charge. But after securing a pass to get as far as Washington, she became entangled in trying to get away from his clutches. There was a dinner invitation from *him*, and requests for introductions from others, all of which she politely declined.

Still, by the time she had settled back into the carriage again, Julia's head ached intolerably and she felt sick to her stomach. The gentle rhythm of the carriage helped her relax, but all too soon, the sprawling countryside gave way to the trim, white tents that marked the outskirts of Washington.

Julia was confident she would be able to proceed without exciting suspicions, but she had yet to undergo the final trial. Folding her hands together on her lap, she attempted to brace for what was to come as the carriage bore her swiftly toward Washington.

The closer they got, the more she had to blink against the burning smoke of cook fires along the sides of the road. Then, through the haze, she distinguished columns of infantry marching into formation, or perhaps going through drills.

Craning her neck to peer through the small window, she noticed a great hustle and bustle among the cavalry as well. Was it her imagination? Or were some of them glancing in her direction with sly interest?

Julia had no time to ponder the matter. The carriage came to a sudden stop and the door sprang instantly open.

"Your pass, miss."

Julia furnished the required paperwork with a polite smile and a steady hand. She concentrated on controlling her breathing as the soldier perused the missive, but the effort made her lightheaded and faint. To distract her thoughts, she studied the officer who had propped his body against the doorway. He possessed dull, droopy eyes, and a countenance that suggested a deep desire for sleep.

He handed the paper back. "One minute, miss."

When he turned to leave, Julia let out the breath she had been holding and tried to regain control. Just then another officer appeared, one of higher rank than the first. He didn't utter a word of greeting. With no regard for courtesy or etiquette, he pointed to her pass.

Julia tendered the document, and then studied him in confused silence as he put on a pair of spectacles and scanned the paperwork at his leisure.

This man meant business. It was plain to see that he would not be turned from his purpose or trifled with, so she did not bother to question his scrutiny. After quite a few minutes, he looked up and stared at her gravely, causing her imagination to run wild.

What was wrong? Why was he taking so long? Had the troops been alerted about her duplicity? Or were they on high alert to stop the Lion?

Julia had failed to notice it before, but as the day had advanced, the heat had increased. She could feel beads of sweat forming on her forehead, but she dared not move or act nervous. The success of this mission was of greater significance than any she had previously undertaken. It was no longer her own life at state. The fate of those she held dearest depended upon her actions. The lives of Landon and her brother relied upon her courage and strength of will.

When her tension had increased almost to the breaking point, the officer quietly handed the paper back, and waved his hand to let Spencer know he could proceed. Julia only resumed breathing when the horses began moving again—but even their fast pace seemed all too slow for her anxious heart. Closing her eyes, she rested her head on the back of the seat, but her tightly strung nerves relaxed only slightly.

Unfortunately, the feeling of security was only temporary.

Within mere minutes, Julia thought she heard the cadence of hoof beats behind her. She convinced herself it was only the wind, and leaned forward for a view out the window. Not a leaf stirred.

It didn't take long to discern the distinct rattle of bit and saber—faint but gaining. The carriage began to rock as the muted sound became a rumble, and then a thundering rush that spread out and enveloped both sides of the road.

"What is it, Spencer?" Julia's voice trembled. She knew the answer by the sound of shouting voices and the puffing of winded horses right outside the coach.

"Seems to be some cavalrymen, ma'am."

Julia took some comfort in Spencer's calm, unruffled tone, but still had to clasp her hands together to keep them from shaking. When the carriage came to a sudden halt, she was thrown forward and had to grasp the edge of the seat to keep from falling. She fought desperately against the dark despair that now threatened to overcome all hope of success.

Breathing slowly but deeply, she realized that even though the nerve-racking thunder of hoofbeats had ceased, the silence was more terrorizing than the noise had been.

Without warning, the door to the carriage jerked open. "Julia

Dandridge, I presume?"

She nodded. "Yes. What is the meaning of this?"

"Your presence has been requested." The Union officer leaned forward and spoke with clipped military authority. "I am here to provide an escort."

Julia forced a laugh. "Thank you for the courtesy." She waved her hand in the air as if to chase away a pesky mosquito. "But I have no need for an escort."

"Nevertheless, you will come with us."

"For what reason?"

The door slammed closed, and Julia heard someone clamor into the driver's seat. The next minute, they were moving forward again, but to what destination, she did not know. She pressed her face to the window as they drove down the streets, trying to determine where they were, and more importantly, where they were going. Her emotions shifted and swung between hope, despair—and utter terror.

A short time later, they stopped in front of a small, nondescript building with a number of soldiers milling about. The door of the carriage opened, and a young captain extended his hand to help her alight. Blinking at the bright sunlight, her gaze fell upon a sign over the door that read: *Judge Advocate.*

"For what offense have I been brought here?" Julia acted offended and outraged.

"Right this way, miss." The captain looked straight ahead, making it clear he was not going to answer any questions. He led her into a large room, where another officer sat at a desk with a tablet of paper in front of him and a pen in his hand.

"What is your name?"

"Julia Dandridge."

He scribbled something on the paper.

"For what reason are you in Washington?" His voice sounded bored and mechanical.

"I reside here. Surely, you know that."

He glanced up at her with an expression of annoyance and then turned his attention back to his paper. "Then why did you leave?"

"Business."

"What business?" He didn't bother to look up, but rather, prepared to write down her answer.

"Mine. Of course."

His head came up slowly, revealing veins in his neck that appeared to bulge to the point of bursting. "It is now *my* business. Kindly answer the question."

Julia pretended to be exasperated as well, and let out a deep sigh. "I was visiting old friends outside the city, and I am now returning. I was not aware that I was breaking the law."

Again, he raised his gaze, but this time, he lowered it without responding.

Julia took a step toward him and spoke loudly and with false bravado. "Since I am here and have been brought before you, it is my understanding that my brother has been falsely arrested." She smoothed her dress impatiently. "I wish to see him as soon as possible."

"And what is the name of the person you wish to see?"

"My brother. Gideon Dandridge."

The man said nothing for a short time. He leaned back stiffly, tapping on the table with the blunt end of a pencil, his keen eyes studying Julia's face. She returned the look unflinchingly, oblivious to the fact that her fate was sealed and lay definitively in his hands.

Suddenly, as if some satanic thought had just entered his mind, he inclined forward with his mouth curved into what could only be described as an evil leer. "And tell me, are you *very* anxious to see him?"

"Certainly, I am. He is my brother."

"Very well." The officer wheeled his chair to another desk and wrote something on a slip of paper. Julia held out her hand, thinking it was her pass to the prison, but he motioned her away and beckoned to a man behind her.

"Now go." He waved them both away.

Julia left the building with the man at her side and walked several blocks before asking where they were going.

"To 14th Street. The Provost Marshal's."

"So he is the one who will give me the papers I need to see my brother?" she questioned calmly.

"No."

Remembering the paper the man carried, she asked. "Does he have to sign the one you have in your possession?"

"No."

"Is that not a pass the Judge Advocate gave you?"

"No."

Finally, the truth hit her. "Am I arrested?"

"That'd be my guess." He expressed the words with no emotion whatsoever.

On realizing her predicament, Julia's first impulse was a mad desire to run for her life. Second thoughts quickly prevailed, convincing her of the utter folly of such an act. Without sleep, and after more than fifteen hours of acute mental torture, she could barely organize her thoughts. Dejection and despair threatened to overwhelm her. But when her mind drifted to Landon and the danger he was in, her resolve was restored. She confronted the tremendous fact of her capture terrified, but determined.

Still, she was wild with shock and panic, ready to go through this test, yet fearful that other—even more treacherous—obstacles lay in her path. Everyone nowadays was a spy upon his fellow man. The most innocent word uttered in jest might at any time be used as proof of espionage or treachery. Had someone reported such a thing about *her*?

Despite being embedded in the very fabric of Washington society for so long, had someone grown suspicious of her true motives? Had Preston Moxley been sent to watch her? To entrap her? Or worse yet, had Priscilla Barton found a way to ensure she would have Landon all to herself once again? Could she have gone so far as to implicate Julia in a treasonous plot, so she would be locked away forever?

Julia attempted to keep her eyes locked straight ahead, yet it was plain to see that the excitement and chaos of the city had not abated since her departure. In fact, it had intensified.

Soldiers stood on guard at every street corner, their loud, belligerent voices shouting out commands, while civilian men— most of them elderly—loafed here and there, talking in strident tones and gesticulating violently. Adding to the din and confusion were the braying of pack mules, the jingle of bits and sabers, and the calls of newsboys as they ran up and down shouting "Extra!"

The quality of the air and the condition of the streets did little to improve Julia's state of mind. Even the footpaths were evil smelling and muddy as the result of a recent rain, causing Julia to watch where she stepped.

"It's right up ahead, miss." Those were the only words the man spoke to her as he put his hand on her arm and directed her toward a dilapidated structure on the left. The sign in front read: *Provost Marshal.*

"Please." Julia gazed up at him, her blue eyes wide and imploring. "There has been some fearful mistake."

He nodded, his expression neutral, and opened the door.

Chapter 40

Julia stepped timidly forward and glanced around at her surroundings. The front parlor of the house, if one could call it such, was dimly lit by an oil lamp, and looked so dirty and uninviting that she hardly dared to cross the threshold.

Once inside, she made out the form of a gaunt, pasty-looking man sitting stiffly behind a dusty desk. He picked up his pen when she entered and looked up at her with suspicion and contempt. "Your name?"

Julia blinked in the shadowy light, trying to adjust her eyes to the gloom. Before answering, she gazed with a mixture of curiosity and horror at a grimy old hag with a scarf over her head, sitting in the far corner of the room, seemingly talking to herself. No one else seemed to take notice, though the sight was not something that could be easily forgotten.

"This is Julia Dandridge." The man beside her answered the question when she did not. The clerk scribbled something on a notepad and then nodded for them to enter the next room.

Julia squared her shoulders, determined to display no sign of the terror that overwhelmed her, knowing it could be mistaken for evidence of guilt. She had no idea of the offence with which she'd been charged, but knew it would require all her strength to maintain self-possession and presence of mind during this harrowing ordeal.

Places such as this were what made honest citizens tremble. Every sign of emotion would be noted, recorded officially, and then used against a person. Guilty or innocent, it was no small matter to be summoned before the provost, whose main interest was to convict, not to acquit.

Large rewards were offered by the government to anyone who furnished evidence prejudicial to the prisoner, so it was not surprising that witnesses were readily found to testify to anything—however improbable or implausible.

When they entered an interior room with no windows and little light, they came upon a man sitting behind a desk, rubbing his eyes as though just awakened from sleep. Julia's escort handed him the slip of paper from the Judge Advocate, which he accepted, but did not examine—or even read.

"Come with me." He stood with much clamor and little grace, and led her down a corridor to another room. There, an overweight, gray-haired gentleman sat at a desk writing, his spectacles perched on the end of his nose. He glanced up over his glasses when she entered, but he did not smile, and he did not rise.

Another man in a soldier's uniform relaxed on a sofa, his crossed leg swinging up and down as he read a newspaper, a cigar creating a circle of smoke around him.

"I have another of Uncle Sam's boarders," the man beside her said with no emotion.

The man still did not return any sort of greeting or display the slightest expression of welcome. Without looking up, he said, "Take a seat, please. I will attend to you directly."

Julia sat down and waited with her hands crossed patiently on her lap, trying to appear composed and unflustered. This was no easy feat, because she felt lightheaded and ill, like some terrible sickness was seeping through her veins. She made no attempt to talk, for no one in the room displayed any sign of being particularly sympathetic to her.

Finally, the man finished writing and motioned to her with a wave of his hand. "You will kindly answer the following questions." He opened a large book resembling a ledger, nearly extinguishing a candle on the edge of the desk that had burned two inches from its socket. Melted tallow dribbled down the sides of the bronze candlestick and dotted the desk, but he seemed not to notice.

"Your name?"

Julia stood and looked around to see to whom he was speaking. "Is it not on the paper there?" she replied innocently. "I have been asked the question a number of times, and am sure they wrote it down."

The man looked up slowly, stared at her a moment, and simply repeated the question more forcefully. "Your. Name?"

"Julia Dandridge."

"Of what state are you a native?"

"Virginia."

She noticed his hand pause, and his lips clenched just a bit tighter before he scribbled the word into the ledger.

"Your age?"

"Twenty-one."

He raised his head then and leaned sideways to talk to someone behind her that she had not heard enter. "This is Julia Dandridge?"

"Yes, sir. The one and only," was the quick reply.

"What is the meaning of this?" Julia's heart skipped a beat, but she managed to keep her voice from shaking. Young as she was, she had long ago learned the importance of maintaining control. "For what reason am I here?"

He looked at her over the top of his glasses. "Why, treason, of course."

With composure and quiet dignity, she listened to the words, though her pulse throbbed mightily in her ears. "If you have evidence against me, I have yet to hear about it."

The men looked at each other and laughed.

"I fail to see the humor." Julia spoke boldly even though she was seized with a sense of despair that bordered on mortal dread. "You may indeed have the power to arrest me, but certainly not the authority."

Again, the men laughed merrily as if she had told them a splendid joke. "My dear Miss Dandridge, there are many confined behind the walls of Old Capitol with less evidence against them than has been gathered against you."

"What evidence? I have committed no crime."

"We have reason to believe you are acquainted with the Lion."

"That's preposterous." She sounded more angry than dismayed and took satisfaction that her voice did not betray her. "I do not know who the Lion is—and most likely, neither do you."

"That may well be the case, but it matters little. There are those who believe you are closely enough allied that he will come for you."

It took every ounce of strength in Julia's body not to fall to her knees and beg…plead for them to have mercy. "Do what you will with me." She raised her head defiantly in an acceptance of her fate, but tried to convey no other emotion. "The Lion, whoever he is, has no interest in me. He will never be caught in your trap."

"Show her to her quarters," the gray-haired soldier ordered as if he had tired of the game.

"Wait." The other one, who wore the uniform of a guard or a warden, took a step forward with a contemptuous stare. "Since you are a loyal citizen, I am sure you will not decline an opportunity to take the oath of allegiance. Such an act will improve your surroundings in the prison and lessen your suffering considerably."

Julia threw her shoulders back and raised her head. "I find that insulting, sir."

"Does that mean you will?" He crossed his arms and stared at her accusingly. "Or will not?"

"That means if my word is not sufficient, neither would my oath be." She endured his irate glare and returned it with one of her own.

"Enough of this." The gray-haired man seemed impatient and angry. "Put her in confinement."

"I would," the man behind her responded, "but them drunken scalawags from last night have taken up the remaining rooms."

"Throw them all together in one cell, and put this one with the girl."

Once again, Julia was led out into the sunlight. After a short walk, they approached a large brick building that she recognized as Old Capitol Prison. She had passed it many times, and pitied the forlorn-looking creatures who would sometimes approach the barred windows, gazing with longing eyes at the grass and trees.

The building had served as a temporary headquarters for the capitol of the United States when the current structure was being rebuilt. It now served as a prison, housing Confederate soldiers and prisoners of war.

Carrol Prison, an adjoining structure, was devoted mostly to the confinement of unfortunate females that aroused either the ire or suspicion of the government. The fact that Julia was being taken to the main prison did not make her thoughts optimistic ones.

While the outside of the complex was reasonably neat and orderly, Julia soon learned that the inside was a dingy, damp place resembling a medieval dungeon. Her escort led her through an empty room and a dark passage that emptied into a large yard. They walked to the other side before entering another passageway with a staircase. Midway through the passage was a door, before which stood a soldier on guard. The sentry was motioned aside with a wave, and the door unbolted and thrown open.

"Walk in."

Julia shrank back when stagnant, humid air pressed down upon her, and she cautiously scanned the filthy interior.

"It's a prison cell," the guard said unsympathetically. "It ain't intended to soothe one's nerves." He shoved her the rest of the way through and closed the door behind her.

Julia froze once inside, breathing heavily, her arms crossed in front of her, afraid to touch anything. She moved only her eyes as she took in her new surroundings.

Two windows on the other side of the cell—without blinds or even glass—opened to the large yard. Outside, a number of men walked mechanically as if for exercise, while others occupied themselves by cutting wood.

Beneath the windows stood large barrels, which she assumed contained kitchen and other refuse matter. Overall, the room was one mass of dirt and gloom. Spider webs hung like silky drapes from the ceiling, and the floor seemed to be alive with vermin of all kinds.

The walls had been papered at one point in time, but dampness had caused it to hang in long, curling strips. A half-burned log rested on a pile of ashes in the fireplace, while the mantel and surrounding area appeared filthy and covered with grease.

Julia heard the key turning in the lock behind her as she continued to survey the room. The furniture, what little of it there was, consisted of an iron bedstead, pillows, a mattress of straw, a pair of sheets, and a brown blanket. Between the windows stood a small table, on which was perched a stone jug and a tin cup.

One wooden chair completed the inventory, on which sat a young girl of about sixteen years of age. She wore a dirt-streaked dress and displayed a startled, frightened expression, as if she suspected Julia had been sent to spy on her.

Julia mistrusted her as well, and stood there for a long time without saying a word. As she tried to recover from the shock of her surroundings, her gaze fell upon the windows again. She shivered and took a step backward in startled disgust when she became conscious of the fact that each man stared curiously at her through the opening before moving on.

Withdrawing to sit on the bed, which lay in shadows on the opposite side of the room, Julia halted when she noticed something moving. Bending down to get a better look, she detected creeping things of innumerable quantities and more signs of unquestionable filth. Seizing one corner of the blanket with the tips of her fingers, she drew it off and threw it as far as she could.

As the shadows outside grew longer, someone began to light the gas lamps in the yard, an apparent signal for the men outside to return to their chambers. To her dismay, Julia discovered that the lights were so arranged as to illuminate the interior of the first floor rooms, so that any prospect of privacy was dashed.

A few minutes later, the door unlocked, and two men entered with meal trays. Julia looked eagerly at the coffee pot. She was also handed a small bowl with what appeared to be about a spoonful of brown sugar, half a cup of milk, two slices of bread, and a little pat of butter that smelled rancid.

Had anything been clean, Julia would have considered eating, but the plates were streaming with dirty dishwater. The fork she had been given had but one prong remaining, and the spoon was missing most of its handle. Both were sticky and contained bits of dried food. Upon closer inspection, she saw black specks of ants crawling through the sugar, topped off with a slight sprinkling of flies. From the odors emanating from the coffee pot, Julia guessed it to be a concoction of tobacco and old coffee grounds.

Exhausted, both mentally and physically, Julia knew she should try to eat—but she could not. She sat down on a wobbly stool and rested her head on her hands on the windowsill, trying in vain to rest. Her body consented, but her mind did not.

She prayed that Landon would re-think his plot, and wished she could warn him of the Yankees' terrible scheme. Staring blankly out the window, she wondered if there could be any way to escape. The yard appeared to be enclosed on three sides by a strong board fence, some twelve feet high. On the top of that stood a platform, upon which the sentinels paced, looking grim and adequately armed.

The fourth side of the yard consisted of a wing of the building. In the upper stories, Julia could see other prisoners moving behind the iron bars. The yard was devoid of grass, shrubbery, trees, or greenery of any kind, so that the men's walking routine had driven dust into the room, which even now was settling on Julia's hair and clothing.

The young girl must have noticed her look of dismay. "The other rooms are much nicer than this, but we are in close confinement."

Although not outright hostile now, neither was the child overly friendly. Julia didn't really blame her. It was clear that surviving in this place involved close attention to whom you called a friend and knowing whom you could trust.

"Why?"

"I don't know, but you see how we are guarded. A soldier before our door and one walking in front of the window at night."

"Is it not so throughout the prison?"

"No," she replied, sounding less timid now. "Upstairs, the prisoners are allowed to walk about and exercise in the yard."

"How do you know all of this?"

"I've been here before."

"You have? How old are you?"

"Sixteen." The girl straightened her shoulders as if that would make her appear older, and then answered the next question she knew was coming. "They say I tore down the flag on government property."

"And did you?"

Before she could answer, a commotion outside caused Julia to run to the window. She, and many others, watched a heavily guarded ambulance being unloaded of its cargo. Even from a distance, she could hear the clanking of iron. Within minutes, a man with hands and feet manacled was helped out by two soldiers and led into the building. He appeared weak, or injured, walking with his head down, listless and feeble, as if he did not have the energy to hold himself up.

"Who was that?"

All around the yard, eyes peered out the encasements and bars, while whispered voices of confusion and excitement filled the air. Julia soon learned that everything here was done sneakily and cunningly, always with a hint of mystery, so as to keep the prisoners in a constant state of nervous excitement.

Her hope for release still flickered, but feebly.

Chapter 41

J ulia closed her eyes and tried to sleep but could not relax. The sights within the walls of this place had been dreadful, but the sounds were even worse. Although she tried to grow accustomed to the frequent and troubling disturbances, she jumped each time the heavy tread of the sentries moved past the window.

Some months earlier, it had not been unusual for gunshots to break her slumber. But this constant activity all around her created a setting so full of sound that it allowed no rest.

Something else soon caused her even greater disquiet, and obliterated her need for rest. Approaching footsteps in the corridor outside her room sent a shiver of anxiety the length of her body.

As she raised her head to listen, the undertones of a conversation reached her ears. From the general clamor of the prison, one voice detached itself and rose above the din. Julia strained to hear, telling herself it could not be. Every nerve was on alert, every muscle tense with anticipation. Although she could not make out any words, her body reacted with panicked alarm in spite of herself.

By the time the key in the lock turned, Julia's forehead was beaded with sweat.

As the door began to open, it hurt to take a breath.

And when Preston Moxley appeared in the threshold, she

thought her heart would cease to beat. The rush of terror and dread that surged through her veins threatened to drive her to her knees.

"My dear friend, Julia Dandridge. I fear I must apologize for your accommodations." Preston gazed around the room, his face creased with disgust, and pulled a handkerchief out of his pocket, which he placed near his nose. "Have you met my uncle, Detective Thorpe?"

A second man, huffing and wheezing like a winded mule, stepped into the small enclosure.

Julia backed as far away from the two men as she could. "So you are the one who sent me here?"

It was hard to believe that just the night before, she had dazzled a crowd with her charm and grace. Now, she presented a pathetic picture of hopelessness, fear, and desperation.

"Only temporarily, my dear. Only temporarily."

Thorpe pointed to the girl who sat huddled in a corner. "The guard outside will see you to your new lodgings."

The young lady practically ran for the door.

"You have no right—" Julia's voice was barely a whisper. For some reason, the exit of the girl left her feeling still more alone and helpless. She was too weary and miserable to pretend a confident deportment any longer. An involuntary chill shook her as she took another step back and felt the cold wall behind her.

Never had she been so frightened and full of despair. Never had she felt so disheartened. Even when she had been requested to carry an important message outside the lines, she had kept her resolve and remained confident. The long journey of traveling by farmer's produce cart down the Maryland shore of the Potomac, with vital information tucked under a comb in her hair, had not been near as trying on her nerves—even though she had been stopped a number of times.

"Now, now, Miss Dandridge." Detective Thorpe spoke sharply and impatiently. "We don't have time for long explanations. We believe the Lion is coming here this very night."

They expected perhaps an outburst of tears, possibly hysterics and wild lamentations—but these were not to be found. Though Julia's lips quivered and were almost blue in hue, her eyes remained tearless.

"Why would you think such a thing, and what has it to do with me?" She lifted her head as a new wave of resolve steeled into her veins. The slightest mistake in look or tone could unmask her, and lead these men straight to Landon.

"Because we have something he wants."

Julia laughed, thinking they referred to her. "You are mistaken. I don't even know who the Lion is."

The men glanced at one another, but Julia could not read the look.

"Nevertheless," Preston said, "we have something he wants." He took a step closer, studying her intently. "You look confused, my dear. Allow me to explain."

"I do not wish to hear your explanations." Julia pretended a calm she did not feel. "I wish to be released immediately. This is an—"

Preston did not allow her to finish. "A Confederate soldier, who had been reported as dead after escaping from prison, was recently discovered by one of our patrols. He was recovering from his wounds in the home of a sympathetic private citizen. He has since been brought here."

It took a moment for Julia to understand what Preston was insinuating, but when she recalled the earlier commotion and the appearance of the man in chains, the realization hit her. She held onto the wall behind her to keep from falling. "Sawyer? Sawyer Graham? Is *alive*? Is h-here?"

The detective clapped his hands together. "Yes, the one and only. Risen from the dead you might say."

Preston spoke again, his tone softer, but with grim purpose. "So you agree that the Lion may indeed be especially interested in the release of Sawyer Graham?"

Julia's eyes darted from one man to the other, trying to comprehend, trying to allow her brain to catch up with what had been stated. For a moment, she didn't speak. She feared her eyes, or her voice, or both, would deceive her—if her outburst hadn't already.

"The Lion is especially interested in releasing anyone who is improperly imprisoned, I believe," she finally said, her voice full of defiance.

"Indeed." Preston took a couple of whiffs from his scented handkerchief before speaking again. "I think it right to give you a word of explanation. Imagine my surprise when I discovered that such an alluring young lady as yourself had given me the honor of following me across the Potomac. If I am not mistaken, however, the purpose of this flattering attention was not for my benefit. I think that I am right in surmising that you may have come to warn that cursed Lion."

Julia started to deny the accusation, but he stopped her with his hand. 'As I am sure you can understand, I was therefore forced to take certain precautions. Hence you were arrested and brought here."

"You have no right to hold me against my will…"

Preston ignored the comment, but reached out to grasp her by the wrist. "As you know, here inside the prison, your brother Gideon Dandridge waits with the other traitors for the arrival of their mysterious rescuer, the scheming Lion of the South. If you scream, if there is a scuffle, if shots are fired, this most impudent devil will no doubt make his getaway to a place of safety, destroying my plans for his capture."

He paused as if to let his words sink in. "If my mission remains unaccomplished, further action will be required. It rests upon your good sense whether or not your brother is permitted to go off with you tonight."

Julia could not utter a sound. His plans were ruthless in design, deadly in capability—and she was now a part of them. Horrible visions of what could happen passed before her eyes.

Preston did not seem the least empathetic or concerned when he regarded her pale, quivering face and trembling hands. "I feel like you are most willing to cooperate with me."

Julia's whole body stiffened in defiance of his statement. "Curse you."

The words came out whispered, but Preston heard them nonetheless. He leaned close and wagged his finger at her.

"Let me be clear. If you scream, if you utter one sound or attempt to move from here, my men, a dozen of them, will seize your brother—and the others—and hang them before your eyes."

Julia listened to her implacable enemy's speech with increasing terror. Numbed with exhaustion, she still had sufficient mental vitality in her to realize the full horror of the options he presented.

She could remain quiet, and allow the man she worshipped to walk unconsciously to his death when he tried to rescue his brother. Or, she could attempt to give him a word of warning, which would signal her own brother's death, as well as the other unsuspecting captives.

Preston stood in the shadows. She could not see him clearly, but she could feel those keen, pale eyes of his fixed maliciously upon her. His callous, whispered words reached her ears like the death knell of her last faint, lingering hope.

"I cannot imagine that you would have any interest in saving anyone but your brother, and all you need to do for his safety is remain where you are and keep silent." He took a deep breath and sighed with contentment. "In any event, no warning from you could possibly save him."

"Go. To. Hell." Julia was so distraught she could hardly force the words from her quivering lips.

Preston laughed majestically and loudly. "My dear lady. Look around. We are already in it."

Detective Thorpe now spoke from where he had stood silently beside his nephew. "And now we will leave you," he said, bowing as far as his rotund figure would allow. "You see, miss, we wish you to be perfectly free to make your choice."

Julia's thoughts whirled. Her temples ached. Her nerves were nearly paralyzed with fear.

She processed their footsteps walking to the door, heard the key turn in the lock. She did not call them back or scream. Weary with mental fatigue and physical strain, she barely had the strength to breathe or hold herself upright.

Oh! Think!

Julia's eyes remained fixed on the door. Her hands were tightly clasped across her breast, and her lips moved as they murmured with pathetic heartbreaking persistence.

What can I do? Oh, God, grant me wisdom.

The minutes flew by in the awful stillness—for how long, she was not sure. When her mind began to clear, she realized that the two men were now discussing their foul plans right outside her cell.

Julia's heart increased its pounding. She leaned into the door, her eyes large and dilated as she struggled to catch the conversation. The more they talked, the more the dreadfulness of the situation struck her. The horror, the disappointment, the dismay, were almost more than she could bear.

"He assured me that your orders have been followed implicitly," she heard Preston tell his uncle. "Word has been spread that Sawyer Graham is alive. All the roads are being patrolled, and the river crossings searched and guarded."

"But they have left an opening? One that the Lion will be sure to find?"

"Yes. Of course." Preston spoke curtly and to the point, each word like a dagger. "Not too obvious, of course. One he will believe we have neglected to cover."

"Nevertheless, the sentinels must keep the sharpest lookout for any stranger who may be walking, riding, or driving along the road or near the river. As soon as any of them sight someone unknown, their orders are to keep him in view while sending another to us with word. They have been told they will pay with their lives for any negligence."

Julia pressed against the door, sickened as she listened to the conversation and learned the whole of the plan to catch the Lion. They would lure him in by leaving a hole in their picket line, giving him false security. Then the valiant plotter was to be surrounded and caught red-handed.

If he did manage to somehow escape their net, those left at the prison would be shot on the spot or given a mock trial and hanged.

Julia slumped to the ground, her head in her hands. All the roads were patrolled and being watched. The trap was well set. The net was wide at present, but drawing tighter and tighter. She had never imagined there could be so much deadly hatred, so much fiendish delight, in one man before.

Preston Moxley and his uncle intended to find and destroy the Lion. Tonight. Possibly right before her eyes. She felt her last hope draining from her very soul.

When she heard someone clap their hands together, she listened attentively again. "One more thing. We must warn the men that the Lion may show fight. Do not kill him outright unless necessary. I want him *alive*."

Julia thought she had already lived through as much horror as one could withstand, more anguish than any human heart could bear. But now the awful reality of this terrible ordeal seized her with new terror. Pain and pure dread seeped in, filling her eyes with moisture that she tried desperately to stop.

Preston's plans were deliberate and strategic. He might well triumph. If caught within the gates of the city, the Lion would be unable to claim protection—not that the officials in power would give him time to do so.

Not a loophole had been left through which even the bravest and most clever man might escape. Every road was guarded. Every corner was watched. And here in the prison, those waiting to be rescued were unknowingly leading the Lion to his death—or to a much worse fate. Preston Moxley was too fiendish to allow a brave man to die the quick, sudden death of a soldier.

No. Preston had nursed the thought of vengeance too long to allow the Lion to die with honor. He yearned to torment the artful enemy who had so long baffled him. He would inflict upon him the utmost in moral and mental torture, in a way that would delight the very demons in Hell.

The capture of this wily foe would be the finest leaf in Preston's wreath of glory. He and his uncle would be hailed as heroes to those who wore blue.

Julia strained to completely grasp the situation. Caught in the elaborate trap were those dearest to her heart. One was the man she idolized—the other the brother she loved. But there were still others here, surely, who were calmly waiting for the Lion of the South to rescue them, even as deadly peril lurked in every shadow.

She must find a way to help. But how? The whole situation seemed more and more unreal. Impossible. This scheme of evil was being as effectively carried out as it had been judiciously planned.

Julia sat alone in the dark, knowing that somewhere, perhaps quite close, her brother also sat. And dear Sawyer, who had endured so much and survived this long, now faced a new threat.

Worst of all, Landon could be unknowingly walking to his doom. Would she do nothing to save him? She had wronged him, and caused the great calamity about to befall him. If he were not warned, he would soon fall into the death trap that his relentless enemy had prepared.

Julia choked back sobs as she abandoned any notion of being able to divert Landon from his mission. Even if she had a way to reach him, it would be useless. Nothing and no one would prevent him from performing the task he had promised to do. And now that it was Sawyer's life on the line, his efforts would be redoubled. She could only wait—perhaps to watch his last moments on Earth.

The thought of losing him absorbed all else...the reality of it too much to endure. If only she could see him again. If only she had the chance to assure him that her love—whole, true, and passionate—was entirely his. Then, perhaps, this tragic ending would be bearable.

Julia caught the sound of distant footsteps, and her heart gave a leap. The tramp of feet was followed by voices—loud, authoritative, and commanding tones that increased in agitation and alarm.

Was it Landon? Or was it the guards? Should she scream right now with a sound that would echo from one end of the prison to the other? Should she cry out a warning that would force Landon to retrace his steps and escape?

Twice the screams rose to her throat, but with them emerged the image of the awful consequence. Her brother and other prisoners shot or hanged before her eyes, practically on her orders. She would be their murderer.

That fiend, Preston, had played on her feelings, taken advantage of her devotion to her brother, and rendered her useless. She could not give the signal. She was too weak. How could she deliberately order Gideon's death, to be killed before her eyes?

Yet, if Landon failed…if indeed the stars lined up with Preston and proved too strong for the heroic Lion, Julia knew her life would not be worth living.

Her breathing stopped as she strained to listen. Everything became as silent as the grave just before the sounds from far beyond her door began to swell. Julia felt, more than heard, the men on the watchtower lining up with their guns. Her senses told her that the guards were crouching in the darkness, ready to spring, prepared to fight.

The voices seemed to increase in number and volume, but in the vast immensity of the prison, it was impossible to say how near or far they were, or from which direction they came. Faint at first, they grew louder, and Julia felt her very life slipping away. She distinctly heard the click of a gun outside her door as a guard apparently prepared to shoot some unseen foe.

Julia's body trembled with hopelessness as she sat in the dark with her torturous secret. She bit her lip to suppress the agony consuming her, wondering if God would help her remain silent, or if anguish would deprive her of self-control and force her to scream, knowing it would kill them all.

Then, a sudden calm overtook her. She convinced herself that she no longer had any choice in the matter. She must drift as fate ordained. Allow destiny to fulfill its course. It was as simple as that.

No! She could not let Landon's blood be upon her hands. She could not be branded his murderer. He, who had sacrificed so much to save so many. She suddenly wished to save him at any cost.

With a wild shriek, she sprang to her feet and darted to the door. She made contact and fell against its thick walls, hammering with clenched fists in a frenzy. "No! No! If you can hear me, you must run! They are waiting for you! Please run! Do what you must to get away!"

The door burst open, and guards rushed in, pushing Julia to the ground. They pinioned her there—two, maybe three of them—but there was no need. Though she had shown commendable fortitude before, she was not making the faintest struggle now. She was barely conscious. She could no longer hear anything, only roaring.

Her attempt to save Landon had failed. The blood of her brother—and Sawyer—now stained her hands.

Chapter 42

J ulia remembered the voices, the shouted commands, the sound of heavy boots, the horses, the gunfire, the urgency. Everything was a mishmash of confusion, commotion, and chaos.

Soldiers, or guards, she knew not which, had pushed their way into her prison cell and hushed her cry of alarm. Then they had tied her hands behind her back, blindfolded her, and spirited her out of the prison.

She had the strange, floating feeling of being carried by infinite strength. Barely conscious and sick with fear, Julia heard a loud voice of command as she was forcefully carried through the prison gates.

"Step aside."

"On whose authority, I'd like to know."

"On the authority of Detective Thorpe, who ordered these prisoners be moved to a more secure site."

Another voice spoke up from behind her. "The Lion is on the prowl. Some say right outside the gates. We're taken these prisoners to a place they'll never be found."

The sound of laughter from multiple sources was then heard. "So Thorpe is out-smarting the Lion is he? Moving the prisoners at the last minute, and with no notice."

"That he is," another voice said, "but watch your backs. The

Lion is on his way, and won't be happy when he discovers he's walking into a trap."

Julia was hustled to a nearby conveyance and thrown unceremoniously onto the floor. The rocking and creaking of the carriage over the rutted roads at a high rate of speed made her nauseous and desperate for fresh air.

She could feel the hot humidity of a sky that was preparing to storm, heard the low muttering of thunder in the distance blending with the nervous neigh of horses, and the rattling of sabers and chains.

They were moving fast, with no thought to her comfort. Perhaps Landon was in hot pursuit. That cheering thought was swiftly followed by heartbreak when she heard more gunfire, more yelling, more chaos and commotion.

"Did we get him?" she heard someone ask.

"Yes. We got him."

"Alive?"

"Barely, but yes."

That was it. Julia could take the agony no more. Her endurance was depleted, and her strength was gone. She fell into a deep black hole from which she wished to never rise.

Chapter 43

The sentries were posted as usual at the outskirts of the city, but tonight a current of increased alertness and anticipation rippled through the ranks. General Carlyle himself had taken control of the troops at the Chain Bridge checkpoint, trusting no one else to the enterprise.

Carlyle felt in his bones that the Lion was going to attempt passage through this very post tonight.

Let him come. The general had suffered tremendously and undergone monstrous mistreatment under the Lion. Tonight he would get his revenge.

To aid the general in accomplishing his task, a strong guard had been posted throughout the city, with additional troops brought in from nearby camps. Every sentry and soldier had been briefed on the crimes with which the Lion would be charged, and all were provided with copies of the reward that would be paid for his arrest. With unusual alacrity, this information had been transmitted from the checkpoints to the outposts, and everywhere in between.

Things looked desperate—if not impossible—for the Lion.

Everyone in blue tonight had been given special orders, and as a result, the line of farmers' carts leaving the city market to return to their homes, clogged the streets at the checkpoints. Each one was examined thoroughly, meaning many of them were dumped by the soldiers in charge, causing the farmers and their wives or children to reload whatever meager supplies they carried with them.

Suddenly, a courier, riding hard, brought his horse to a sliding stop. "General Carlyle?"

Carlyle struggled to his feet. "That's me. What do you have?"

"A report from yesterday, sir. With all the excitement, the account was late in getting through."

The general ripped open the missive and scanned its contents. Then he squeezed the paper into a ball and threw it to the ground.

"Another sighting of the Lion, sir?"

Carlyle began wheezing and coughing as if his throat were closing up. "No wagons through this gate until they are inspected. I don't care what they contain or how long it takes!"

"What was it this time?" one of the guards asked.

The general stared out into the darkness as if envisioning the scene. "I'll tell you what it was," he said, his voice cracking with distress. "It seems a wagon, driven by an old hag, pulled up to the far gate—"

"Surely it was stopped by the guards," the sentry interrupted. "That's the rules."

"Oh yes, they stopped it." Carlyle muttered something under his breath that was unintelligible. "But the old lady insisted she had to get to the doctor—that her grandson in the back had smallpox."

All those gathered round took an involuntary step back. "Smallpox?"

"So they let her through?"

"Yes, they let her through—and turns out, it wasn't smallpox." Carlyle's voice rose above the clamor of wagons. "They say the hag driving was the Lion himself. And who knows what cargo was in the back!"

As he was speaking, a farmer's wagon pulled up to the checkpoint, loaded down with a dozen coffins that appeared to have been thrown upon the conveyance quite haphazardly...or perhaps by someone in a hurry. General Carlyle gazed at the men around him with squinted eyes, and squared his shoulders. "I'll handle this one."

Sauntering over to the young driver, he leaned against the wagon casually. "Hello," he said in a cheerful, good-natured tone, pretending to be duped by the charade. "And where might you be going with these, my lad?" He elbowed the man who had walked up next to him. "Look here, Captain. Coffins heading out to the countryside."

It seemed to everyone witnessing the scene that Carlyle had suddenly developed a sense of humor. Only a few attributed the general's sudden joviality to the liquor they'd seen him confiscate from one of the wagons. In any event, it was fun to watch. And if Carlyle was successful in nabbing the Lion, which his confidence and exuberance suggested he was going to do, all the better for them.

"I'm off to Camp Defiance, on orders of Gen'ral Franklin." The boy seemed impatient, but tolerant of the delay. "They have some sickness among the officers."

"Oh they do, do they?"

Carlyle's tone suddenly became a bit more threatening and loud. "Surely, the Lion does not think we will fall for such a trick as this!" He motioned for the men. "Open them. Be quick about it. But be ready."

The boy began to show signs of annoyance and unease. "The general is waiting," he said. "His orders said to hurry."

Carlyle laughed. "Well, now, I trust you, my lad, that I do. But we'll just have to check." A half a dozen soldiers, some with pistols drawn, began roughly lifting, tilting, and searching the wooden boxes.

They were little more than halfway through the operation when a loud noise was heard, followed by a general uproar of wagons banging into one another, and horses and mules revolting.

The melee was followed by a moment of intense silence, which was then broken by yells and shouts and running feet.

"What is that ruckus?" Carlyle implored.

"The horses are getting fidgety not moving, sir. Some of the wagons are trying to turn around and move to other gates."

"Oh, they are, are they?" The general imagined the Lion slipping through his grasp again by moving to another gate where the guards were more lax. He looked around for more men to help, but there were none to be seen who were not already busy at some task.

His mind began to wander, and then to race, as new possibilities presented themselves. Perhaps this was a decoy! All of his attention, and that of his men, was centered on this one wagon. Maybe the Lion was using this opportunity to sneak through another gate! Had he fallen for the trick so easily?

"Let this wagon through," he growled, as he stared at the three remaining coffins, yet to be searched.

Carlyle swiped at the sweat running down his face, as again he had second thoughts. The temperature was hot, and the dust was thick. So was his mind. He could not think with all the commotion, and the knowledge that time was of the essence. He may never get another chance to nab his detested foe, and save the country from the Lion's despicable acts of courage.

The general studied the street where wagons were backed up as far as the eye could see. If the Lion was in one of them, Carlyle must be the one to find him. The mysterious rebel's reign of superiority must end, and it must end tonight. "I said, let it pass," he yelled, certain—more or less—of his course of action. "Bring up the next wagon."

Things calmed down considerably after that, providing General Carlyle a sense of relief that the line was moving again. But not fifteen minutes later, the general distinguished the approach of horses' hooves. At first it was just the faint ring of steel on the cobblestone, but soon, the full thud of a steady canter fell upon him. This turned into a stampede of sound that made the earlier provocation seem minor. A unit of cavalry, their horses' necks stretched out full-tilt, galloped toward the gate. The tall officer in the lead pulled his impressive mount to a sliding halt, close enough to spatter Carlyle and some of the men of the guard with pellets of mud.

"Tell me." He spoke in a hurried, commanding voice. "Has a wagon of caskets passed through here?"

"Caskets?" A chill passed from Carlyle's head down to his feet.

"I *said* caskets, didn't I? Are you deaf and *dumb*?" the man thundered.

"Y-y-es, sir." Carlyle trembled as he stared past the gate. "I mean, no sir," he said, turning back to the man who addressed him. "I mean, yes, it passed this way, but we checked it, sir. They were empty."

"*All* of them?"

"Yes, sir." His eyes looked up to the officer. Though he wore his hat down low, the figure was impressive and decidedly that of a man in command—a man who would tolerate no deceit. He sat ramrod straight with no expression on his stony face, yet Carlyle could sense his ferocity and agitation.

"Well, sir, maybe all but a few."

"You damned fool! Two of our most valuable prisoners were in those caskets, and likely the Lion himself!"

"I'm sorry, sir. We tried to check them, but the line was—"

"Never mind that now. Have your men stand aside. We can still catch them." He turned around in his saddle. "Spare no effort to overtake them. Send the ambulance along. I have orders to bring the Lion back alive!"

Carlyle stood speechless, the pallor of deadly alarm distinct on his face. He took a step back to avoid being run over or crushed, as the officer spurred his horse through the gate. A dozen blue-coated soldiers followed with a spirit and determination worthy of all praise. Most of them rode with one hand on the reins, the other on their rifles, which rested on their thighs. An ambulance, pulled by four mules, proceeded through the gate at an impressive pace as well, and disappeared into the cloud of dust created by the horsemen.

Their forms vanished into the darkness long before the sound of them did. The clanking and crash of dozens of shod feet, the rattle of steel, and the jingling of bits, resounded for quite some time. Then, after a few minutes, came a flash and a loud report in the distance, followed by another and another.

At last, silence was restored.

Chapter 44

Julia heard the crackling of a campfire in the distance and the sound of muffled conversation. The neighing of horses and tramping of feet added to the low hum of activity around her. Touching the rough wood on which she lay, and feeling the ache in her back, she reasoned she was in the bed of a wagon. But why?

When she remembered what she'd just gone through, she didn't care where she was. Even if she were condemned to live the rest of her life in a dark, horrible cell, it was a fate she could accept. She moaned softly when she thought of those she had left behind, probably to their deaths. Gideon, dear brother. Sawyer, dear friend. Landon... She stifled a sob.

Had they survived? Been hanged? God in his mercy had allowed her to miss it all. And now, she wished only to lie very still with her eyes closed, so that she might listen to the pounding of her own heart and will it to stop.

A tear trickled out of one closed eye as the soft hum of conversation continued around her. But after another brief moment, one voice stood out from the others.

"All is well, my lady. Do not abandon hope."

The sound of that voice coming through the haze comforted her in a way that no other voice could. Straining to see through the fog of sleep and darkness, Julia blinked to clear her vision.

She could not see the face of the rider—he was in deep shadow and stood some distance away. But she recognized the form and the features of the gallant cavalier who sat upon his horse with military erectness in the moonlight. His coat was buttoned to the chin and was stretched tightly across his broad shoulders. The light from above illuminated the brass buttons on his uniform, the pistols on his belt, and the gleam of his dark eyes, as brilliant as any lightning she had ever seen.

But he was wearing blue.

Julia blinked, thinking she was dreaming. Perhaps she was dead. Or perhaps *he* was. But instead of dissolving like a shadow as she expected him to, the man approached, appearing more substantial than ghostly—more solemn and grand than any spirit.

It was Landon.

Something inside Julia turned clean over, nearly choking her and making her feel shaky and weak. Yet in its wake came a flooding warmth and a sense of peaceful certainty. She exerted every effort to preserve her self-control, but the struggle was for naught. Her breath came faster, her hands began to shake, and her emotions changed from utter surprise to incredulity, and then to ardent relief and joy.

The next instant, the tall horseman had impelled his steed to within feet of her and bowed with cavalier grace over the pommel.

"At your service, miss."

Her eyes locked on his, and it was if he breathed new life into her. Julia blinked, thinking it could not be real. She turned her head slightly, the pain of the movement causing her to wince, and saw men standing and laughing around a small campfire nearby. All wore the uniform of the enemy.

Landon dismounted, and in silence, drew near. He stood over

her for a moment, not talking, only studying her with a concerned and protective gaze.

Julia reached up and touched his arm, feeling the course fabric of his uniform in her fingers. Even though he displayed an appearance of magnificent bearing and authority, she still thought him a mere apparition. Her emotions toggled between dread and breathless anticipation, hope, and fear, that it was really all just a dream.

"You are real?" she whispered.

Everything was out of focus. Even her memories of that through which she had just passed had an unreal quality, as if it had all been just a dream.

"The Yankees think so." He shot her a twisted grin, the first she had seen since her return to Virginia. She felt his hand move to rest reassuringly on hers. He appeared colossal highlighted in the moonlight. Perfectly heroic.

"But I...I heard someone say they had caught you."

Landon's brow wrinkled in confusion. "But as you can see, they did not."

"Landon...I..."

The mystery in his eyes beckoned to her, and the passion burning within them made her lose her train of thought. He was perfectly striking, stalwart, a model of soldierly grace and strength; yet his expression seemed troubled and distraught.

Julia longed for the protectiveness of his arms, and as if reading her mind, he bent down and drew her to him, lifting her as gently and as carefully as if she were a day-old kitten. "Quiet now. No need to talk."

She drank in the comfort of his nearness, trying to grasp that a man who so rarely showed any visible emotion was saying soft, soothing things to her. She felt his hot breath against her cheek, his powerful, reassuring arms. Her senses were overwhelmed with a feeling of security as he infused her with his persuasive, compelling, indomitable strength.

"No. I must." She struggled in his strong arms. "You don't know—"

He held her closer. "I know everything, dear one. You need to rest." His touch was strong, firm, protective...possessive. Beneath his bulldog resolution and courage, Landon Graham had a kind soul, and gentle, comforting hands.

Julia relaxed a little and then pulled away so she could look up at him. "You...know...everything?" She reached up to touch his weary face, where suffering and torment had unmistakably left their traces. "But can you forgive?"

"There is nothing to forgive," he whispered. "It was an impossible situation."

The warmth and certainty of his expression brought tears to her eyes, and the words that followed made them flow. "I only hope you don't think of me too harshly." His voice was gravelly. His hands trembled. And his steady gaze bore into hers in silent expectation.

Before she could answer, someone walked up behind him and spoke. "Is she awake?"

Julia recognized the voice, and her eyes filled instantly with tears of joy. "Gideon?"

"It's about time you woke up," her brother said. His words were lighthearted, but the tone of his voice revealed his true emotions.

Landon stepped back and allowed Gideon to take his place. He held Julia close to his heart, squeezing her as if he'd never let go.

"Gideon. You're safe! I was so worried about you." Julia

leaned back and put her hand on her brother's cheek. The dark circles under his eyes spoke of many hours without sleep, and his face appeared heavy with strain. Otherwise, he seemed to be in good health.

When she did not stop staring at him, he brought his hand to his face and rubbed the whiskers on his chin. "I must look a sight—"

"For sore eyes," she finished for him. But then the bandage on his arm caught her attention. "Oh, dear. What happened?"

"It's nothing." He glanced at the soiled dressing as if he'd forgotten all about it. "Just a small wound."

"It's nothing?" Julia's voice grew shrill with concern. "Let me look at it."

"You can do that later," he answered. "Rest now."

"Better that he was hit halfway down one arm than halfway between two of them," a familiar, cheery—but weak—voice interrupted.

Julia's eyes widened as they fell upon Sawyer standing beside her brother. Had a ghost risen before her, she could not have been more shocked or surprised. He was pale and thin, almost unrecognizable but for the crooked smile on his face.

"Do you have a hug for me, too?" He wore an expression that was both tired and determined.

Julia excitedly drew him into her arms. "Oh, Sawyer. How good it is to see you."

"Yes, I've come back from the dead."

Indeed, it appeared that he had, with great, dark smudges under his eyes and looking like a ghost.

Julia sat dazed, looking from one beloved face to another, still not quite believing it was all real. It slowly began to sink in that when she'd heard someone say, "did we get him?" they'd been talking about Sawyer. "But how did you—?"

"I'll let Landon explain that."

"Why don't you get some sleep first?" Landon leaned close as if to observe more closely the exhaustion stamped on her face. "We can talk once we get back to Welbourne."

"Back to Welbourne?" She looked around at the three sets of eyes that were upon her. "But won't they find us there?"

"They have no reason to look there."

"No reason? But Preston knows…"

"Preston and his uncle are on their way to Richmond to be shown some very special Southern hospitality."

"And General Carlyle?"

Landon glanced over at Gideon. "He knows nothing, and even if he does, no one will listen to him. He will be shunned and avoided until the day he dies."

"Don't worry, Julia," Gideon said. "Detective Thorpe and his nephew wanted all the glory, so they didn't tell anyone else the specifics. The Yankees are no closer to catching the Lion than they were a month ago."

"Except now they are perhaps a bit more hesitant to attempt to discover his identity." Sawyer laughed and elbowed his brother.

"Here." Gideon came back from talking to one of the men by the fire. He leaned over, and handed her a canteen. "Take a sip of this."

Julia did as instructed and grimaced when the liquid ran down her throat. She found the whiskey to be both calming and stimulating.

"Not too much." He took the container back. "Feel better?"

"I'm not sure." Julia put her hand up over her eyes. "I feel like I'm dreaming. How did you—?"

"All right. I can see you are not going to go back to sleep."

Landon helped her sit up, and then lifted her out of the wagon and carried her over to the fire.

"I'm not sure where to start."

"At the beginning, of course."

"Very well."

He helped Julia get comfortable leaning against a large rock and lowered himself next to her. A kind of pleasant stupor stole over her as she looked around at the smiling faces of the courageous warriors who had helped in the rescue. One of them leaned down with a tin cup of water. "Thirsty, ma'am?"

Landon waited until she'd taken a few sips, and then began. "You see, I have been planning this little escapade for more than six months now."

Julia regarded him curiously over the rim of the cup. "But none of us were there back then."

"No. But many innocent people were, and perhaps, somehow, I knew it would be necessary in the future. In any event, one of my associates in the city was able to gain entry as a prison guard."

Julia's eyes grew round as she thought about the complexity of the Lion's network of spies. She thought her heart would overflow as he carefully recounted the inventive manner in which he had snatched the fugitives away, right from under the noses of Detective Thorpe and Preston.

She could not help but marvel at the wonderful ingenuity of Landon, and the pure audacity of those who had taken part in his daring plan. Indeed, Landon seemed more inclined to give credit to the valiant deeds of his men, rather than take any for himself.

Julia studied his face as he spoke and saw the fine lines of weariness around his eyes. If ever a commander was tried by overwhelming and continuous peril—and effortlessly rose above it—Landon had. He triumphed by sheer moral power and force, no matter the odds or chances.

As she swept the faces of those listening to the tale, she could see how they idolized their leader. Even now, in spite of his fatigue, he appeared focused, attentive, his body crackling with an energy that he must have held in reserve.

Julia was so happy, she could have sat there forever, listening to his kind, gentle voice, seeing the twinkle in his eye once again, and watching the other men mill about and talk.

"He was there mainly to serve as eyes and ears." Landon continued the story. "To learn the routines, placement of the guards, et cetera."

"And then some of the men were arrested two days ago in a drunken brawl," Gideon interjected.

Julia shook her head as she remembered the officer having to move other prisoners because of the number of drunken brawlers who had been brought in. "On purpose?"

Landon nodded. "It gave me a head start. I already had soldiers on the inside. My prison guard unlocked the cell of our so-called drunken colleagues, and provided them with weapons and uniforms. They created quite a chaotic scene, giving commands that sent the real guards on a wild goose chase.

"How did you know I—?"

"He knew I'd been arrested." Gideon interrupted again. "And I heard the commotion when you were brought in."

"But I screamed, and was tackled by guards." Julia shook her head, not understanding. "Held down."

"Begging your pardon." Landon said as his brow creased with concern. "They were my men. Once the chaos on the inside started, we moved in from the outside in Federal uniforms."

"They pretended to be a unit of elite guards brought in to

move the prisoners—under express orders of Detective Thorpe." Gideon laughed. "I almost got into a fist-fight with one until my eyes fell upon Landon."

"You were there, too?" Julia gazed up into Landon's eyes, trying to imagine the danger he'd placed himself in. A prison heist, surrounded by the enemy, in the middle of the capital city—and he the most hunted man in the country.

"He made sure you were safe," Gideon explained, "and then went looking for Sawyer."

"Oh, so that's how it was?" Sawyer commented from outside the circle as he rested against a tree. His voice was weak, and his pale, wax-colored lids were closed, yet he wore a faint smile on his face.

At that moment, Julia's eyes locked on Landon's. If not for the other men staring at her, she would have burst into tears at the thought of his sacrifice and suffering on her behalf. He loved her. He must. He had saved her before he had sought out his own brother, whom he adored and esteemed more than life itself.

Instead, she reached for his hand in the darkness and found it waiting. Something warm and vital and urgent passed from him to her, a burst of energy so intense, she wondered how others did not see the sparks.

"So, that's how you got in," Gideon said. "Tell her how you got out."

Julia turned her head toward Landon. "Yes, I heard their plan. They had every road patrolled and guarded. It seemed impossible."

"The extra patrols only made our job that much easier."

"I don't understand."

"I paid a young lad to take a load of coffins to a camp outside the gates."

Julia looked around, obviously not seeing how that was significant.

"It held up the line and created a scene of impatience and annoyance. There was a general uprising among those in the line that diverted the guards' attention, and then we proceeded as planned."

"Proceeded as planned?" Julia shook her head. "I still don't understand."

"You see how we are dressed, my dear. We operated as a special guard to get out of the prison, and then as a cavalry detail dispatched to catch up with the Lion, who had supposedly escaped the city in one of those coffins."

Julia looked down at her own dirty clothes. "But how—"

"You were placed in the ambulance that followed behind, along with Sawyer who was in no shape to ride. We were instructed to bring the Lion in alive, you know."

"We ran into some Union cavalry who wanted to provide us with an escort," Gideon added, "but Landon told them they could be of better use if they stayed back and helped secure the prison."

Everyone in the group laughed at the image. Instead of stopping the Lion—the Union troops had offered to give him an escort through their lines.

"I'm so sorry I didn't tell you everything when I had the chance." Julia rested her head on his strong shoulder.

"I should have trusted you, as you deserved to be trusted." He paused when his voice cracked, as if waiting to get it under his command again. "Then you would not have been forced to try to help a man who had done so much that needs forgiveness."

They were sitting side by side, leaning against a rock, safe from the grasp of the enemy, though not yet home. The exploit the men had carried out, seemed so simple, yet so vastly complicated. Julia could only marvel at the steady leadership and courage that had led to the success of the bold plan.

"We have much to talk about," she said quietly as she gazed straight ahead.

He leaned over and wiped a tendril of hair from her cheek. "Yes, as soon as we get back to Welbourne." He lifted her hand to his lips and pressed a warm kiss upon it. "I am at your service."

Chapter 45

J ulia walked toward the dining room at Welbourne with a
smile on her face. She had been back just a week, but in that
time, she'd created a lifetime of new memories.

Gideon had returned to his old self after a few days of rest
and a handful of home-cooked meals. Though he was still a little
gaunt from his tireless duty, it was comforting to hear his familiar
voice in the mornings and his laughter ringing throughout the
house.

Julia had spent every waking minute with him, walking and
riding around the beautiful grounds, catching up, and reminiscing
about the past. She had laughed more in the past few days than in
all the previous six years.

Sawyer, too, had improved considerably in a short span of
time. Suffering mostly from malnourishment and fatigue, he'd
gained color in his face, and a pound or two from Aunt Mazie's
cooking. Sallie waited on him hand and foot, and Landon barely left his side. Both treated him as if he were royalty, which he
seemed to enjoy, but everyone knew it wouldn't be long until he
was back on his feet and fully recovered.

Julia entered the vast dining room and paused. A storm had
rolled in, hastening the arrival of dusk, but Spencer had already
lit the candles of the overhead chandelier. Instead of appearing
gloomy and dark, the room sparkled and glowed in the soft light.

In the center of the room sat a table of royal proportions, long enough to host dozens of diners if the occasion arose. Five places were attractively set with the most exquisite fine china and silverware, both of which had been handed down through generations of Grahams. A vase that overflowed with fresh lilacs served as the centerpiece, the fragrance of which filled the room, and added to the magical appeal. The spectacle was breathtaking in its classic style and refined elegance.

This was the most impressive space in the mansion, and as such, was used only for formal occasions. The rug on the floor was plush and unworn. The ornate fireplace mantel appeared to have just been polished, and the candlesticks on the table gleamed like shiny mirrors.

In her younger years, Julia had not been allowed to set foot in this room, but tonight the ban had been lifted. Landon, for unknown reasons, had invited everyone to gather here for the evening meal. Julia had been both happy and confused by the request, but did not venture to guess Landon's motives. She'd barely seen or talked to him since they returned to Welbourne, both of them occupied with spending time with their siblings.

As Julia's gaze drifted around, enjoying the sight of familiar objects, the smile on her face faded. A lightning flash had caused the figures of Landon and Gideon to emerge from the darkness in stark relief. They stood off to the side in the shadows, their heads close together, as they conversed in hushed tones.

Neither had apparently heard her enter, but Landon must have sensed her presence. He turned around as she stood there, and nudged her brother in warning.

Gideon was the first to speak. "Little sis. Come in. Come in."

"I-I was just going to light the candles." Julia nodded toward the candles on each side of the table, and then proceeded to pull a matchbox from the drawer of a small cabinet. After fumbling with the box, she struck the match and watched it flare to life. She couldn't stop her mind from racing with questions, theories, and assumptions as to what the two men had been discussing.

But deep down, she knew. Landon would not remain idle long—and neither would her brother. The war was not yet over. In their minds, their duty was not yet complete. Had they been planning their next excursion into enemy territory?

The notion was so alarming that a feeling of sickening dread crept over her.

The Yankees had just been humiliated and disgraced, and would be ready—or at least expecting—another daring venture. The thought of the two men she loved the most leaving again caused Julia to become distracted. At first, she was angry. But then came fear, followed closely by dismay. Why couldn't things stay as they were right now? The past had been painful and bleak, but the future looked suddenly darker. How dare they be so fearless and tenacious; so reckless and rash.

Julia's hand trembled so noticeably that Landon walked up behind her, wrapped his fingers around her wrist, and helped her complete the task of touching wick to flame. Before either could say anything, there was a screech from the doorway.

"The table looks bee-u-tee-full," Sallie exclaimed when she walked across the threshold holding onto Sawyer's arm. "Doesn't it, Sawyer?"

"Just like the old days." He gave a weak grin that showed the two small dimples that had not disappeared despite his weakened condition. He had been scraggly and unshaven upon his arrival at Welbourne, but now he was neatly dressed and well groomed—and had apparently regained his good humor.

"Go ahead and take a seat." Landon motioned to everyone

in the room as he took the chair at the head of the table. Julia sat to his left, with Gideon beside her, and the twins relaxed into the chairs on the opposite side of the table.

"Why are we eating in here?" Sallie's eyes were bright and questioning.

"Yes," Sawyer chimed in. "What's the big news?"

All eyes turned to Landon, who shifted uneasily in his chair. "First of all, I'd like to say that it is a pleasure to have the Dandridges here. It feels like we are a whole family again." His eyes swept each face with a look of calm, but his voice was thick and unsteady. "Bonds have been forged that even war cannot tear asunder."

"Yes, finally, everyone is back together," Sallie nodded enthusiastically, completely oblivious to her brother's discomfort. "Is that why we're eating here? Is that the big news?"

"No." Landon cleared his throat. "The reason we are here... The reason I called you all together...here, to the dining room..." He turned his attention to Gideon as if seeking help, but seeing none forthcoming, he tried again. "What I wished to say is..." He picked up a fork and moved it a few inches before placing it back where it had been. "I just finished talking to Gideon, who agreed—"

Julia closed her eyes tightly as if she could block out his words by doing so. She held her breath, expecting him to say that he would be leaving again soon and taking her brother with him. The mission would be important no doubt, and the consequences clear. It would be dangerous, and they may not return.

She could tell from the sound of Landon's voice that no more painful struggle ever tore the heart of a patriot—but that did not lessen her own pain. How could she let him go to perform his dangerous deeds when they had already been separated for far too long?

She should have known this was all too good to be true; that such good fortune was not to last forever.

Taking a deep breath to quell her selfish emotions, Julia feared she would burst in the effort to control her private anguish. She tried, without success, to keep her mind agreeably engaged, to enjoy the present and not worry about the future, but she felt like the universe was playing a cruel trick. This perfect evening with those she held dear was destined to end with devastating revelations.

Candlelight sparkled and reflected in the chandelier overhead, making everything appear serene and secure. Yet this small slice of happiness was perhaps to be the last one for a long time—possibly forever.

"What he's trying so unsuccessfully to say," Gideon finally broke in and came to his friend's aid, "is that after passing through some very tough trials, we have all learned the precious gift of time…" He paused to look over at Julia, and then he too faltered. An uncertainty crept into his expression, and his gaze darted back to Landon for help.

"I don't understand what either of you is trying to say." Sallie tilted her head and looked from one to the other. "Will someone just tell us, please?"

Julia wanted to scream, to run and hide, and be spared from hearing the words. She was certain they were planning to leave— perhaps as soon as tomorrow. They wanted to announce it in an official, dignified way—though nothing, not even this beautifully orchestrated meal, would ease the hurt of it.

Who could tell what type of perilous scheme Landon had conceived for the Lion's men to undertake? He was brimming with energy, intolerant of idleness, and determined to fight to the end. Each of his ventures had been bold and daring, yet he refused to rest, aimed ever higher, attempting to outdo and surpass the seemingly impossible endeavor he had already accomplished.

How could she make him understand that blood enough had been shed and treasure wasted? It was time for others to stand.

The reconciliation that Julia had dreamed of and hoped for… the future that could have been joyful and renewing, was not to be. No principle of law or logic would require Landon to continue this mad game, but Julia had no doubt he would.

She stared at the flickering flame of a candle, lost in her own thoughts, barely hearing the conversation any longer. Even though Landon's prayers had been answered by getting Sawyer back, and her dreams fulfilled by getting Landon back, he intended to tempt fate and deny her true happiness.

Landon tried again. "What we're saying is that, although we're not related by blood, we've always been like a family." His gaze swept the table and then came to rest on Julia as if to analyze her reaction. "All of us." He was a little more composed now, and spoke in the same low tone one would use to ask about the weather or comment socially on the taste of a fine wine.

Yet still his explanation did not make sense to those at the table, particularly since it was communicated by a man known for his perceptiveness and control. Today, he seemed uncharacteristically uneasy and apprehensive.

"I don't understand," Sallie said, under her breath in an exasperated voice.

"Allow me to explain." Gideon spoke while staring at the chandelier overhead, as if the answers would come from there. "Since I am, by rights, Julia's legal guardian…"

Julia felt Landon reach over and place his hand over hers, an action that expressed what words could not. She opened her eyes and stared at the tanned skin standing in stark contrast to the snow-white tablecloth. His touch was strong, firm, possessive…

protective, causing her mind to race and her head to spin. Did he think this was enough to ease the blow? That a simple touch could shield her from the severity of the words to come, or calm the dreadful suspense?

How very considerate of Landon and Gideon to discuss the implications of their perilous plan on *her* life, knowing it could conceivably leave her deprived of a brother and most likely robbed of a future with Landon. How very considerate, and how very cruel. But then again, men never saw things in the same light as women did, nor did they understand the emotional ramifications of their reckless deeds. Did they think mere words would heal a lifetime of heartache and loneliness?

Julia glanced at both her brother and Landon. There was no mockery in either of their eyes, no sign of teasing. They both believed she would settle back into a normal life after their shocking news, when the truth was, she could barely find the strength to breathe.

As if nerved to sudden action by the expression of distress on Julia's face, Gideon continued. "What I mean to say is, Landon has requested—and I have granted—permission for him to seek Julia's hand."

Shadows and silence fell upon the room, as a hushed expectancy sparked like the lightning that still flickered in the background.

"It looks to me like he already has it," Sallie responded blandly, nodding to their hands on the table. She took a casual drink of water and then stared at her brother and her friend across the table to see what would happen next.

Julia sat unblinking, gazing straight ahead as her mind struggled to catch up. It took some time for her to discard all of the things she thought were going to be disclosed, and replace them with the words that had been spoken. Like the sun bursting out from behind a cloud, the revelation at last pushed through her fear and doubt, sending a tingling surge of warmth to every nerve.

"I think he's waiting for an answer." Gideon nudged her arm with his, and nodded toward Landon.

Julia lifted her eyes to meet Landon's and found them waiting—not solemn or troubled anymore, but yearning, with an intense look of love and reverence glimmering there. The expression was unnerving, coming from a man who rarely showed emotion, particularly any relating to the heart. "I-I'm sorry," she said sincerely. "I didn't hear the question."

A soft stirring of shuffling feet and suppressed nervous laughter stopped instantly at the sound of Landon's husky voice.

"Not a day goes by that I'm not consumed by the thought of you, Julia." He squeezed her hand more forcefully than he could have possibly realized. "Will you do me the honor of becoming my wife?"

Julia's heart swelled with happiness as she scanned the faces of those who were dearest to her in the world. "Of course." A single tear of joy slid down her cheek, which Landon brushed away. "As long as you promise to never leave Welbourne again."

She thought she saw the color leave Landon's face somewhat, but he didn't have time to make that pledge or refuse it.

"Now we really are sisters," Sallie exclaimed clapping her hands. "I can't wait to plan the wedding. We'll have—"

"Something simple," Landon finished for her.

"Yes, something simple." Julia nodded in agreement. Her whole world had just changed in a way she hadn't thought possible. She was so happy after so much pain that it almost frightened her. She didn't think—had never thought—it possible to feel so much elation. Yet every look, every gesture, every face in the room, was confirmation of a bright future.

"I'd like to propose a toast." Gideon held up his glass. "To the future Mr. and Mrs. Landon Graham." The glasses clanked noisily in the center of the table as the dining room at Welbourne reverberated with the laughter of old friends.

A strange mixture of emotions raced through Julia. Familiar faces and surroundings mingled with the devotion she felt for the man beside her, created an unexpected sense of delight—yet mixed with a touch of apprehension.

Seeming to read her mind, Landon entwined his fingers with hers, providing a sense of reassurance and strength. Julia could feel his affection and devotion flow into her and over her like a comforting mantle, yet his hand too, trembled perceptibly.

When things had quieted down somewhat, Sallie held up her glass. "And here's to the Lion, whoever he may be, for bringing our family together again."

Not wanting to risk looking at Landon, Julia kept her eyes focused on a clock on the mantel, as once again the glasses clinked together. But as she stared at the timepiece, her attention became more focused. She remembered the constant ticking of the device from her youth, yet had never really taken notice of it. While winding it once, Landon's father had told her it had been brought to America from Scotland by his grandfather, as a reminder of the family's ancestral courage and resilience.

Julia studied the extravagant heirloom with new awareness. On each side of the face of the clock stood winged lions, lunging toward the dial.

Julia lifted nothing but her eyes to the portrait of the first Graham to come to America. He sat in a stately, refined pose, his arms crossed, his dark, mysterious gaze staring into the distance. And on his finger, he wore a ring, large and intricately engraved with the head of a lion.

Landon picked up his own glass and held it with a steady hand, gazing at Julia with a meaningful look that acknowledged the secret they shared. "Yes, here's to the Lion." He wore a lopsided smile, but his eyers had a smoky, smoldering look to them that affected Julia like an intimate touch. "Long may he live."

Julia lifted her own glass again, and tried to appear as composed as her future husband. No privilege on Earth could make her as proud as being asked to become this man's wife.

"Yes, to the Lion. A courageous warrior and a man of great character." She stopped to catch her breath at the sight of Landon's disarming smile and eyes now lit with a sensuous flame. "Long may he live."

Also by Jessica James

"Rivals Gone With the Wind as my favorite novel of all time. I can think of no better way to describe it."
— Reviewer

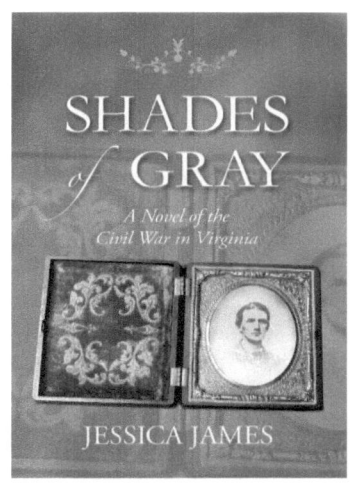

"I think it is the best Civil War fiction book since Cold Mountain."
— James D. Bibb, Sons of Confederate Veterans, Trimble Camp 1836

"A classic love story as much as it is a war story." *— Civil War Book Review*

"This is not a contemporary retelling of the Civil War as much as it is a sympathetic and loving portrait. A page-turner and quick read." *— Historical Novel Society*

www.jessicajamesbooks.com

What Readers Are Saying

"If you want to read a book you will never forget and will think about for months after reading it, read *Shades of Gray*. It took my breath away. Honestly, you will not sleep."

"My house is a mess, my sink is piled high with dishes and my husband ate watermelon for dinner because I could not put down *Shades of Gray*. Could. Not. Put. Down. Honestly, this book completely captivated me and left me emotionally drained. I loved it!!!"

"I've not been much of a reader and was given *Shades of Gray*. I've read it five times and fall in love every time I read it. Because of you I have developed a love for reading."

"It is now 1 a.m. cause I couldn't put down my I-pad with your delicious novel. Thank you for the pleasure you afforded this 81 year old."

"Wonderful, fabulous book! I seldom reflect back on a book, but this one has haunted me since I finished it at 2 a.m."

"Could hardly work or sleep until I read the last page."

"Lost a lot of sleeping reading this one. Too good to put down! Made me laugh. Made me cry. Awesome book!"

"I loved this novel. Still crying, but I laughed just as much as I cried."

"Bravo! One of the best books I have read on the Civil War. Absolutely could not put it down. Please do not stop writing."

"Excellent book. Well developed characters. Edge of your seat suspense."

"I can't remember having such a heavy heart and crying so much since reading *Gone with the Wind*. Thank you!"

"Loved. Loved. Needs to be made into a movie."

"I'm not usually one for Civil War era books, but I've got to say you really got me on this one. I LOVE it!"

"Oh my, I let the world go on around me and could hardly put it down. Every free moment, every break at work. LOVED IT!!!"

"As a history buff I have never read a more compelling novel with a Civil War setting. Brilliant. I was SEEING events rather than reading words."

"I was completely lost and spellbound by the realistic story. Without hesitation I must say *Noble Cause* now ranks equally with *Gone With The Wind.*"

"Though a male I liked it, and recommended it to my wife."

"I stayed up until 2 a.m. two nights in a row because I couldn't put it down. It was a book that I couldn't wait to read, yet I didn't want it to end!"

"This book has touched me more than any other I have ever read. I cried, laughed, and then cried some more. Thank you for such an amazing and touching story."

"If someone said I could only ever have one book for the rest of my life either of these [*Shades of Gray* or *Noble Cause*] would be my pick. Thank you."

"I know a book is very good when I think about it after I complete the book, and I cannot start another one right away. Five star rating for sure."

This book absolutely ripped my heart out. Superb. Thank you for such a moving, believable love story."

"I have not read a romance novel in probably 10 years. Your book was so good for my soul."

Other Historical Fiction Books by Jessica James

Sign up for Jessica James' Newsletter to receive a free copy of **From the Heart: Civil War Stories and Letters**

www.jessicajamesbooks.com

About the Author

JESSICA JAMES is a multi-award winning author of historical fiction and military suspense. Her novels appeal to both men and women, and are featured in library collections all over the United States, including Harvard and the U.S. Naval Academy.

By weaving the principles of courage, devotion, and dedication into each book, she attempts to honor the unsung heroes of the American military—past and present—and to convey the magnitude of their sacrifice and service.

Connect with the author at jessicajamesbooks.com
Signed copies of every book are available upon request.

Jessica James Awards

2017 IndieBRAG Medallion Winner
2016 Gold Metal Military Writers Society of America
2016 Readers' Favorite International Book Award
2016 BOOK OF THE YEAR Finalist/Foreword Magazine
2015 NJRW Golden Leaf Award
2014 Valley Forge Romance Writers Sheila Award Finalist
2014 John Esten Cooke Award for Southern Fiction
2014 Reader's Crown Award Finalist
2014 Next Generation Indie Award Finalist in Fiction/Religious
2013 USA "Best Books 2013" Finalist in Fiction/Religious
2012 Bronze winner Foreword Magazine Book of the Year in Romance
2011 John Esten Cooke Award for Southern Fiction
2011 USA "Best Books 2011" Finalist in Historical Fiction
2011 Next Generation Indie Award for Best Regional Fiction
2011 Next Generation Indie Finalist in Romance
2011 Next Generation Indie Finalist in Historical Fiction
2011 NABE Pinnacle Book Achievement Award
2010 Military Writers Society Award in Historical Fiction
2009 HOLT Medallion Finalist for Best Southern Theme
2008 Indie Next Generation Award for Best Regional Fiction
2008 Indie Next Generation Finalist for Best Historical Fiction
2008 IPPY Award for Best Regional Fiction
2008 ForeWord Magazine Finalist for Book of the Year in Romance